PRAISE FOR ED LIN

"Lin is an astonishing talent. "
— JUNOT DÍAZ

"Lin's unsentimental, purely realist—not naturalist, not socialist, not postmodernist—novel raises hopes that American fiction may yet grow up. "
— BOOKLIST, STARRED REVIEW, FOR *Waylaid*

"...darkly comic... "
— PUBLISHERS WEEKLY, STARRED REVIEW, FOR *Ghost Month*

"Hold on for a breathtaking, multi-cultural ride. With some good luck and a few well-placed joss sticks, you just might survive."
— MARTIN LIMÓN, AUTHOR OF *Nightmare Range*, FOR *Ghost Month*

"Stellar..."
— PUBLISHERS WEEKLY, STARRED REVIEW, FOR *99 Ways to Die*

"A stylish, smart thriller for the mind, heart, and gut. Sex, music, history, politics, food, humor, and just a touch of violence and death—you get it all. And when you're done, you'll beg for more."
— VIET THANH NGUYEN, PULITZER PRIZE–WINNING AUTHOR
OF *The Sympathizer*, FOR *Incensed*

"A unique blend of tension, charm, tragedy and optimism, with characters you'll love, and a setting so real you'll think you've been there."
— LEE CHILD, FOR *Ghost Month*

DAVID TUNG
A GIRLFRIEND
HE GETS
IVY LEAGUE

CAN'T HAVE

UNTIL

INTO AN

COLLEGE

A novel by **ED LIN**

David Tung Can't Have A Girlfriend
Until He Gets Into An Ivy League College
Published by Kaya Press
www.kaya.com

Copyright © 2020 by Ed Lin
23 22 21 20   4 3 2 1

Cover and book design by: spoon+fork
Artwork by: Richard Hahn

Manufactured in the USA
Distributed by D.A.P./Distributed Art Publishers
155 Avenue of the Americas, 2nd Floor
New York, NY 10013
800.338.BOOK | www.artbook.com

ISBN 9781885030627
Library of Congress Control Number: 2020939036

This publication is made possible by support from the USC Dana and David
Dornsife College of Arts, Letters, and Sciences; the USC Department of
American Studies and Ethnicity; and the USC Asian American Studies Program.
Special thanks to Stephen CuUnjieng and the Choi Chang Soo Foundation for
their support of this work. Additional funding was provided by the generous
contributions of: Akhila Ananth, Tiffany E. Babb, Manibha Banerjee, Neelanjana
Banerjee, Partha Banerjee, Rahul Banerjee, Thomas G. Beischer & Lily So, Melissa
Chadburn, Lisa Chen, Anita Chen, Jade Chang, Anelise Chen, Floyd Cheung,
Jen Chou, Stephen CuUnjieng, Kavita Das, Lawrence-Minh Davis, Steven Doi,
Susannah Donahue, Sesshu Foster, Chris Eng, Julianne Hing, Jean Ho, Huy Hong,
Anvi Hoang, Ashaki Jackson, Andrew Kebo, Parag Khandhar, Vandana Khanna,
Juliana Koo, Sun Hee Koo, Whakyung Lee, Andrew Leong, Edward Lin, Mimi
Lok, Leza Lowitz, Abir Majumdar, Jason McCall, Chris Moad, Faisal Mohyuddin,
Risyiana Muthia, Jean Naylor, Viet Thanh Nguyen, Gene Y. Oishi, Chez Bryan
Ong, Eric Ong, Teraya Paramehta, Leena Pendharkar, Amarnath Ravva, Alexander
Rocklin, Audrey Shi, Andrew Shih, Paul Henry Smith, Nancy Starbuck, Wendy
Tokuda, Kay Tsuji, Jonathan Wang, Monona Wali, Patricia Wakida, Joseph Wei,
Duncan Williams, Koon Woon, Sachin Adarkar & Amelia Wu, James Spicer &
Anita Wu, Jessica Yazbek, Shinae Yoon, Mikoto Yoshida, Joyce Yu, and others.
Kaya Press is also supported, in part, by: the National Endowment for the Arts;
the Los Angeles County Board of Supervisors through the Los Angeles County
Arts Commission; the Community of Literary Magazines and Presses; and the
City of Los Angeles Department of Cultural Affairs.

DAVID TUNG CAN'T HAVE A GIRLFRIEND UNTIL HE GETS INTO AN IVY LEAGUE COLLEGE

KAYA PRESS   **LOS ANGELES**

For all the Saturday crews

CHAPTER ONE

As precious minutes ticked down in homeroom, I was anxious to get to my first class, biology. Yet I also desperately wanted more time to study for the quiz that I and only I knew was coming. I couldn't hold my legs still as I tried to memorize everything in my book and notes.

I took a deep breath and tuned out all distractions. The homeroom announcements sounded like pleasant fish-tank bubbling noise. I envisioned my class rank rising.

It was a Thursday in mid-March, and sophomore year was almost over. I was ranked eighth out of a class of 240. If I could end the year in sixth or seventh place, that would be a major win. One or two steps up may not seem like much, but for college applications from Shark Beach High, a higher rank would mean the world.

My school is a public institution based in a landlocked town in northern New Jersey known for receiving 20-25 Ivy League college admissions offers every year. That's one of the highest for any public high school our size in the state, even if the figures are skewed by seniors who receive offers from multiple schools.

In reality, only six or seven students per year from Shark Beach High end up attending Harvard, Yale, Columbia, Princeton, Penn, Cornell, Brown, and Dartmouth. In that order of preference. Only six or seven. I was on the wrong side of the cutoff.

Luckily for me, the top 10 students in my grade are separated by only 0.25 grade points. This also means, however, that we have to battle amongst ourselves for every hundredth of a point.

With two more years to go, any one of us could be valedictorian. Though, to be honest, it's actually more important to be at the top of the class at the end of the first grading period of senior year, when the applications go in.

Cutthroat competition exists in high schools all across the country, but you'd be hard-pressed to find students as bloodthirsty as the ones at Shark Beach High. We're the only school on the East Coast where about 80% of the students are Asian American, nearly all Chinese, and many with immigrant parents. Twenty-eight percent of the student body are themselves immigrants. And immigrants are competitive as hell, if you don't already know.

Shark Beach's school system wasn't always like this. When I was really small, in first grade or so, there were so few Asians that I would still occasionally get ching-chonged in the hallways at school. That sure doesn't happen any more. About a decade ago, other Asians began moving in from across the country and from overseas, drawn by the stellar schools and the town's proximity to New York City. Shark Beach offers an elite education that's tuition-free for whoever can afford to live and pay taxes here. It's like catnip for ambitious parents, immigrant or otherwise.

Nowadays, the hallways are filled with Chings *and* Chongs.

This fact about our town has attracted media attention in recent years. CNN came to Shark Beach High to interview students when Harvard was being sued for allegedly discriminating against Asian American applicants. The non-Asian reporter they'd sent tried so hard to push us equivocating kids into saying something substantial, but nobody had wanted to jeopardize their own upcoming applications. Yes, every Shark Beach High student acknowledged, any sort of bias is wrong, but it's up to the courts to decide.

CNN should have known better than to put "success"-focused kids on the spot, but, hey, our faces, not our voices, were what they wanted most.

Shark Beach High students might make for bland talking heads, but throw a minor pop quiz at us, and we'll rip each other to pieces for every point. We'll also take on every bonus question and any extra credit made available to us to lift that B-plus to an A-minus to an A. We even sometimes resort to sandbagging the competition.

Consider our current class valedictorian, Brett Hau. Everyone knows he has a sweet tooth. So on the days when there's a big test, Brett's rivals ply him with free candy and soda, hoping he'll have a sugar crash. During the last big in-class essay we had for Honors English, Brett had to make a run for the bathroom, but he managed to get back in time to finish. Still snagged a 100%. Maybe we should all drink four Cokes before tests.

Some idiots get too carried away with all of this, of course. One junior was suspended last year for slashing someone's car tires in the school parking lot. How stupid. You're supposed to slash their tires *before* they can get to school.

Most students stick to expensive but more socially acceptable methods, including private tutors and extra test prep. Whispers have gone around about parents who've gone so far as to bribe college officials for an admission, but that route is definitely closed off nowadays.

My family isn't part of that moneyed world. We own and operate the mid-priced but solid Tung's Garden, located in the southern part of Shark Beach, an area that's just starting to see more redevelopment. So no extra academic help for me. My parents expect me to get better grades by listening to them yell at me. Then again, even if they were willing or able to pay for a tutor, I wouldn't have time for lessons anyways. I work at the restaurant after school and on the weekends— basically, nearly all my waking non-school hours.

In any case, everyone knows that academic success alone isn't good enough for Ivy League admissions. If anything, intangibles might matter even more than grades. If the Harvard lawsuit revealed anything about that school's admission process, it's that all A's and nothing else is a major turnoff. The other Ivies can't be that different.

For a while, I was hoping that becoming an emerging track star would help me stand out. I was the fastest ninth grader in the school in the 200 and 400, and though I haven't yet beat any school records, I've come close.

I hoped to do even better this year, but I've had to withdraw from track meets and practices after I got shin splints in December. We'd been running indoors, not on grass, and I'd been pushing myself hard—too hard, it turned out.

My lower legs no longer hurt, but I couldn't risk aggravating them again. Making first or second team for all-state boys in the fall would be a great way to help dress up that college application. But for the moment, all I can do is try to raise my class rank by focusing on classes such as biology, in which I am only an A-minus student.

Biology at Shark Beach High is taught by Mr. del Pino, who imagines himself to be thinner than he really is. His ill-fitting clothes are always just a smidge too snug, and from the side, his body looks like a capital "P," with his belt right under the carb bulge. A million years ago he himself had been a student at Shark Beach High. He often laments how we can't do the same labs that he used to do back in the day, when two boys could pick up dead dogs from the kill shelter for class dissections. Now he has to use worms instead, or, even worse, virtual frogs on school tablets.

Word on the street, though, is that a stellar recommendation letter from him can crack open the doors of an Ivy. So doing well in his class is a must for me.

I want to be a doctor, after all. The kind that displays my diploma proudly on my office wall.

All this is easier said than done, though. Mr. del Pino's notoriously tough pop quizzes can elicit whimpers from even the most confident student.

One day, when I was doubled over from pain upon hearing his third question—he always dictates his questions—my eyes were drawn to his feet under his desk. His exposed socks were mismatched.

I'd noticed this before but had chalked it up to just another one of Mr. del Pino's many quirks. Something about seeing this in the midst of taking a pop quiz, though, made me wonder about the correlation between the two. After a few weeks of close observation, I came up with a theory. Mr. del Pino wears mismatched socks on days that he has to do laundry, which puts him in a bad mood, which makes him more apt to spring an impromptu quiz.

I don't know how close to the truth my theory is, but our last five pop quizzes have taken place on odd-socks days.

All this has led to me making a point of looking for

Mr. del Pino in the hallway before homeroom so I can secretly take pictures of his feet. My iPhone is an old model, but it still has burst mode.

Upon reviewing this morning's photos, I saw that one sock was black and one was brown. A Thursday pop quiz was for certain!

I looked around my homeroom. No one else from my biology class was studying, much less cramming. They had no idea what was coming down the pike.

So while the popular kids chatted amongst themselves about parties and other outings that I wouldn't be invited to, I stared at my bio book and focused on the taxonomy of humans and other animals.

When the bell rang, I bolted out of the room. I wanted to get to Mr. del Pino's class early to maximize every possible moment of additional study time.

As always, Mr. del Pino stood at the doorway of the classroom, greeting us individually in a mock formal tone as we walked in.

"Mr. Wong, good to see you. Ms. Ko, thank you for coming today. Ah, Mr. Tung, you look like you're up to no good."

"Why?" I asked.

"I can see the mischief in your eyes," he threw back at me before moving on to his next target. "Ms. Lee, we've got a seat just for you in the front. Mr. Lin, let's try to stand up straight, your bones aren't that heavy."

I slid into my seat and dealt myself books and notebooks from my bag. I took a breath and dove in, trying to stuff in one more essential detail before the bell rang. I already had the taxonomy mnemonic "King Phillip came over from Germany, swimming" firmly lodged in my head, but the Latin classification names were harder to get down perfectly. Mr. del Pino never did multiple choice, and nothing was worse than getting an answer wrong because you ended something with an "a" when it should have ended with "ae."

"Family hominidae," I repeated to myself. I made up another mnemonic: "The family will be home in a day."

The bell rang. Mr. del Pino closed the door promptly and headed to his desk.

"Today, I have a lovely little film I'd like to show you," he declared, pausing to dramatically drum his fingers on his desk. "But first, let's have a little quiz."

As most of the class tried to swallow their sighs, I lit up with glee.

There were 10 questions on the pop quiz, and I was pretty sure I got nine of them right. Based on the twisted feet and rocking upper bodies of my fellow students, I'd say I did pretty damned good relative to everyone else.

After the test, we saw the promised short film, which was about extinct primates. Then, in order to run out the clock, we took turns reading aloud from the main textbook. I flipped back a few pages to check on the one question I hadn't been sure about. My chest swelled with pride. I'd gotten a perfect score.

I glanced at Hanson Ding. He, too, was checking his answers, and seemed to be silently cursing. Since he was ranked #3, this was good for me only in a long-term sense. No matter how poorly Hanson did, I still wouldn't be within striking distance of him because of this one quiz alone. There was a decent chance, though, that today I could slip by one of my more immediate rivals, Christina Tau, who was currently right above me in seventh place. I squirmed at the thought. She had seemed just out of reach all year.

Christina's a girl that you know you're supposed to think is hot because everyone says she is. She looks like the slinky cat women who hang around the bad guys in movies. Too much mascara and lipstick makes her frequent scowls look sexy, and her form-fitting, upscale clothes show off the curves around her widening hips. Sometimes she sways her shoulder-length hair around like she's in a shampoo commercial.

Yet she's somehow managed to keep me out of the top seven for the entirety of our freshman year until now. How could someone who puts so much effort into the way she looks also have the time and energy to get a slightly better grade point average than mine? Was she really smarter than me? I hoped not. I hoped no one ahead of me was.

One thing was for sure at least: nobody, not even Christina, could beat my perfect score for the day in biology. Too bad for her that she was in Mr. del Pino's second section of biology. He made their quiz a lot harder on the assumption that they'd have advance notice that a quiz was on its way.

I walked to my next class with my head held higher than usual. The satisfaction I felt from nailing that biology quiz was enough to sustain me through the whole weekend.

As I turned down the hallway, I almost ran into some lackeys from the student council slapping up notices for the upcoming Dames Ball. I gave one flyer a cursory glance, then immediately forgot about it. No way would I be going, after all. For one thing, the Dames Ball required the girls to do the asking, and no one was going to ask me.

Mainly, though, I'd been told in no uncertain terms by my mother that I couldn't date in high school. My father may not have felt the same way, but he had said nothing. What she said overruled him, anyway.

How did I feel about all this? Well, I did think about girls from time to time, but never consciously or for very long. Maybe that was my mother's ultimate goal all along.

Because of ongoing construction to expand the school, I still have the same locker I was assigned to on a "temporary" basis at the beginning of my freshman year. It's in a hastily assembled bank of lockers in a dead-end hallway that leads to what used to be the music practice room.

Shark Beach High no longer has a music program, but that's no big deal because nearly all the Asian kids take private piano and violin lessons. By way of contrast, when the school tried to institute a lottery to determine who would get into the overcrowded AP physics class, the Greater Shark Beach Chinese School organized parents to harass the principal and the local board of education with phone calls and emails until a second section of AP physics was added.

The area around my locker is generally emptier than other hallways, as it's a bit out of the way. Given that my school strategy is to get through the day efficiently while earning straight A's, though, the relative solitude suits me just fine.

As I was swapping some books, I felt someone bump my shoulder.

"Oh, sorry," said Scott Sima. "I didn't make you drop something, did I?"

"No," I said. "Everything's cool."

Scott is a junior, a football player, and one of the biggest kids in school. He's also one of the most popular. The only commotion I ever see near my locker is when a line of giggling girls comes by to ask Scott how he's doing. Or if some of his teammates drop by to act out various viral sports videos.

Harvard's football coach supposedly sent him a letter asking if he planned to apply. If true, he remains remarkably modest about it all. Unlike some students, he isn't stuck up about whom he talks to or not. Though I'm pretty sure he doesn't know me by name.

"Yo, Scott!" someone yelled.

Scott turned to me and rapped the door of his locker.

"Take care, David," he said.

Wow, he does know my name!

"Later, Scott," I managed to reply in an even tone.

Even if Scott's not a friend, he's always friendly. He acknowledges everyone equally, like someone running for president.

At lunch I bought a plate of vegetable lasagna and a box of soymilk at the self-serve line. Halfway through the day, and all was good. No test or quiz in Algebra 2/Trig class, as it turned out. French class was kind of a joke. World History was as basic as it sounded.

I took a mental inventory of my remaining classes as I set down my tray at my usual spot, the sparsely populated half-sized table near the exit. Gym/Health was next. Then there was Honors English, which I wasn't worried about, either, though Mrs. Humboldt could always throw a curve ball by making us write an in-class essay. Still, as long as you argued your case well, it was a fairly easy A. My day would end as always with Honors Dialectics, which was actually fun, especially when the class got into heated arguments. In short, no papers were due or upcoming in any of those classes. The rest of the day promised to be a cakewalk.

Satisfied, I wolfed down my lasagna, then slowly sipped my soymilk as I read a practice MCAT question on my phone.

Now, for the short-term thinker, it may seem more logical for a high school sophomore to study for the SATs rather than the MCATs, since one presumably needs to complete undergraduate studies before applying to medical school. But I've always figured that any head start that I can get will help me in the race to grab one of those top seven Ivy League spots. Think about how much more knowledgeable my application essays and interviews would be!

Plus, I had already taken the SATs, and while I

missed getting a perfect score, I planned to mount another attempt when I was a junior. Until then, I was going to blast away at the more-difficult MCATs. Kind of like taking practice swings with three bats so I could really knock it out of the park when I was down to one.

Here's an inside tip on cracking MCAT questions: Read as much as you can. I've found that the test rewards those who already understand what's known and accepted in the medical community.

Following my own advice, I've made a habit of going through the free abstracts of online journals; they're usually the least opaque parts of a scientific paper. I've already begun to reap the benefits of this strategy, as well. For example, the problem I was working on had multiple questions that followed a few paragraphs of dryly written text about how the human kidney filters out toxins. For someone—like me!—who already understands how dialysis works, knocking out the answers is much faster and easier than someone trying to figure it out for the first time. After all, there's no chance the right answer will contradict what has already been medically established.

I ticked off the correct answers, received a congratulatory message (and an offer to buy the site's app for 10% off), and put away my phone. My day was only getting better.

Just then, Benson Gong stopped by my table. "Would it be all right if I sat here, David?" he asked.

"Yeah," I said. "Have a seat." I stretched my legs and put my arms behind my head to show how relaxed and casual I was. I wasn't some stressed-out academic grind that nobody wanted to sit with.

"Thank you," he said with a little head nod. Benson was a fairly recent arrival. The Gong from Hong Kong, I heard someone call him. It sounds like a disparaging tag, but how racist can it be if the guy who said it was Asian?

I flattened my newly emptied soymilk box and looked over at the popular students sitting at tables along the back of the room that had views of the parking lot. They all could admire each other's new cars.

When I was younger, I would have been embarrassed to be sitting with someone like Benson. I'm ashamed to say now, but in grade school I used to try to raise my own social stature by making fun of the new fobby kids and how they always smelled like Tiger Balm.

This short phase of intolerance ended when I made someone cry at recess, and I realized how mean I had become.

Over the years, as our school has become more Chinese, Taiwanese, and Hongkonger, I've learned that being fresh off the boat is a complex issue for many Asians, including those of us born in the U.S. We cringe a little when we hear new kids mangling English. It reminds us of the older generations wrapped up in the old traditions, people who don't get it. The fashion-handicapped and the socially inept.

In any case, it wasn't as if I could act like I owned the town when my family owned so little, relatively. Most of the kids in Shark Beach High come from families much wealthier than mine. Girls wear real diamonds and gold, and Jimmy Choo flats are as popular as Nikes. Boys wield the latest phones, ones that don't even fit in the pockets of their Burberry shirts, and plug their ears with AirPods that they stash just before their next class.

How do I usually dress? I tend to favor a green-and-black checked shirt tucked into brandless jeans. In class photos, I'm always underdressed as hell.

Many families in my town have two parents each of whom work management-level jobs in New York City. Some have lofty-enough titles that they take chauffeured cars into Manhattan, dropping off their kids at school on the way. They live in multilevel smart homes outfitted with renewable-energy systems that qualify for federal tax breaks.

My family? I can't remember the last time we even turned on the heat. We stay warm in the winter by wearing sweatshirts inside.

It's a good thing that learning is free. I don't raise my hand in class much, but whenever teachers are anxious to get a right answer and move on to the next question, they call on me.

So why am I only ranked eighth? Our guidance counselor Mr. Wald said we were the most evenly matched class he'd seen in a few years, and that basically the top 10 were all tied. That's just made me even more determined to claw my way up.

The way I figure it, having a lower social profile gives me the added advantage of stealth. But the real reason I don't have a big crew of friends at Shark Beach High is probably because I go to a Chinese school in New York on Saturdays, while nearly everyone else in my high school attends the local one.

Not that I would have time for socializing regardless. School, work, Chinese school. That's my life.

Of the three, Chinese school is the only one with any upside to it. Sure, as a concept, any Chinese school, even in the city, is definitely annoying, but Chinese school doesn't come with the pressure of grades or report cards, and thus has no bearing whatsoever on my college applications. I still learn when I'm there, just not necessarily what they're teaching.

The only problem is, Shark Beach High, and the town itself as a matter of fact, only really has one big clique with two minor variations: the kids who go to Greater Shark Beach Chinese School on Saturday, and the ones who go to church on Sunday. There's a lot of overlap between the two. Both meet in the same building, after all.

I'm not in either group. I haven't gone to the Greater Shark Beach Chinese School since I was eight, when my mom mysteriously decided one day that she didn't like the people who ran it and pulled me. Who knows. If I *had* continued to attend, I might well be goofing off and laughing with the cool kids at lunch during the week and not just on Saturdays in Chinese school.

I understand that the families of my Shark Beach High classmates hit the country club on Sundays after church, but that's not a part of our lifestyle, either. We don't have the time—or the clothes—to go golfing. We work Sundays.

The thing is, friendships at my age are forged in places where grade pressure is off. Connections are reinforced through summer camps, Chinese school outings, church, and adjacent lawns kept as neat and trim as cemeteries. Over a series of retreats, camping trips, and benefit car washes, not to mention weekly sermons and texting in Sunday school, that core of Chinese American kids becomes more and more tightly knit.

Meanwhile, I spend my summers at the restaurant, working full-time every day and night.

Looking up from my phone and my reveries, I couldn't help but admire how easily Benson seemed to be reading Chinese characters. What was he looking at? The news? A porno story? Is Benson a U.S. citizen or does he even want to be? Maybe his long-term plan was to get back to Hong Kong and fight for democracy.

My familiarity with characters was awful, despite the years of Chinese school, and I certainly couldn't read them upside down no matter how hard I tried.

I didn't want to ask him questions, though. He seemed busy, with his head buried in his phone as he picked at the raw vegan option, a cold bean salad.

I must have drifted off again a bit while watching him, because I felt a tap on my shoulder and looked up to realize that someone had sidled up to me. It was Mr. Wald, the guidance counselor.

"David Tung," he said, "just the man I wanted to see."

"Hello, Mr. Wald," I said.

Mr. Wald is probably about 60 years old, but there's

something young about him. He likes to comb his yellowish hair tight against his scalp, making his head look like a big rippled potato chip. He's only slightly out of shape.

"I want to start talking to our rising juniors, David, and I expect you to make an appointment soon. You can do it online, of course." Benson stared at Mr. Wald, looking slightly afraid. I was a little uneasy myself. After all, Mr. Wald was the guy who sent out high school transcripts and sometimes wrote recommendations for college applications.

I'd first met with Mr. Wald back in January when I went to his office for information about an internship at the oncology department of Harmony Health Systems, a large hospital in Summit, N.J., one town over from Shark Beach.

Harmony Health had recently hired Dr. Vivian Lee, an award-winning cancer doctor, luring her away from prestigious Memorial Sloan Kettering in Manhattan. It was no secret that Harmony Health was hoping to model their game after MSK's, and now they had the queen piece, Dr. Lee herself.

The internship was only open to sophomores, which meant that the applicant pool was somewhat restricted, but there was no way it wasn't going to be super competitive nonetheless. How many other kids from the surrounding counties—ones with mothers and fathers who *were* doctors—were likely to apply? Hundreds? Thousands? Hundreds of thousands?

Getting that position, which reported to Dr. Lee, would make my college application shine like Venus at sunset.

With such dreams in my head, I submitted my internship application shortly thereafter and had been checking the big bulletin board outside of Mr. Wald's office at least once a day for updates ever since. Summer positions at law firms and banks had already begun to get filled in, but there was still just a big blank after "Harmony Health Systems." I wanted my name in that blank so badly.

"Mr. Wald," I asked, "Have you heard anything about Harmony..."

"David," he said through a chuckle, "They're going to take a while on this. Relax. You'll hear something when you hear something. Anyway, we can talk about it some more when you come see me."

The bell rang for the end of lunch. Mr. Wald nodded at us and walked away.

I'll hear something when I hear something. I'd been hearing that line or some variation of it my whole life. It was annoying, but there was nothing I could really do about it.

Benson and I got up and walked to the cafeteria door. As I held it open for him, I looked back at the kids strolling up from the back tables and noticed Fred Zhao talking to his friends while carelessly gesturing with the latest and most expensive iPhone model in his right hand.

I wouldn't exactly call Fred a friend, but we've known each other since elementary school. He even invited me to his birthday pool party back when we were both in the sixth grade, probably because we'd once had a deep conversation about UFOs and the Loch Ness Monster.

That birthday party showed me the huge financial gap between my family and the lives most of my classmates were. I couldn't even appreciate the heavy cardstock that his invitation was printed on, but I begged my mother so hard to let me go instead of working at the restaurant that day that she eventually relented.

Fred lived in what was then the tony section of Shark Beach, the northern part. I'd never even seen a house like Fred's before—semicircular driveway, chandelier in the foyer, no plastic on the couches. What really intimidated me, though, was the relaxed and unhurried way the other children and parents acted around one another.

They seemed totally and utterly given over to ease, comfort, and wealth. These people looked familiar, but their leisurely manner was foreign to me. I was accustomed to being tasked with something all the time. My weekend mode was rolling up my sleeves and working. Done with homework? Then bus these tables. Then rinse off these plates and put them in the dishwasher. Then trim these vegetables. Then sweep this floor.

I walked through the house, dropped off my gift with the housekeeper, and went through the back door to the pool.

Knowing that it was a pool party, I had shown up in generic swim trunks and one of my father's old t-shirts. The other boys were also wearing swim trunks and shirts, but everything was branded, even their flip-flops. Some were playing games on iPads in waterproof cases. One of them controlled the music on the wireless speakers surrounding the pool. The girls were wearing expensive swim parkas, gold jewelry, and carried accessory bags that held towels and sunscreen. Everyone was holding something. The only thing I had brought with me was a present. And now I was empty-handed.

I was glad to slip into the water, which hid my cheap swim trunks. While the girls lay under umbrellas on the deck recliners, I played chicken with the other guys. Sometimes I was the guy on top, sometimes I was on the bottom, but my team tended to win. Maybe working at the restaurant, filling and unloading the dishwasher, had helped me develop more upper-body strength than the other boys. I almost got lost in the fun.

The only problem was that my mom said she would pick me up at 3:30 p.m. on the dot when prepping the restaurant for the evening would take priority over everything else. So after about an hour of splashing around in the pool, I found myself turning to the outdoor clock above the pretend lifeguard stand. Knowing I would have to leave before anyone else made it impossible for me to enjoy myself fully.

At some point, Fred's father fired up the massive barbecue grill and began churning out burgers and hot dogs. The other men stood around him, drinking beers and joking about stocks.

Fred was half-finished with his hot dog when his mother came out of the gazebo and made him and his cousins go into the house. They emerged on the second floor rear balcony of the house carrying string instruments, which they handled with aplomb, their bare bony knees and elbows poking out of their Ralph Lauren swimwear. Fred looked as if he wanted to cry or had been crying, but he, too, continued to saw away at his violin.

Those kids played for what felt like more than an hour. Everybody at the party seemed familiar with the melodies; I only recognized the ones that went with furniture commercials. Fred's aunts and uncles, in their billowing linen shirts and blouses, clapped enthusiastically at the end of each of the songs. The kids in the audience, who were probably learning the same tunes themselves, snickered loudly at the mistakes.

Worst of all, no one was allowed to swim while they played. Too noisy. I shivered uncomfortably in my damp trunks as I listened. All the other boys had swimwear made from quick-drying fabric.

Before the concert was over, it was time for me to leave, so I headed back to the house to leave the way I had come. Fred's dad walked over to cut me off. He told me that since I hadn't showered, I should walk around the yard to the front to meet my mom.

Just as I was closing the wooden gate behind me, I heard kids jumping back into the pool. I turned around and surveyed the scene I was leaving one last time. Afternoon sunlight dappled the water's surface with little flashes of fire. All those kids splashing and shouting—they never had to worry about anything. Not in the way that my parents and I had to. They could go on vacation to the Old Country, a 12-hour flight each way, and spend two, three weeks there, no problem.

There was none of that for my family. We never had any vacations. We didn't know what it was like to do nothing while awake. I was at a birthday pool party just a few miles from my house, and knowing that I'd be at Tung's Garden soon enough, I couldn't even let go and have fun. And how did we celebrate my birthdays? At break time, I would blow out the candles and share the cake with the kitchen staff and delivery guys.

Then again, I would never be forced to give a humiliating recital in my swim trunks. That was a rich-kid problem. They learned early on how important it was to look good in public and perform on cue.

As was to be expected, my mother was right on time. Luckily for me, everyone else was still by the pool in the back, so no one saw that our car looked like crap compared to the Infiniti models parked along the street or in the driveway. When I opened the passenger-side door to get in, I saw that my mother was still wearing a dirty apron. She had no idea how embarrassing it would have been for me if the other kids had seen her looking like that.

She asked me if it had been worth the time for me to go, and I said yeah.

That night I worked wearing my own dirty apron wrapped around my swim trunks.

I still get angry now when I think about that pool party, even though I'm not sure why. I was invited. I went. I was treated decently. The whole time, though, I felt like I shouldn't have been there.

I certainly didn't grew up entirely friendless and alone

here in Shark Beach, though. Over the years, however, it's become harder to keep up the social side of life as school and work have become more intense.

I had one friend, Tim, with whom I would swap Xbox 360 games at recess. He was my main source for new games. He also had a disc-cleaning system at home that he would use to fix my games when they started to skip. We drifted apart after his dad cracked down on him for getting Bs in seventh grade and sold the game console. Tim's family is white, but that was totally a move from the Asian Dad Playbook. I lost interest in playing them after that.

Another friend, Yaro, I met in middle school. He's half white and half black. We bonded over our love for the game 20 Questions. He'd already exhausted the patience and deductive-reasoning ability of most of the other kids, so he'd been impressed when I was able to correctly guess the circumstances under which six people died in a cabin on a mountainside.

His parents made him go to Catholic school for eighth grade, but Yaro and I reconnected when we found each other on the high-school track team. These days, we usually play 20 Questions through texts because we don't have any classes in common: Yaro's in different honors sections than me, and I'm learning French while he's taking German.

Now that I'm sidelined from track, I rarely see him at all.

I would also classify other track members as pals, by the way. Being away from the team has ended a major social component of my life. I can't wait to get back at it in the fall. Without me, Yaro and the guys are losing meets.

I left the cafeteria, and saw Benson just ahead of me in the wall-to-wall mass exodus. When we hit the first intersection, however, an unlucky few of us split off for gym class.

Today wasn't a strenuous day, fortunately. Our gym teacher Mr. Scanlon, a former Home Depot manager, let us take free shots at the hoops the entire period while he sat on the bleachers, reading a manual and stroking his perma-crewcut. This is something he usually does when we have a health module coming up and he needs to figure out how to teach it.

After class, I changed out of my gym clothes before going to Honors English. I hadn't even broken a sweat.

"Put everything away under your desks," Mrs. Humbolt said as the bell rang and Honors English began. All 25 students groaned airlessly like ghosts. This could only mean one thing.

Mrs. Humbolt is old, in her mid-40s, but trim, probably as a result of practicing yoga, something she likes to mention with some frequency. Apparently, it's a great way to de-stress.

"Don't worry," Mrs. Humbolt said as she passed out lined pages to the first person in each row to pass back. "This isn't a test. It's a written exercise in rhetoric."

There was a collective sigh of relief.

"But it will count toward your grade."

Our guards went immediately back up.

"Today, we're going to write extemporaneously about relationships. Human relationships," she continued. Mrs. Humbolt was fond of giving us broad topics that were open to interpretation.

As I glanced up from my desk, I saw Christina Tau, who sat four rows ahead of me, eyeing me warily before turning away. Aha. That was a tell. She must've flunked the biology quiz.

"Everything is contextual," Mrs. Humbolt added as we got to work. "You have the entire period. Let's see what you come up with."

I decided to write about how the Nationalists lost the Chinese Civil War to the Communists by mistreating the general population and even their own soldiers. This is something I knew about from having watched a multipart documentary on the subject on my iPhone one sleepless night.

Mrs. Humbolt didn't really care what you were arguing as long as you could provide logical, supporting statements. About halfway through the period, though, I found myself caring more about my topic. I was frustrated with Chiang Kai-shek. Not because I necessarily sided with him but because he didn't have honest and competent leaders in the field. How could he have given Mao a fair fight?

I know how Chinese people think. Your reputation precedes you everywhere, as far as 10,000 li in every direction. If people hear you're crooked and, worse, that you're losing battles, they'll switch to the other side without knowing anything else about you.

The ringing of the bell was met with a number of

anguished sighs. Mrs. Humbolt walked down the rows and snatched papers away.

"One thing you're going to have to learn is when and how to finish," she said to the class.

I handed her my paper and joyfully collected my things. That paper felt like an A.

Christina Tau was still looking at me as I left the room. She must've really eaten shit on that quiz.

I trashed someone else's argument in dialectics, my last class, to end a day of victories, and boarded the bus home on a high. At my stop, our ageless Civic was already waiting there with the engine running.

My mother, who is in her late 40s, sat at the wheel, stoically looking out the front window. She reserves nearly all her smiles for customers. I hopped into the car.

"How was school?" she asked with a lilt that implied she was expecting bad news. She's always looking for hints of an imminent catastrophe.

"I got a hundred on a biology quiz," I said, offering up some red meat to her sensibilities. My mother was satisfied to hear this succinct evaluation of the school day.

"Good, good," she said distractedly as we pulled away from the curb. Her mind was now set on getting her youngest employee—me—to Tung's Garden for another night of work.

Many Shark Beach households seem to designate Thursday as delivery night, and for the most part everyone wants their food between 6:30 p.m. and 7:30

p.m. Friday and Saturday nights, kids and parents have their own plans, and meals are more casual and not as time-dependent. Orders come in from 6 p.m. through 10 p.m., steady but spread out. Most customers who dine in come for the buffet.

My mother and I are half of the restaurant's regular cast members. The other two are my father and Auntie Zhang.

Almost six feet tall, and a little on the heavy side, my father has a pudgy, boyish face that assures customers that the food is good. Dad keeps his hair in place with water, and it curls at the gray ends when dry. My mother and father take turns playing host and serving tables for the non-buffet special orders.

Auntie Zhang, who's at least several years older than my parents, cooks nearly everything single-handedly. She lives above the restaurant and has been around for as long as I can remember. The title is an honorific, as she isn't truly a relative, though I think I once heard that her grandmother had been a good friend of my great-grandmother's. Something like that.

I have many little jobs at Tung's Garden. I clean and chop every vegetable. I haul trash out to the dumpster, too. Whatever I do, I tend to throw myself into wholeheartedly. If there's one thing I've learned from being at the restaurant, it's that working hard makes time pass more quickly than trying to do as little as possible.

During the brief lulls, I do my homework at the employees' table in the dining room. It's the one that has two chairs with duct-taped upholstery.

I was finishing up my Algebra 2/Trig homework when

I heard my father lock the front door to customers. Now all that was left to do was to clean up the dining room and kitchen and head home.

CHAPTER TWO

The next morning was Friday. I woke up at 6 as usual and walked out of the house 20 minutes later eating a white-bread sandwich of cold stir-fried beef from the restaurant. I finished an apple and chucked the core down a storm drain.

As I got closer to the bus stop, I slipped on my primary defensive weapon, my headphones. Avoiding human interaction is my primary goal each morning, so I focused on reading through my RSS feeds, which were set for the latest news about Harmony Health, cancer, and Ivy League admissions.

Four kids who live in the nearby new developments were already at the stop. Fred and Grace. Percy and Jean. The four stooges.

Different kids are always showing up at the bus stop depending on the year and the weather, but it was these two Chinese American couples that I had to watch out for.

Jean Chu in particular. Jean was a relatively recent arrival, having moved here from L.A., and she always seemed unhappy despite being conventionally pretty and coming from a rich family. Not that those things are reasons alone to be happy. Plus, as nice as the golf courses and shopping are in this super-Chinese corner of the Garden State, we don't have a Hollywood sign or a Walk of Fame. The only filming we have around town are security cameras.

Maybe Jean was mortified at having to ride the bus at all. Being only 15, she was old enough to crave the status of driving to school but too young for a license. The only problem was that her boyfriend Percy crashed his Audi shortly after getting his license last fall. The two of them had been gone from our stop for a total of only about two weeks before his parents decided to punish him by making him, and consequently Jean, take the bus again.

Fred Zhao, whose pool party I had once gone to, also has a car—a Tesla, I've heard—but he keeps failing the road test for a probationary license. Grace, the nicest if least memorable of the bunch, successfully passed her test for a driver's license last summer, but rumor has it that Fred won't allow her to drive to school until he has his license, too. The four friends probably all deserve one another.

This fine spring morning, Percy and Fred were wearing A.P.C. coats in heather and navy, respectively, and Alexander Wang-designed Adidas shoes. They'd both used product to style their hair into Daniel Dae Kim curls. Grace and Jean had pulled their hair back into glistening ponytails and wore Citizens of Humanity jeans and lululemon winter coats in colors that matched those of their mates. They looked like the same team in home and away uniforms.

There was also another kid at the stop, a short white boy who'd moved to Shark Beach before the start of the school year. I didn't know his name, and so much time had passed since he'd arrived that it was now too embarrassing to ask.

The white kid had his face in a paperback that he was reading with fingerless gloves. Percy and Fred were watching a video together and cracking up. Grace was scrolling through something on her phone. Jean gave an evil smile when she saw me approach. It was time for her favorite pastime: taunting me. She pocketed her phone and approached.

"David, what are you wearing?" she asked loudly and performatively for her intended audience of three to hear. I slipped off my earphones and put them around my neck. I'd already learned that the best way to deal with Jean was to give short, simple answers.

"As you can see, Jean, I'm wearing a hoodie and corduroy pants." She crossed her arms.

"I've never seen you wear anything nice, David," she said with disgust.

"I've never heard you say anything nice, Jean." Her boyfriend Percy cracked up at this, but Jean was livid. I had messed up her attempt to mock me. She pointed at Percy.

"What are you laughing about?"

He shrugged. "It was funny."

Jean turned back to me. She sighed and tossed her bleached ponytail, then waved her right hand in a big circle from my head to my knees to indicate that my attire was wholly unacceptable. "You dress like a delivery boy, David. Seriously."

Why did Jean have to be so malicious? Her family is a part of the 1%, which probably only means 10% in Shark Beach.

Then again, Jean was only in the high teens in class rank, probably too far down at this point in the game to have a chance to break into the top tier. Clearly being besties with Christina Tau hadn't rubbed off enough on her, grade-wise. Maybe that added to her life's frustrations.

"How'd you do on that bio quiz, Jean?" I asked. Her eyes flashed.

"I did just great, David," she said. "How about I quiz you about why you don't have a life? Do you even know anything about girls?"

"I know that girls like you love riding buses to school."

Percy laughed again. Jean gave him the look of death. "What?" he asked her.

Jean turned back to me and spat, "Thanks for taking a shower today, David." Her three friends offered some scant laughs. Somewhat satisfied, she walked over to convene with Grace.

Jean's barbs were always pretty weak. What burned me up was not so much what she said as the way she was always trying to elicit raucous laughter or at least silent acquiescence from her crew at my expense.

On the plus side, this early morning engagement with Jean was generally the only openly annoying treatment I encountered during the course of the school day. Once over, I could essentially go back into academic attack mode.

I looked down the street in vain. Where was that damned school bus already?

You'd think that someone in my situation would have figured out by now some way to spend as little time at the bus stop as possible, since the bus is always at least five minutes late anyway. But of course, the one time I strolled up a little tardy, a schedule-abiding substitute driver had been on duty, and everyone at the stop was already long gone by the time I'd arrived. My mom had to drive me to school that day, and it was the worst ride ever.

I was relieved when I finally saw a yellow reflector twinkle down the road as the bus pulled in for the stop before ours. The two couples moved down to where the doors would open so they could get on first. They always had to be first.

Upon entering Shark Beach High, I managed to beat Fred and two other sophomores on my bus to the bulletin board outside of Mr. Wald's office. My prowess at running still served me. They caught up later, and we crowded together, all eyes on the blank line next to Harmony Health. I knew my grades were better than theirs, but how was my essay? More of my classmates began gathering in front of the board. As I looped around them to leave, I almost slipped on a flyer for the

Dames Ball. They were putting up so many notices for the dance, they littered the floor.

Taking out my phone, I headed towards Mr. del Pino's favorite bathroom. He always went there for a morning piss at 6:55, 10 minutes before the homeroom bell. When I saw Mr. del Pino coming, I walked toward him, waving a greeting with my left hand. With my right hand, I shot pictures of his feet in burst mode. Sure, we'd just had a quiz yesterday, but it's never a good idea to be complacent. He's worn mismatched socks two days in a row before, and he also happened to give us two quizzes in a row.

I reviewed my pictures as I continued down the hall. No quiz today.

When I got to homeroom, I saw that Percy from the bus stop was sitting backwards in my seat, talking to a boy who was a near-mirror image to him. Percy and Percy II were laughing about something.

"Percy, I need my seat," I said.

"Just chill out for a minute, doggy," Percy said to the floor. I said nothing and put my books on my desk. He let out an exaggerated sigh and stood up. His friend brought out something in a bag from under the desk, but Percy held up his hand as if to say, "Hold on to it." I heard a clank against the tube-steel chair leg and knew it was a flask.

Percy dismounted from my desk and popped a piece of gum in his mouth. He then cracked his knuckles before shoving off. I wondered if the gesture was meant as a warning to not tell about the booze.

I dropped into my seat, and Percy II tapped my shoulder.

"Want a swig?" he whispered. I was surprised by this random act of intentional kindness.

"Naw, I'm all right," I said. Percy II's eyes narrowed as the good vibes melted away. I wasn't to be trusted because I wouldn't partake in the spoils.

"Keep your mouth shut about this, little Davy," he said, kicking the bottom of my chair for emphasis.

Drinking and partying means the same thing for most kids at Shark Beach High, and there's always at least one party a month, usually after a major test. After all, everybody needs a safety valve. Alcohol in homeroom was new to me, but not surprising. Unlike smoking and vaping, drinking was considered socially acceptable to Shark Beach teens.

Percy II made a big show of throwing Listerine strips in his mouth. But he must've reconsidered his earlier behavior because a moment later he leaned in and whispered to me, "Seriously, Dave, please don't tell." I nodded.

The guy had nothing to worry about. Even if I decided to tell on him, it's not as if any of the teachers would believe me. They were all middle-aged white people who thought for the most part that every one of us was smart and that we all got along. I was often told to work with "your friend X" on a group exercise when X was nothing near a friend and either ignored me or impeded my learning the entire period. Some teachers, in an effort to keep our Asian names and us straight, clung to their seating charts throughout the entire year.

I flipped open my MCAT study book and tried hard to understand. Percy, the original, was sitting in the front talking to a girl who couldn't stop playing with her hair. I opened a spiral notebook and began to copy a random question, its answer, and the explanation of its answer. Doing this word-for-word was my force-fed method of study. It was a good way to get something into my subconscious by bypassing my uncomprehending but conscious mind, which would otherwise keep that information out.

The only time I got distracted from my work was when I got a text from Yaro that read, "A man jumps off the roof of a building. As he is falling, he hears a phone ring, and he dies before he hits the ground."

Yaro takes 20 Questions seriously enough to punctuate texts correctly. I wasn't able to solve this one, but I did determine that the man had died of a heart attack brought on by a surprise that was both good and bad.

As soon as I walked into biology class, I saw an overhead projector on a wheeled cart next to my desk. Mr. del Pino hated computers and technology in general, and refused to use the Bluetooth projection system mounted on the ceiling.

I put away my notebook; Mr. del Pino allows us to take pictures of these presentations.

He killed the lights and was about to lay down the first page of the presentation when he said, "Whoops!" He'd slipped the incorrect paper into the lower tray of the cart. I could just make it out by the light of the projector lamp.

It was a list of students applying to the Harmony Health internship. Mr. del Pino had written an "N" next to most of the names that I could see. Maybe he wasn't planning on writing recommendation letters for them?

I had a "Y" next to my name. The only other "Y" was next to the name Christina Tau.

As soon as I entered Algebra 2/Trig, I saw a folded crane on my desk. That meant it was my turn at the front of class. Miss Muntz, who hated the sound of "Ms. Muntz," ran her class unconventionally. Her modus operandi was to stand one kid at the dry-erase board to figure out problems throughout the whole period while she monitored the rest of the class, ready to pounce on anyone not paying attention.

I think she uses this technique as a defensive tactic. By teaching in this way, she never has to turn her back to the class. Or maybe it's actually just a strategy to get us to study harder so that we won't look stupid on our day at the board. Whatever the case may be, there's no denying that it's morbidly fascinating to watch that one student at the front of the room, struggling to learn in real time.

As a consolation, however, Miss Muntz's daily victim always gets a candy bar at the end of the period along with kind words of praise.

That day, I was the chosen one. Good. Now I'd be able to forget about the internship and my continuing rivalry with Christina for one period at least. I just needed to concentrate on not choking in front of everyone. I handed the crane to Miss Muntz and said, "Let's go."

"That's the spirit, David," she said.

Miss Muntz has a gold-plated throat, one that could sing an oldies song from the 90s and make you like it. Her face generally has the focus of a runner about to bust out of the blocks, and her hair is impossibly black, Asian black, even. So much so that I've heard girls whispering that it must be a wig. Us boys never really think about such things. We're all mostly just inclined to be wary in the presence of a powerful woman with disarming eccentricities. Everyone respects her teaching, though. We hadn't realized how much she'd taught us until we took her tests.

I picked up the blue marker. Its felt tip was still in decent shape because everyone else always chose the black marker. I popped off the cap and wrote my name and the date at the top of the board.

At the beginning of the year, we had all been scared shitless to stand in front of the class. We mostly learned to get over it, though. Still, nothing would be more satisfying to me than figuring out a problem before anyone else.

Once everyone was seated, Miss Muntz paced the back of the room. "How many people want to see David crash and burn today?" she asked. Nobody overtly confirmed the sentiment, but I heard snickers. Miss Muntz was known for voicing unspoken thoughts with little regard for whom it might possibly embarrass. This was outrageous behavior according to Chinese culture, which values subtlety and silence. As a result, Miss

Muntz had something of a reputation of being crazy, especially to the newer arrivals. But no one complained about the performance of her students, current and former, on standardized tests and AP exams.

I never took her remarks personally. For one thing, I knew Miss Muntz was only reaching for comedic effect. For another, I was smarter than most of the other kids in my section of Algebra 2/Trig. I stretched my arms and reminded myself to draw large graphs and write big numbers. There was a tendency, especially amongst the boys, to draw insecurely small shapes on the board.

"Are you ready, David?" asked Miss Muntz, her tight mouth slightly off-center.

I cracked my shoulders and nodded.

First off, I bisected a scalene triangle into two right triangles and calculated the area of each. On the second problem, Nancy Lin raised her hand to challenge me, but Miss Muntz confirmed that I had the right answer.

I crossed my arms and smiled hard at Nancy.

"Don't gloat, David," chided Miss Muntz.

"I have the right to," I said. "I'm out on a limb here in front of the class."

"Look out for the marker. You're staining your shirt."

The top of my marker had jabbed into my left elbow, and its blue ink was seeping through my off-white shirt. The class laughed, Nancy the loudest.

"Looks like you 'blue' it, David," said Miss Muntz, winding the class up again. She tapped her book. "Now for the next problem."

At the end of class, Miss Muntz told me that I had done

well, and I duly followed her to the file cabinet for my treat. She unlocked the top drawer, jerked it open, then slapped the side in frustration.

"Sweet sugar shapes, I forgot to restock," she said. "David, come to the faculty lounge before lunch, and I'll get you something from the machine."

"It's all right, Miss Muntz," I said as the bell rang. "It doesn't matter."

"No, I insist." She shoved the drawer shut and locked the file cabinet with flair. "We have to hold to our traditions," she said. "Otherwise time wins." Of all the problems she'd thrown at me, this was the only head scratcher.

Mr. Cohen, my World History teacher, looks like a balding Abraham Lincoln minus a stovepipe hat

He believes that studying history requires a sympathetic eye and to have empathy for people who fully believed they were Doing the Right Thing.

In fact, Mr. Cohen once showed us a few edited scenes from the movie *Do the Right Thing* in class and then encouraged us to watch the rest on our own. According to him, it was a modern retelling of the story of America. I'm sure most people didn't bother. I certainly didn't. It didn't count toward extra credit, and I'm never in the mood to watch old movies, anyway.

As we walked into class, Mr. Cohen was sitting at his desk, engrossed in a book. On the board he had written, "Take one chip and sit down." Plastic blue and red poker chips were piled in equal amounts on the shoulder of the whiteboard.

Each of us did as we were told. By the time the bell rang, both piles were nearly gone. We looked around tentatively to see who we would potentially be teamed with, if that's what the chip colors were about.

Mr. Cohen stood up and tapped his desktop.

"Everyone with a blue chip, raise your hand." I raised my hands along with my teammates. "You guys, you're the so-called democracies. Everyone else, you're the so-called Communists.

"You'll notice that I say 'so-called.' Why do I say 'so-called'? Hey, Mr. Wu, why do I say 'so-called'?"

Charlie Wu shifted in his seat and answered carefully. "Because there are no democracies or Communist nations that truly live up to their respective ideals."

"Yes, very good, Mr. Wu. Actually, that's a bit too academic." That was how Mr. Cohen disparaged answers, even though he was himself a teacher and thus an academic. He paced the front desks, inspecting the troops. "Now, Miss Meng. Can I call you 'Miss' or is it 'Ms.'? I know you can't be 'Mrs. Meng,' yet."

He seemed to be flirting with Amy Meng.

"'Ms.' is fine," she said.

"Ms. Meng, please tell me how Communism is different in China and North Korea."

"People in China are allowed to own private property and essentially enjoy a free market."

"I don't like how you use the word 'enjoy.' You're showing a bias there. You can't 'enjoy' a free market when you work a backbreaking, dead-end job, now can you? I think we should say that Chinese people have access to a free market. Okay?"

Amy nodded and fiddled with her red chip. Mr. Cohen returned the nod, covering for a tit-ward glance, and walked to the back of the room. Some people turned to follow his progress.

"Now, ah, Mr. David Tung."

"Yes," I said. He liked to use my full name.

"Please tell me how democracy is different in Canada and the U.S."

"We directly elect our President, while the Canadians appoint one."

"That's a legacy of what sort of government?"

"A monarchy."

"So is Canada a democracy?"

"Overall, it is, although the country also incorporates a number of socialist conventions, such as its nationalized health system." Still, Mr. Cohen wasn't satisfied.

"Which country is more democratic, the U.S. or Canada?"

Mr. Cohen was killing me with these follow-up questions.

"It's debatable because issues vary depending on one's age and class."

"Not to mention sexual orientation and physical ableness. Canada legalized same-sex marriage in what year?" We all looked at him, dumb as cows. He met our mute faces and said, "C'mon, people!"

"Two-thousand and five!" declared Gina Yip. "That's when Canada legalized gay marriage." She brandished her phone without shame. The only thing Mr. Cohen disliked more than being interrupted is kids checking their phone during class for any reason. He punished people by giving them active roles in the class discussions.

"Ms. Yip," he said, "get up and go stand at the board. You're going to judge who wins the arguments."

She headed to the front of the room and flattened her skirt.

"That's not fair!" objected Ryan Chu. "She's from a Communist country! She's biased!"

"Hong Kong isn't Communist," said Gina.

"It's a part of China! Mr. Cohen, you should be the judge!"

"Oh, no, not me. It's all Gina. And if she feels that there's a particular student who isn't participating enough, she can call on them to make the next argument. Got that, Gina?"

"Yes, Mr. Cohen!"

Needless to say, she called on Ryan mercilessly.

After World History, I chucked my books into my locker and headed to the cafeteria for lunch. After taking a few steps, I remembered that I'd promised to go claim my candy bar from Miss Muntz.

I approached the door to the faculty lounge with caution. The metal handle felt heavy, forbidden, as if it were the gateway to Adultland with all its problems.

In Chinese school, we are always being told that teachers such as Confucius are to be revered. There's no higher calling than obtaining knowledge, and those who help you learn can never be adequately thanked.

From what I can tell, the teachers at Shark Beach High are doing a good job. Our SAT scores regularly trounce those of the two puny private schools in Shark Beach.

On the other hand, it's well-known that our teachers aren't paid so great. I mean, relative to others in the profession, sure, the town takes care of them. They don't seem to have a problem with meeting their mortgages or car payments. But only a few years ago, before I was in high school, our teachers went on strike for better wages.

Since almost all of them live outside of Shark Beach, I have no idea what sort of houses they have, but their modest cars can't compete with the students' Beemers and Benzes, many of which are armed with thumping audio systems. The joke going around is that teachers always have the right of way in the parking lot because they're less worried about damaging their cars. Their sensible Hondas wouldn't look any worse for the wear with a few more scrapes.

Every once in a while, I see a few of the teachers at Tung Garden's weekend buffets. Mr. Cohen and his wife are semi-regulars. My mother always insists on giving them 10% off. And this one time, Miss Muntz came in on an awkward date. I stayed in the kitchen for as long as I could, but she smiled and waved at me as she was leaving.

I tend to see more teachers at our restaurant during the summer when we are all liberated from the rigors of the school day.

Many of the teachers hold down seasonal temp jobs to supplement their incomes. Mr. del Pino is a rent-a-cop who helps keep the peace at nearby Cheesequake Park, which always has problems with people drinking and littering. One summer, Mr. del Pino tried to break up a fight, and all three men had to go to the hospital for stitches. The incident made local headlines.

My French teacher, Ms. Fullilove, has a real-estate side gig. She has video ads on the *Shark Beach Gazette* site that can't be skipped. Anyone checking out the local police report or classifieds is forced to encounter Ms. Fullilove's smiling face, all caked over and rounded, as she talks up her real-estate credentials. She actually says a decent "xie xie" at the end, a pander to prospective Mandarin-speaking clients.

I continued to hesitate just outside the door to the faculty lounge. I couldn't just barge in there—the sign read "Faculty ONLY." That seemed pretty unequivocal, and I'm not one to disobey an official sign so readily.

On the other hand, if a teacher tells you to come to the faculty lounge, that's where you go. I'm a practical guy. I planned to hit up Miss Muntz for a college rec, and she might hesitate if I didn't show up at the appointed place on time.

"Son, you have to pull down the handle," said Mr. Lyons, who'd come up behind me. He was the AP Physics teacher. Although he wore button-down shirts and ties, he apparently didn't wear an undershirt. A patch of sweat had rendered a part of his white dress shirt semi-transparent, and I could see the hair on his chest.

"I've got this," I said, cranking the door open.

"Of course, you must have a good reason for entering our private space," he continued.

"Miss Muntz told me to come," I said stupidly.

"Oh, that nutty dame," he said as he pushed the door open all the way and motioned for me to enter first.

I walked in. The place looked like the break room in "The Office" but not as brightly lit. It was odd seeing teachers sitting together in little clumps just like students. They must have their own cliques, too. Ms. Fullilove and Mr. Cohen were playing a board game on an iPad. Miss Muntz had the attention of two fat and ugly men. Mr. del Pino was fiddling with the coffee machine.

"I'm going to show you guys the answers this shithead put down on his quiz!" Mr. del Pino said as he punched a button and turned around to better address the room. His smile melted and dripped off his face when he saw me standing there, the only non-white person in the lounge. He cleared his throat and pointed at the door. "You shouldn't be here, David."

Miss Muntz stood up, and one of the gross guys she'd been chatting with leaned to one side and stared directly at her ass.

"David, I'm glad you made it," she said. I went over and she patted my shoulder.

The slob who wasn't ogling her said, "Hey, that's inappropriate physical contact, Janet." Only his partner laughed.

Miss Muntz grabbed her purse and steered me to the snack machine.

"Pick anything you want, except for the dental floss. Well, you can get the floss, too, if you really want it." She unsnapped her wallet and poked around.

I looked over the offerings. It was almost all nervous snacks and candy for frazzled faculty. Except for that dental floss. Well, nothing's more annoying than getting stuff stuck in your teeth, especially if you're trying to command respect in a classroom. A bright fluorescent-lit glare wiped out the reflection of our faces in the vending machine's glass.

"What's your favorite?" I asked her.

"Payday," she said.

"What about Mounds?" asked one of the slobs, the other one cupping his breasts and chuckling. God, what was their problem? It didn't even make sense because Miss Muntz didn't have big tits.

"I've never had a Payday before, so I'll take that," I said.

"A man after my own heart," she said sadly as she fed in four quarters.

"Better save those for the laundry! Unless the kid can wash your clothes for you!"

I turned to the two slobs—I wasn't sure which had just spoken—and said, "We don't have a laundry. We have a restaurant." It came out harder than I had intended.

"Whoa, calm down, kid!" said the fatter one. "We're just having our funny time. What happens in the lounge stays in the lounge!"

"David's family runs a wonderful restaurant," Miss Muntz declared to the room.

She touched me with some affection on my shoulder blade. "David, don't pay any attention to them," she said quietly. "If the union weren't so strong, those two would have been fired long ago."

I looked at her face, seeing for the first time a person and not just someone I needed to get an A from.

"Thank you," I said as I held up the candy bar.

"You're most welcome."

Now that I'd completed the task that I had been summoned for, it felt strange being there. I didn't like the way the teachers were looking at me. I was a threat. I could post embarrassing pictures of them or write about the unflattering things I heard.

Clutching my candy bar, I left.

Benson Gong sat with me again at lunch. I offered him the Payday bar, and he took it.

When I went to my locker to swap books, I was surprised to see Christina Tau standing there. I figured that she was waiting for Scott, so I nodded at her and turned to my locker.

"Hey David," she said, "I want to ask you something."

I turned to her and leaned against my closed locker door. Christina was wearing a dark blue blouse and a matching skirt. Her eyes widened.

"Sure," I said.

"Will you go with me to the Dames Ball?"

What? What did she just say? I heard words but I couldn't process what they meant. So I tried to sound out each one to myself. Will. You. Go. With. Me.

What was she saying? Will? Who's Will? Go? Where is he going?

The world was tilting. I crouched slightly and leaned more of my body weight against my locker. It was either that or slide to the ground.

"What?" I managed to croak out loud, my throat suddenly parched. She shook her head and smiled in exasperation.

"David, will you go with me to the Dames Ball?" Christina was more insistent this time. I could feel her perfume filling my nasal cavity as waves of blood rushing through my head crashed in my ears. I saw her in a double-image, two faces of Christina anxiously anticipating something.

Whoa! She was asking me out! To a dance! To *that* dance!

Even as her smile widened, Christina looked worried. She wanted to hear me say something!

"Yeah, sure," I heard myself say.

She squealed, and her dangling earrings shivered.

"Oh, David, you actually had me a little nervous," Christina said. "My friend Jean said I shouldn't ask you." Oh right. She was besties with my bus-stop nemesis.

"Why?" I asked, though knowing Jean, I could well imagine all the trash she'd talked about me.

"She said you were a little weird, whatever that means, and that you probably weren't allowed to go on dates, anyway."

I totally wasn't allowed to go on dates.

"That's silly," I said. Christina smiled conspiratorially as she handed me her phone after pulling up an entry for new contacts. My left hand shook, but I made sure to type my number in correctly. I handed back her phone and gave a little gasp. I had forgotten to breathe for a moment.

"What's wrong, David?" she asked.

My mother's going to kill me, I thought. Shit, why

did I say, 'Yes'?

"Oh, nothing," I said. "I mean, I can't believe you're asking me! You could have asked anyone to go with you!" The words flew out of my mouth. If I'd been thinking clearly, I'd have said something like, "Christina, there's no way I can go to this dance with you, but thank you so much for asking me."

"I'm so glad I asked you," said Christina. "We'll talk later." She brushed against me slightly as she left. I turned to watch her and felt my phone jump. She had sent me a kiss emoji. Christina turned back to register my reaction. I smiled awkwardly, trying to show her every tooth I had.

I was dead. Yet my heart was pounding harder than ever.

The first time my mother told me to stay away from girls was around the same time she told me to stay away from electrical outlets. By seventh grade, when some kids were starting to couple up, I already knew that that was one rite of passage denied to me.

Now, even I know that a school dance isn't the same thing as a serious one-on-one date. Really, attending the Dames Ball probably just meant hanging out in small groups of people with theoretical sets of partners.

Still, I couldn't be certain that my mother wouldn't view the dance as equivalent to conceiving a child. "That's how it starts!" I could imagine her yelling.

I'd known for a long time that I couldn't ask out any girls, that I had to keep my hands in my pockets so to speak.

What I'd never even imagined was that a girl might ask me out.

Not that this kind of fine distinction would matter to my mom. She'd probably say that I must have done something to make Christina ask me.

I knew this because about a year before, my mother had gone batshit insane when my classmate Sharon Chung had come to Tung's Garden with her extended family on a Sunday. They had all gone to some wedding where the food wasn't so great, so they'd come to our buffet afterwards to eat up. I certainly didn't know they were coming.

Everyone was formally dressed, especially Sharon, who was wearing a somewhat low-cut dress. We saw each other briefly in the dining room, and we said casual hellos without any of our body parts touching. Then I went into the kitchen.

My mother followed me in and declared that Sharon was my secret girlfriend. I started to laugh, but she wasn't joking. She growled that I had no business "carrying on" with that girl in public and that I had brought shame upon my whole family. My father happened to come in just then, and she had some sharp Mandarin words for him as well. He was just as befuddled as me. Auntie Zhang worked away as if she hadn't heard a thing.

I shivered at the memory, bringing myself partially back to my surroundings.

Other people were walking by, oblivious to the fact that I was slipping into shock. I certainly had all the symptoms. I was sweaty, light-headed, and my blood was carrying an electric current.

Christina Tau. Former rival. Current lover.

Aw, she hadn't fallen in love with me. Maybe she could, though.

I almost allowed myself to be carried away by such thoughts until I realized that I lived at home and that my mother was always within screaming distance. She could really make my life hell. My only hope was to hide everything related to Christina and the dance from my mom.

Somehow, my legs carried me into Honors Dialectics, my last class of the day. I eased into my seat feeling sick.

Oh, Christina, what have you done?

Mr. Norton is a middle-aged white dude with salt-and-pepper hair and a handlebar mustache. Some teachers spring pop quizzes. Mr. Norton springs pop debates, appraising us based on how much we talk, which makes up 20% of our final grade. Those students who exist in the "quiet Asian kid mode" carefully cultivated by their parents soon find themselves with a string of zeroes in class participation.

Unfortunately, as the latest discussion got underway, I was completely unable to concentrate.

"David," Mr. Norton called out. "David Tung, don't you have any objection to Carrie Pang's assertion?"

"Assertion that what?" I asked. The class laughed at me. I was lost. I would have laughed at me. Mr. Norton shook his head and called on someone else. The argument continued. I focused on what other people were saying and tried to get back in the game. States' rights versus federal rights. OK, got it. I raised my hand.

"Yes, David?"

"Asserting states' rights has been used in the past to undermine civil liberties guaranteed by Constitutional amendments," I declared. Mr. Norton rolled his eyes.

"Oh, you mean just like we said in the opening contention?" Students erupted into laughter again. I was on track for a belly flop, and this was usually one of my best classes.

When class was over, Mr. Norton took me aside.

"David, you deserve a zero today."

"I know," I said. "The truth is...I don't feel very well." He looked at me askance.

"You do look a little pale."

"I feel all clammy," I said. It was true. "I would have gone home, but Honors Dialectics is my favorite class."

Mr. Norton sighed. He wasn't prone to flattery, but he knew I was usually one of his most enthusiastic, on-point students. He put the tip of his index finger on my shoulder and said, "Feel better soon, David."

I did indeed feel slightly better, knowing that I had dodged a goose egg.

I had a sudden thought. Maybe asking me to the dance was Christina's effort to sabotage me academically! Could she be that diabolical?

I trudged aboard the school bus and rested my head against the cool window. Replaying the scene at my locker a few times in my mind, I knew that Christina had been sincere. She hadn't been trying to harm me. If she were, she wouldn't have been afraid that I'd say no.

"David? What's wrong?" I turned to see Jean Chu. Usually, she was too consumed with new grievances by the end of the school day to bother with me on the way home. But not today. "Aren't you happy that Christina asked you to the Dames Ball? She ignored my sage advice and her better judgment to do so. But what's done is done." Jean sighed and walked to the back of the bus with exaggerated disappointment, her ponytail bobbing with each step.

Sharing any kind of space with Jean was always a chore. It suddenly occurred to me that I'd probably have to hang with her at the dance; that is, once I managed to get there.

The bus drove out of the parking lot and picked up speed. The sound of the laboring engine kicked my thinking into gear. Maybe I could go to the dance and get back without my mother noticing. The Dames Ball was still three weeks away, the first Saturday night of April. Saturdays were pretty big nights for our restaurant, but I could say I was sick and go home. A sore throat or runny nose never shielded me from work, so it would have to be something bad. Maybe something involving pretend vomit.

Since both my parents would be more tied up at the restaurant than usual without my help, they'd be too busy to check up on me. Though Tung's Garden closed to customers every night at 10, we usually never got out of the place until 11 at the earliest. I could sneak out of the house, bike to the school, meet Christina for the dance, and be back home way before my parents returned.

By the time the bus arrived at my stop, I already had a decent outline for Operation Christina plotted.

As I walked down the bus aisle, I sniffed my shirt. No trace of Christina's perfume. Good. I left the bus and hopped into our car with studied nonchalance.

"How was school?" asked my mother.

"No tests today," I said.

My mom didn't seem to notice, but I had to cross my arms and legs to hold still for the 15-minute ride to Tung's Garden.

Luckily, it was a Friday night, hectic as ever. As a result, I was too busy to worry about Christina for most of the evening.

First up was washing an aluminum tray for the buffet table. This had to be cleaned by hand whenever the washer was filled with dishes. I put a little too much muscle into the task, though, and hot water sloshed on my shoes. After I finished cleaning the tray, I put it on the drying rack and wrung out my socks in the utility sink on the floor next to the back door.

I sat on a stool, pulling on my damp socks. Don't you know this is how I live, Christina? How my family lives? This is me every day.

Christina still had ski lift tags on the zipper of her winter jacket from a Christmas trip to the Alps. I'd never even been on a plane, never mind a vacation. Me sneaking out for the dance would be my first night off from Tung's Garden since my last winter track meet. The sheer incongruity of the whole situation caused me to redouble my efforts at blocking out all non-academic thoughts.

By the end of the night, my still-damp socks had pickled my feet, but I'd also managed to make a huge dent in my weekend homework during breaks. My parents and I said good night to Auntie Zhang and drove back to our modest house on our unexceptional block. I went upstairs to my bedroom.

After I washed up and lay in bed, I emerged from work mode. I couldn't get Christina's face out of my head. The last thing I remember thinking before falling asleep was me promising her that I was going to make this happen.

Not that I actually knew *how* to dance, but that was the least of my worries.

CHAPTER THREE

Saturday mornings always begin early for me and my family. By 6:30, Mom, Dad, and I are back in the car, and by 6:47 we're usually at the restaurant with Auntie Zhang, who whips up eggs and scallion pancakes for our breakfast.

After eating and thoroughly scrubbing our hands, all four of us sat at the employees' table, trimming piles of vegetables with small knives. We tossed stems into a bowl in the center. Our task was tedious and repetitive, but we were skilled enough to do it quickly without cutting our fingers.

"I heard New Pavilion is doing good," my mother declared. Thinking about the competition helped my mother to psych herself up for the day.

New Pavilion is a Chinese restaurant in New Tappen, a few towns north of Shark Beach. In my mother's mind, it's a rival to Tung's Garden, although our delivery zones don't even overlap. She's always a little paranoid that any Asian customers she doesn't personally know are spies for New Pavilion.

"Umm," said my father. In general, he tries to say as little as possible. Even a simple, innocuous reply can always be misconstrued as a challenge to one of my mother's judgments, resulting in a tongue-lashing.

This time, my mother chose to seize upon even this noncommittal grunt. "That's all you have to say about it?" she snapped.

Oh, man, it was too early for this. I'd already turned off my ancient phone. If my mother saw that someone labeled "Christina" was trying to text me, she'd probably cut my head off like she was trimming a vegetable stem.

The image made me laugh hard once before I could catch myself and clamp my mouth shut. Too late. My mother seized upon what she believed to be my flippant reaction to her New Pavilion worries.

"New Pavilion is about to put us out of business, and you're laughing, David?" she said, enraged. Now, I know from experience that any attempt to talk my way out of a confrontation will just make her madder, so I decided to tackle the matter at hand. Hey, it beat telling her about Christina and the dance.

"How are they going to put us out of business, Mom? They're so far away."

"They could open another location in Shark Beach," she said. "When banks see how well New Pavilion is doing, they'll want to loan them money and convince them to expand!" She glared at me, annoyed that I couldn't see what was obvious to her.

Auntie Zhang jumped in to defuse the situation by mentioning in Mandarin the latest twist in a Chinese soap opera. This was a stroke of tactical brilliance. Or kindness. Or both.

"The father is so handsome!" Mom said joyfully. "The son, too! The niece is so pretty!"

I glanced at the clock. Still just 7:15. In about an hour, I'd be out of my mother's range on the 8:19 New Jersey Transit train to Manhattan's Chinatown with my dad. That was our Saturday routine. We would ride together into the city, him to buy supplies for the restaurant, and me to attend Chinese school.

At 8:00, I washed off the shreds of vegetation from my hands, making sure to get all the green out from under my fingernails and trying not to look too cheerful.

I know that for a lot of people, Chinese school is nothing a big pain in the ass, but for me, a kid with no recreational outlets, it's practically the only fun I get to have in any given week.

My father and I left the restaurant for the 10-minute walk through two blocks of closed storefronts. We shielded our faces because the morning sunlight was right at eye-level. Dad yawned without covering his mouth and white breath spouted out of him like a geyser. He was already priming himself for his customary nap on the way in.

There weren't many other people at the train platform. There never are. It was still early, and most people who head into the city from Shark Beach for dim sum tend to drive in so they can load up the car with groceries for the trip home.

Christina wasn't there, naturally. Not that she would be. But I've found that just thinking about someone can sometimes conjure them up. One day, when I was in the restaurant, for example, I was thinking about what a jerk Mr. del Pino was for giving a surprise quiz when guess who walks in through the door. Yes, the man himself. Before he could see me, I ducked into the kitchen and hid there until he'd gone.

Remembering that incident made me uneasy. Don't think about Mr. del Pino! Or Christina!

A train rolled in, and we boarded, taking an empty three-seater in the second car. My father slid into the inside seat and immediately slumped against the window and closed his eyes. I sat on the seam between the middle seat and the aisle seat. Sitting right next to him would have made me feel like a kid, and sitting a full seat away would have caused him to open an eyelid and say, "Too embarrassed to sit with your family, huh?"

I regarded my father as a rectangle of sunlight slid across his closed eyelids and open mouth. He liked to point out his prominent brow bone, which he claimed was a sign that he shared blood with Mongolians, the toughest people in the world. The man was proud that he could work all night on his feet and cart out the garbage to the dumpster in the middle of winter without wearing a coat.

As I settled in for the ride, I pulled out my phone to try to do some practice MCAT questions, but my mind kept drifting.

What was Christina doing now? Maybe she was still sleeping. From what I'd heard, her mom was a corporate lawyer and her dad did something at a hedge fund. Their house had been featured in an architecture magazine for its solar-powered HVAC system. Maybe Christina's house was toasty because the heating was free. Maybe she didn't have to wear much. Maybe she was in bed right now wearing only panties.

Realizing that nothing good could come from continuing this line of thought, I forced myself to think of something that could induce mild panic instead: the Harmony Health internship. What if Christina got it instead of me?

Since the internship position reported directly to the renowned Dr. Vivan Lee, I had made a point of doggedly researching as much as I could about her. Thus far, I'd found out that she never updated her Twitter, and she didn't have Insta. This morning was no exception.

I decided to look up her Harmony Health bio page once again to see if they had fixed the typo I had discovered there.

The first line underneath the posed photo of Dr. Lee smiling read: "At an early age, my parents encouraged me to study hard and get good grades." Unless Dr. Lee's parents were "at an early age" when they were encouraging her, the sentence was grammatically wrong. Maybe it would reflect well on me and my application if I took the initiative to write her and point out the mistake. After all, it would prove that she needed me. No, wait a second. Correcting her might piss her off!

I searched the latest reviews for Harmony Health and was rewarded with a new five-star review that mentioned her name. With her "professionalism and resilient empathy," Dr. Lee had given one family hope in the face of tragedy.

What would it be like to have someone like that as a boss? Her "resilient empathy" must be giving her a hell of a time as she tried to reject all those intern applications.

I stared at Dr. Lee's headshot and tried to read into her eyes. Hire me, I muttered to her picture. She looked as though she could be my mother's sister. Come to think of it, maybe Dr. Lee wasn't so nice, after all.

A text window slapped itself over Dr. Lee's face. It was from Christina Tau, and it began with "I've been thinking about you..."

I anxiously opened the full text window.

"I've been thinking about your look," her message read. "Something like these?" She included two links, one for best-dressed men at the Grammys, and one for the Golden Horse Film Awards in Taipei.

The Dames Ball was a fancy dressed-up thing? I hadn't even thought about that, but of course it made sense for Shark Beach. Could I ride a bike in a tux?

"Oh, cool," I wrote back to her. "Will check out."

I immediately went to the Men's Wearhouse site because it was the only place I knew that rented tuxes. Outfits started at $100. I didn't have even that kind of money, and based on the links Christina had sent me, relatively basic outfits probably wouldn't cut it.

My phone service was cut off as we plunged into

the darkness of a tunnel. After a few minutes the train slowed for the final stretch into New York's Penn Station.

As we eased into the platform, my father's eyes sprang open. "David, let's go," he said. It was the first thing he'd said to me the entire trip.

We took an escalator up to the station's below-street-level main floor, and walked east down a long corridor with posters of expensive and unhealthy food choices. Saturated color close-ups of melted cheese, eggs, and glistening meat looked like edible paused porn.

Wait. Why was I having such impure thoughts? Maybe this was how smart kids fell off the path to the Ivy League. They made the fatal mistake of reaching for more personal freedom, and as a consequence their GPAs slipped below 3.5.

I had been so good until now about focusing on grades and school activities that could combine for the strongest possible college application, keeping my nascent libido on serious lockdown all the while. Yet staying busy at school and work could only take my personal development so far.

Didn't John Milton write that reason couldn't develop without choice? If there was no devil, and no way to choose to commit evil instead of good, then our brains and morality were useless. Maybe it was necessary for my moral and ethical development to see what it was like to go out with Christina. Surely, going on dates weren't the evil acts my mother saw them as.

Honestly, if I had been free to date girls, I would never even have thought about asking out Christina.

She was one of the rich and beautiful. My family was just getting by, and I was basically a manual laborer. I wasn't beautiful, either, though I was taller than her, thanks to a two-inch growth spurt the previous year. I was now about five feet nine. Which meant I was almost fully grown. Which meant that I should be allowed to start seeing girls, even if I had to sneak out to do so.

I straightened up as I continued walking with my father.

What I really needed was an advocate, someone my mother's age to reason with her somehow. Tell her, hey, kids his age go on dates. It's not a big deal. That's the way things are done in America. Something like that.

I watched the back of my dad's head as we went up the escalator. I knew he couldn't be my champion. Silence was his defense against my mother. He couldn't even stand up for himself.

He'd been an engineer once, but when the Great Recession hit, he'd been laid off. As a result, my parents had gotten in touch with Auntie Zhang and the three of them had started up Tung's Garden. That was back when I was just a toddler. I'd learned to walk on the rugs of the restaurant dining room.

My father and I rode the D train to Grand Street in Manhattan's Chinatown and climbed out of the narrow, dungeon-like station exit.

We walked west across the Bowery, then split at Elizabeth Street.

"Study hard," he said, like always. As if that's what

you do while you're in Chinese school.

"I will!" I declared. Then he went north and I went south.

CHAPTER FOUR

I walked down Elizabeth and crossed Canal. A double-wide tenement housed my Chinese school. The building itself was a survey of Chinese immigrant history. In the 1800s it had been a retail store. It became a warehouse during World War I, and then a boarding house just after World War II. A fire in the 1950s brought down the tenements in the back, and some enterprising Chinese people had gutted the remaining building and restructured it to take advantage of the cleared space. This newly expanded structure was turned into a multistory sweatshop or garment factory. What you called it depended on whether you were a worker or one of the owners. In the late 1990s, as cheap manufacturing in China took over, the building cleared out and became the new location of the local Chinese school.

The facade of the building still boasted original brick arches over its windows, and the entrance bore a stone mascaron of a creepy face made of leaves.

The flag of the Republic of China, with its white sun over a blue rectangle, fluttered from the roof. To older Chinese people, the display of the de facto flag of Taiwan probably signaled a defiant stand against the People's Republic of China, whose allies now dominated Chinatown politics. To me, it signaled that I was about to step into my Saturday persona as one of the cool kids who didn't worry about grades and was prone to mischief.

My phone buzzed. A text from my friend Chun. "Think fast."

I ducked immediately. His arm went over my head and his shoulder collided with mine. I shoved him into a stone pillar by the gate.

"Dave, you could have killed me!" he cried. Chun shook his left arm to make sure it was still intact. He was wearing his cold-weather outfit of an insulated blue vest over a long-sleeved black sweater.

"Next time, I will!" I said.

He stuck out his chin at me. "Just try, you lousy northerner!"

Chun has a long, smooth nose that ends in wide nostrils that nearly press down on his top lip. His eyelids are heavy, his cheekbones, nonexistent. He has the face of a light-brown cartoon grasshopper. Clean cut and lean, and a little on the shorter side, he likes to comb Japanese wax through his hair to keep it down, giving himself an old-school Chinatown waiter hairstyle.

Raised in Chinatown by a single mother who worked in a restaurant, the ever-restless Chun has probably shoplifted from nearly every Chinatown store and market at one time or another. Needless to say, he has a love/hate relationship with the neighborhood. Chinese school is probably the only thing Chun really likes because it's one of the few Chinatown venues that he's still free to roam. Like me, he's an ABC, only he's Cantonese, the people of the deep south of China and Hong Kong, while I'm a "northerner."

We stepped away from the stream of kids shuffling into the building and did a one-arm bro hug.

"Dave, man, I finally looked up Shark Beach on Wikipedia!" He showed me the page on his phone.

After all these years of Chun teasing me for coming from a "rich" town in Jersey, he had finally put in the least amount of effort necessary to research it.

"What made you look up my town, Chun?"

"I saw an ad for 'Shark Week,' and I thought, that sounds like the name of the place where Dave lives, so I punched it in!" Chun pointed a finger at my left armpit. "You were saying you weren't rich, but that's a lie!"

"My family *isn't* rich, Chun."

"Get outta here!" He held up his phone. "It says people there make $200k a year!" I sighed because most Wikipedia readers don't know the difference between median and average household incomes.

"The median is $200,000," I said. "That means more people earn that much than any other amount. The average is a lot lower."

He waved his hands as if none of that mattered. "Well, there are people in your town who make that much, that's my point. Here's something else, though."

He checked his phone again before continuing. Seriously, he was going to read the entire entry to me? "Your town is only 40% Chinese, but you said most people in your high school were Chinese."

I had to correct him again. "That 40% figure for the general population includes a lot of non-Asian empty nesters. Most people under 30 are Asian. Developers have been knocking down old houses and redeveloping blocks into mini mansions."

Chun pocketed his phone and smirked at me, unbudgeable. Now I knew how his teachers must feel. Anyway, what was the point of arguing with him? In a few minutes, he'd just move on to something else and forget whatever he'd been reading about on his phone.

"So why again do you come to Chinatown instead of going to Chinese school in your richy-rich town? Tell me, Dave."

"Chun, I've been coming to this school for eight years, man, and I've told you lots of times already. My parents don't like the woman who runs the Chinese school in Shark Beach, so they send me here."

He nodded. "They had a big fight or something, right?"

"Yeah, I guess so. But I remember our families used to be friends when I was really small."

"Chinese grudges run deep," he said. "We hold our resentments all the way in our bone marrow. Especially against family members. No bullshit. When you go to a relative's funeral, you'll see a bunch of strangers there. Those are the parts of the family that don't talk to your branch anymore."

I wondered if there could come a day when my mother and I wouldn't talk anymore. Shit, if she busted me for going to the dance with Christina, would she throw me out of the house? Would I have to move in with Auntie Zhang above the restaurant?

"Chun, you're bringing me down, man," I said.

He came in close enough for me to smell the coffee on his breath. "I'm speaking with knowledge. You'll see when you get older."

"I'm already older than you, Chun."

"No you're not!"

"I'm one year older than you. See?" I gave him the finger, and we both laughed.

Chun and I sobered up quickly after we stepped inside the building and nearly knocked over hapless Principal Ho. What an unfortunate name. Principal Ho wore a cheap suit that was too small and a cheap tie that was too loud. He was only a little taller than us, and he wore his sparse hair strewn across his scalp like dead, inky tentacles, his eyeglass lenses thick enough to shrink his eyes to blurry blueberries.

Americans—white Americans, at least—probably wouldn't get a good impression of my Chinese school by meeting Principal Ho, but Chinese parents would never be so simple-minded as to judge him based on his appearance alone. Principal Ho had a PhD! From Harvard! An Ivy League school! He was smart! Maybe he could do something for my kid!

"Lao shi hao," Chun and I both boomed at Principal Ho. Hello, teacher!

Thank God a sarcastic tone sounded as though you were trying to speak Mandarin properly.

"Hao, hao," said Mr. Ho with a tilt of his head. He was always nice to me in particular because I was the only kid in the school who came from that richy-rich Jersey town. Some of this halo also illuminated Chun when he was with me. "Tong xue men hao." Hello, students!

"Hao, hao," we said as we ditched him and headed for the stairs. Chun jumped ahead, taking two steps at a time. For kicks, he tapped people on the opposite shoulder as he passed them, making them look the wrong way. I was sort of the opposite, saying hi to the younger kids while jogging up.

Our class was on the fifth floor. It was really on the fourth floor, but it was labeled the fifth because Chinese people are superstitious, and "four" in both Mandarin and Cantonese sounds like "death." Very few buildings have fourth floors in Chinatown. No one would willingly go to their death.

Me and my crew always took the stairs. There was an elevator, but it was slow as hell. Besides, taking the stairs had fringe benefits. At each landing Chun would try to look up girls' skirts or look down at their cleavage.

On the second floor, he grabbed my shirt and forced me to the banister to get an eyeful of Brandy Chew.

"What do you think of those tits, Dave?"

"Oh, yeah," I said, more for him than for me.

Someone behind us yelled, "You guys are disgusting." We both turned to face our accuser.

Betty Jung stood there, arms folded. I've also

known Betty for eight years. Betty is half white but has the darkest skin of anyone in the school. Her nose is narrower than most, but her black hair, cut into a bob that goes just past her ears, looks all Chinese. Betty's light brown eyes, now narrowed to slits, made me nervous.

"Chun made me look," I stammered. Betty's scowl deepened.

"You didn't have to go, 'Oh, yeah!'"

Chun opened his arms wide to Betty and tilted his head. "Hey, Betty, we're boys, what's the problem? We're not harassing anybody, we're just looking." Betty pointedly turned away from him and stared me down.

"Wow. I expect this kind of behavior from Chun, but not from you, David." She seemed to spit out that last word with particular disappointment. As she turned to continue up the stairs, I realized I felt a little funny.

I'm a nice guy, really. I wouldn't have ordinarily stared at Brandy Chew's chest, but Chun had forced me to. When it comes to grades, sure, I'll gloat over someone going down, but there's nothing personal in it. Really, in the end, I'm just competing with myself.

The stairs were crowded, but I found myself pushing through the other students, trying to catch up to Betty. I wanted to tell her something, even though I wasn't sure what it was I was going to say. It's not as if she and I were friends, exactly. In fact, I didn't think she had many friends, though she was more than capable of holding her own in Chinese school. Her Mandarin was better than some kids who had been born in China. She was also never afraid to speak up. Betty was usually the first girl to raise her hand in Chinese school. Sometimes she was the only one.

"David, slow down!" Chun yelled after me. "Who cares what she thinks!"

I couldn't ignore her. Now I realized I felt embarrassed. Betty had totally called me out on my behavioral slip, and I didn't want her to have a low opinion of me.

I finally caught up with her near the third-floor landing. I tapped her lightly on her back. She whirled around and batted her eyes at me. I was a little staggered by how hard they hit me. I opened my mouth slightly in wonder.

Betty didn't wear makeup or jewelry, and her unisex outfits typically consisted of solid t-shirts and pants. Today she was blue on top and beige below. In a lot of ways, Betty Jung was the opposite of Christina Tau; in that respect, Betty and I had something in common.

"You have something to say, David?" Betty asked in a bored tone.

"Yeah, I do." I said. "I just wanted to tell you that you have the wrong idea about me." Betty gave me a mocking smile.

"What *is* the right idea?"

"That I'm not a bad guy."

"You don't even know what I'm thinking."

"But I can imagine, Betty."

"Okay," she said slowly. "If what I said hurt your feelings a little bit, then maybe you really are a nice guy."

"Thanks," I said.

"Even though you *were* checking out Brandy Chew's tits."

"Hey, like I said, Chun forced me to look."

Betty laughed. "Does he also force you to smoke with him and those other guys? Out on the fire escape?"

Well, it's true that we were only modestly discreet about that. We didn't care if people knew. Principal Ho had never caught us, anyway, though he was aggressively against vaping in the school, and confiscated all related equipment he came across.

"I'm not nice because I smoke?" I asked.

"No, but you think you're being cool, when you're just acting like a loser."

I was trying to come up with a retort when I felt a hard slap against my ass.

"What the hell!" I yelled. I whipped my head around in time to see my friend Andy smile faintly, daring me to retaliate. Andy's about 30% bigger than me, and his fuzzy hair goes all around his round head like fur trim on a coat hood. He looks like a cheerful bear trained to wear jeans and flannel.

"C'mon, Andy!" I said. "We told you before not to slap people's asses. Americans don't do that."

"I *am* an American," Andy declared in his accented English as he cracked his knuckles. This is true. Andy was born in the U.S., in Sunset Park in Brooklyn to be exact. But before he was even a year old, he had been put on a plane and sent to Wuhan, a big city in central China, where he was raised by his grandparents while his parents continued to work menial jobs in New York.

Andy is one of a generation of kids born in the U.S.

and raised in China before coming back to the States, which he did with his grandmother when he was about eight years old. She was the source of the Chinese cigarettes that we smoked. In return, we were always careful never to use up more than two, otherwise she'd get pissed at Andy.

"Then act American," I said to Andy. I turned back to Betty, but she'd already left without even telling me. How annoying.

Andy and I continued up the stairs. Chun caught up to us when we were close to the fourth floor.

"You missed it, Andy," panted Chun. "Brandy Chew was wearing this low-cut sweater." Andy shrugged.

"You can see anything you want online."

Chun started to say something, then stopped. It was a remarkable show of restraint for him.

As soon as we got to the fourth-floor landing, we saw a group of smaller kids gathered around Yuet-keung, or YK, who was selling game cards again. He flipped through the plastic sheets to show off his wares, never letting the actual binder out of his hands. The point was to dazzle his potential customers with abundant supplies of the rarest cards.

YK has small, elflike features and stands a few inches shorter than Chun and myself, while Andy towers over us all. The last to have joined our group of four, YK came to New York from Hong Kong about five years ago. He wears eyeglass frames that are so ugly they have to be expensive.

"These three cards are a set," he told Carl Ching,

a boy who was about 10 years old and wearing a light-blue church suit. "Nightmare Moon, Princess Twilight Sparkle, and the Rarity card. They're going for $70 to $80 on eBay, but you've been a good customer, Carl. I'll sell you these three for half that: $35."

"That's still a lot," Carl said slowly. "I haven't paid more than $10 for a card before." YK nodded his head as he measured his mark. The transaction could still go through at the higher price. Carl's family wasn't badly off.

"I understand why you're reluctant, Carl, but these cards are tough to find." YK paused. "I don't want you to pay more than you want to, though, and I do have other customers…" He began to shut the binder.

"No, wait!" Carl cried. "I want them!" He took out his wallet and YK gave him $5 in change before Carl could hand over two $20 bills. Carl opened his wooden carrying case and YK placed the cards, still encased in plastic holders, carefully inside.

"You're making a really smart purchase," YK cooed. "These are going to double in value in no time." Carl walked away giddily with two of his friends in tow. Chun clicked his tongue.

"Don't you feel bad for ripping off little kids, YK?" he asked. YK stood and shoved his closed binder into his armpit, shedding his smooth salesman persona.

"He got a bargain," YK spat.

"Admit it, all your cards are fake," taunted Chun. YK pushed Chun aside.

"Not fake!" Then YK added something in Cantonese that made Chun give him the finger.

Chun always seems to enjoy giving YK a hard time. Andy says it's because they're from the same tribe, so they have to battle each other as a rite of manhood. Andy and I aren't Cantonese, so we sometimes felt a little left out when the two would snipe back and forth like that. About half the kids in the school speak Cantonese, but Chun and YK accounted for nearly all the arguments that take place in the dialect.

Mr. Chen, our music and stage teacher, shook his head in disgust as the four of us strolled in late to our first class. He's in his 30s and balding, but also has a thick mustache and beard. A long-time staple at the school, Mr. Chen also directs musicals for these little theater companies in the city. It was a little awkward last year when he invited the class to see one of his shows playing on a Sunday night in the New York Fringe Festival. I don't think anyone went.

"Let's all please remember to come in on time," Mr. Chen admonished us in English.

"Sorry, Chen lao shi," the four of us all said as we walked to the back of the classroom, looking anything but sorry.

I believe Chinese school strategically forces its oldest kids, aged 13 to 18, take the performance class right off the bat in order to sap our energy and break our will. That way, we'll be worn out and obedient for the rest of the day.

As my friends and I took our seats, I noticed Betty giving me the evil eye. I raised an eyebrow at her, and she turned away. Was she still judging me?

"I'm going to repeat the announcement I made earlier for those who failed to get to class on time," said Mr. Chen as he looked into the distance. "This time around, all groups will have to have at least one boy and one girl. That will force us out of our comfort zones and help us grow a little. Thank you, Betty, for that suggestion."

The four of us looked at one another in alarm. Chun, YK, Andy, and I had come to rely on being able to do half-assed skits that would be more for our entertainment than anyone else's.

Mr. Chen's classes are responsible for performing in the auditorium for school assemblies, which take place a couple of times a semester. During last month's Lunar New Year showcase, Chun had tripped and crashed through a wall, bringing the entire show to an abrupt end.

It's a good thing there are no grades in Chinese school.

Now that we were required to have a girl in our group, such shenanigans would probably no longer be possible. The girls in our class tended to be more serious about these shows than we were. Actually, everybody in our class was more serious than us. Since we had to perform, even we couldn't get away with not putting in some minimal effort, despite being the worst students in the class. Now the baseline was going to be much higher.

"All right now," called Mr. Chen. "Let's stand up, everyone, and get ready to sing. We'll start with 'The Moon Represents My Heart.'" He fired up the karaoke machine, and we followed along with Teresa Teng's popular version of the vapid song, reading the onscreen lyrics in pinyin and characters. Halfway through, Mr. Chen paused the video. "Chun, I'm having trouble hearing you. Come up front and sing to the rest of the class," he said.

YK, Andy, and I were dying as Chun shuffled to the front of the room. Mr. Chen started the song up again, and Chun sang angrily, loudly, and off-key. Betty put her fingers in her ears.

The period between Mr. Chen's class and snack time was Chinese dance with Ms. Bai for the girls and Confucian philosophy with Dr. Wu for the boys. Nobody had dictated this dividing up by gender per se, but our own internal gauge kept us hewed to the line of old cultural tropes. A few girls had once tried to brave the double-speak of the philosophy class, but Dr. Wu's drone eventually overcame even the most enthusiastic among them. Worse, he only used male pronouns in his lessons, and when a girl asked him to use "she" and "her" sometimes, he stomped his foot and declared that Confucius had no female disciples. Dr. Wu's harsh bigotry eventually drove all the girls back into the long-sleeved costumes that the school had stockpiled for Ms. Bai's class. Chinese dance is all in the arms, apparently.

None of the boys wanted to be in Dr. Wu's class, either, but anyone who ever attempted the switch to dance always came crawling back. Apparently Ms. Bai loved to torture any boys who came in by forcing them to try to do splits.

Dr. Wu has one eye that's clouded over with a cataract that looks like a trapped ghost. As he passed out the day's handouts, he regarded us with his good eye and puffed out his chest.

"The Book of Poetry has three hundred pieces," Dr. Wu declared, "but the design of them all may be embraced in one sentence 'Having no depraved thoughts.'" He looked up at the ceiling. "Tell me, class, what does this mean?"

Andy leaned over to me and whispered, "I don't want to be Chinese, anymore."

I propped up my head and pretended to be studying the handout.

After class, we trudged down to the first floor for "snack time." I always thought that was such a stupid name. The Mandarin word used at school, xiaochi, literally means "small eats," hence the "snack" interpretation. But xiaochi is in fact way more substantial than that. It's more like a small meal. What's more, it's always served right at lunchtime. Rumor had it that the reason why Chinese school couldn't call it "lunch" because it lacked certification to serve meals.

We filed into a hall outfitted with folding chairs and banquet tables. Tables at one end held trays of warm food including lo mein and dumplings as well as room-temperature entrees such as sesame noodles and spicy tofu. Sometimes they would switch up vendors, but the food was uniformly the same and of the same minimal quality.

We four guys always cut right to the front of the line, and not even the waiting teachers would object. We loaded up on fried rice, spare ribs, and sesame noodles, and took a table near the exit. I never ate much. Compared with Auntie Zhang's cooking, what they served us in school would have caused a rebellion in ancient China.

YK opened a notebook and began to sketch.

"I feel inspired," he said, adjusting his eyeglass frames with his right wrist.

"He's possessed," said Andy. Chun decided to bypass the discussion at hand entirely. He looked more agitated than usual.

"Can you believe we need to let a girl into our performance group?" He slapped the table. "It's all because of that Betty Jung. She needs to shut her mouth. And if Mr. Chen is taking suggestions from the class now, then I have a few for him."

I searched for Betty in the hall and saw her sitting at a table with Kathy Wong, the Chinese school's resident vegan punk rocker.

YK stopped drawing. He began to stuff his mouth, but also managed to ask, "What's so wrong with having a girl in the group?"

Chun's right knee began to jiggle up and down. "There's nothing wrong with it, y'know, as a suggestion, but the girls in our class are so lame! It's totally gonna ruin our thing."

"I'd rather not do anything at all," I said.

"Yeah, me, too," said Chun, "but the administrators need us to fill up programming time. Know what I'm saying?"

"In real Chinese opera, men play all the women's parts," said Andy.

"Let's put a wig on Andy and say he's the girl in our group," said Chun.

"He's the least girly of us," I said.

"Oh right, sorry, I forgot about you. You're the most girliest of us all," said Chun.

"You mean "most girly,'" I said.

His eyes lit up. "Ha! You admit it!"

I had actually been wondering whether or not to tell the guys about what had happened to me on Friday with Christina Tau, but Chun's latest outburst convinced me not to. Though we spent a lot of time talking shit together, we never actually got too personal, and had certainly never talked about dating or girls, even if tits were broached once in a while by Chun.

That guy was such a wild card. What if Chun decided to make fun of me in a public way? It was totally not beyond him to yell out something like, "Dave's scared his mommy's gonna find him with a girl!"

"If you think he's so girly," said YK, "then give him a kiss, Chun."

"He's not my type," said Chun, who was becoming uncomfortable.

"Wait," I said. "Let me get Brandy Chew over here. Chun likes ogling her." I stood up. Better that I get him rather than he get me.

"Hey, stop it, Dave!" said Chun.

"Brandy!" I yelled across the room.

"I said stop it," Chun hissed.

Andy stood up and pointed to Principal Ho entering the hall.

"It's time," he said.

By this he meant that now that the principal was done making his "security check," we could head for the third-floor fire-escape door, which he always managed to leave unlocked and ready for us to access. The entire school—students and administrators—would be downstairs for the last 20 minutes of snack time; meanwhile we could convene for our weekly illicit smoke break.

"Andy," said Chun, as he leaned against the exterior brick wall of the school, "Is your grandmother still smoking two packs a day?"

Andy reached inside his coat and produced a pack of Zhongnanhai-brand Chinese cigarettes. "She's a little over two," said Andy as he shook one into his left hand and lit the end with a lighter.

Our smoking thing had started about a year ago when Andy's family was trying to get his grandmother to quit. That led to Andy walking around Chinese school with a whole bag of Zhongnanhai packs, which he was hiding for his grandmother while his parents searched the apartment. Seeing them, Chun had grabbed a pack, lit one up, and challenged the rest of us to try something real Chinese people smoke.

Despite all the practice I've had since then, I never really let the smoke get past my molars. Chun still coughs when he tries to hold it in. But YK can take the longest drag and then blow out smoke rings. Even Andy can't do tricks like that.

"Andy's grandmother shouldn't stop, especially at this point," Chun said as Andy passed the cigarette to me. "She's been smoking all her life. If she makes a drastic change now, it will only hurt her health. It's the change that kills you, isn't it, Dave?"

I took a puff and handed the cigarette to Chun. "If the body's so accustomed to a certain amount of a stimulant, such as nicotine," I offered, "a sudden change in the daily dosage *could* cause withdrawal symptoms. In an elderly person, this might lead to adverse effects."

"Like death?" asked Chun.

"Only in extreme cases," I said.

"Damn, son, you already talk like a doctor!" said Chun.

"Dave is already on his way to medical school," said YK. He blew out a ring of smoke and the wind took it away.

"That's right!" said Chun. "Hey, for real, when you're a doctor, Dave, can me and my mom come to you free for checkups and shit?"

"Could you at least get health insurance?" I asked. "If you're covered it won't cost you anything out of pocket, and I'll still get paid. That would be a win-win."

Chun gritted his teeth and chuckled. "Listen to this guy! Hey, Dave, health insurance is harder to get than a job! Andy, are your parents covered at their work?"

"No," said Andy.

"What about your parents, YK?"

"They have some coverage, but it just started in January."

Chun pressed him. "And they're managers at that eyeglass store, right?"

"Well, not managers," YK said carefully. "More like long-time employees."

"Now let me ask you guys this: When was the last time either of you saw a doctor?" Both YK and Andy laughed at the thought. "See this, Dave? I'm not bullshitting you about this. If you want to make it as a doctor, you gotta move far away from large populations of Chinese people. We don't take our kids to the doctor, even when they're sick!"

"Chun, are you going to take your mother to the doctor when she's sick?" asked YK. Chun pretended to be offended.

"Hey, don't talk about my mother, you loser!"

Loser. That's what Betty had called me for coming out here and smoking with the guys. Yeah, it wasn't a productive sort of thing, but it was an activity that enforced solidarity. I wondered if her family had health insurance.

Then I remembered that a few years back, Betty had been out for a while because her father was really sick. There'd even been an online collection going around for her family. If she'd been more popular, or if her family had been more tied to the world of parents that circled around the Chinese school, I'm pretty sure more money would have been raised. Still, I remember hearing that her dad had eventually recovered. I didn't know much more because I'd never actually asked her about it.

The bell rang inside, signaling the end of snack time.

YK passed around pieces of gum to end our little ritual.

The last two classes of the day at Chinese school were calligraphy and tradition. Both were grueling experiences for different reasons. Calligraphy was effectively an art class. We used brushes and ink and nice sheets of bamboo paper, not copy paper.

Mrs. Ma, the teacher, is short and fat and has infinite reservoirs of patience. There are some characters I haven't been able to get down for years, yet every week she gently reminds me again that they aren't quite right. The class basically consists of Mrs. Ma walking up and down our rows, making sure we're holding our brushes properly, that we're using the proper amount of ink, and that we follow through on our strokes to the end.

In other words, this was another class you couldn't snooze through.

Today, Mrs. Ma seemed to find something amiss. She began to make loud sniffing sounds when she got near YK. "I smell smoke on you, Yue-qiang!" she declared, using YK's name in Mandarin. He sat up a little straighter and hunched his right shoulder.

"My family went to Korean barbeque last week," he said. "I tried washing this shirt, but it still smells."

Mrs. Ma closed her eyes and shuddered. "Korean," was all she said.

At the end of class, after Mrs. Ma left, Betty came up to me.

"You guys almost got busted," she said. "When are you all going to stop smoking?"

"Betty," I said. "When are you gonna gimme a break?"

"Why do you deserve a break?" Betty really wanted to know. She wasn't taunting me.

I shoved my hands in my pockets. "You probably don't know this, but I work really hard all week."

She rubbed her chin. "I know you have a restaurant."

"I mean, I also study hard in school."

"There's no way you study as hard as me, David."

I was incredulous. "I go to a really competitive school, Betty."

"So do I."

Chun broke in.

"Say, Betty, why won't you leave my man Dave alone? Methinks the lady does complain so much."

"Oh, I get it, Chun," she said. "You're randomly parroting something you dimly remember from Shakespeare."

"I thought you'd appreciate it, being half English."

"I'm half German American," said Betty.

"Well, all right," said Chun, temporarily at a loss. He decided to hit her back from another angle instead. "Oh, and by the way, Betty, thanks for screwing us over in performance class."

She glared at him. "Do you guys know that Mr. Chen has been taking a lot of heat from Principal Ho because you ruined the last show?"

"Who gives a shit?" asked Chun.

"Not you, obviously," said Betty. "It's already bad enough that I have to see you in high school."

"Wow, you guys go to the same school?" I asked.

"Chun is only nominally there," said Betty.

"I nominally don't give a shit," said Chun.

We retreated to our corners for the next and final class, tradition, which was held in the same room as calligraphy. A few weeks before, while out on the fire escape, I'd joked that tradition class should be called New Dimensions in Boredom, and the acronym had stuck.

"NDB!" Chun boomed out as Mr. Szeto entered. Mr. Szeto isn't a bad guy or anything, he just doesn't really register in any way. The guy has no personality and no looks. Average height, average build, nondescript face. He's the man who isn't there. In a videogame, he wouldn't even be one of the mini-bosses. In a film, he'd be the older brother asking to be avenged as he died.

Mr. Szeto prefers to lecture uninterrupted with little to no input from us students, and certainly no questions. He doesn't care if you're on your phone, though, and probably wouldn't even mind if you dozed off. All that mattered was that you not interrupt him droning on and on about The Warring States Period. As long as you didn't snore, distracting him from his "flow," you'd be fine.

Maybe it sounds cool, having a class that you can totally disengage from, but trust me, it's a big-time drag. You could do almost anything you wanted, but after about five minutes, all you wanted to do was bolt.

Half the class was already on their phones as Mr. Szeto began his lecture, and I decided to join them. Instead of playing games or texting, though, I read through a new MCAT question. Test preparation was my mobile comfort zone, not fun little distractions. I am a smart guy, after all.

The thing is, though, I was having a hard time with this latest question. Which is weird for me. I usually pick things up quickly. I've had to. But now, as I read and re-read about a kind of bacteria, none of the information would stick.

I knew the problem couldn't be Mr. Szeto's voice, because it had never derailed me before.

Then I realized that I had Christina Tau on the brain.

She had surfaced a few times in my thoughts already, most prominently when I was weighing whether or not to tell the other guys about her. But my anxieties related to Christina and the dance were clearly beginning to take a toll on ability to learn.

I mean, apart from staying one step ahead of my mother, how should I start acting on Monday? Was I supposed to start holding Christina's hand? Would one dance date mean that we were boyfriend and girlfriend? Or did that take two dances?

All this was impossible for me to think through. I've always been able to figure out my way through academic problems because ultimately there are solutions. Even when MCAT questions aren't well written, there are ways to a clear answer.

I had no one to talk to about this problem, and I had no experience to go on. Christina, on the other hand, was already way ahead of me. I knew for a fact that she'd had a boyfriend for like a whole month last year, a guy named Tom Tsai. He was a year ahead of us, and they'd met through the local Greater Shark Beach Chinese School.

I clearly remember this one day when Christina's

friend Jean started harassing Tom in the hallway, practically screaming in his face, "Christina shouldn't have to put up with your shit!" I don't think Christina was around when this was happening. Jean seemed to act like her fixer.

Christina's world had multiple layers. I closed my eyes to contemplate it.

Andy roused me by roughly shaking my shoulder. Most students in NDB class were already gone, and my three friends were standing around my desk.

"You fall asleep, Dave?' asked YK.

"His eyes were open," said Andy.

"Are you all right?" asked YK. "Maybe you need more protein in your diet."

"He's the doctor," said Chun. "He would know."

"I was just lost in my MCAT studying," I mumbled.

"So that's what they call dreaming in Jersey, huh?" said Chun.

Chinese school was over. We jogged down the stairs together, did our bro hugs, and split up, each going our own way.

Chun had to go meet up with his Chinatown buddies, who were just now waking up. Not that Andy, YK, and I weren't his buddies. Just that his high school crowd was on an entirely different level. At least that's what he intimated. The fact that they didn't have to go to Chinese school indicated that they probably weren't subject to much parental supervision. Apparently, they stayed up late most nights gambling. Chun also strongly implied that his Chinatown friends might be involved in various other nefarious activities, but he assured us that he himself absolutely, definitely wasn't.

Like me, YK had to go off to work for his parents. His job sounded more interesting than mine, though. He rode the subway loaded down with backpacks stuffed with frames, heading from the Chinatown eyeglass store to a lens-grinding factory in Brooklyn, then bringing them back again after the proper lenses had been installed.

Andy had to...I have no idea. None of us really did. YK told me he once saw Andy after school in the library, going through a public database of real-estate property records. YK had asked him what he was doing, and Andy had simply said, "We live in the information age."

As for me, I had to head back north past Canal Street to Broome Street, just off Bowery. Once there, I would look around for the cleanest truck in Chinatown and make my way to it.

Mr. Yeung, the driver, kept his vehicle nearly spotless. Sure there were dings on every corner. You couldn't help that in the city. But even the dents shone. He said the secret to keeping his truck pristine was to spray oil all over the side panels before parking it in the garage. No spray paint or other graffiti could stick to that.

Every Saturday, Mr. Yeung would take my dad and me back to the restaurant with a load of fresh veggies and other stuff in his truck. He'd been doing this for a few years now.

This afternoon, Mr. Yeung's truck was illegally parked next to a fire hydrant. The motor was running and the front wheels were already turned out, ready to shove off if a parking cop tried to creep up on him.

My father was sitting in the middle of the cab. Seeing me head over toward them, he passed an antique Game Boy to Mr. Yeung, then leaned over to open the street-side door for me. The two of them always passed time waiting for me to finish Chinese school by playing electronic chess against each other.

"You say 'Hello' to Mr. Yeung?" my father asked as I was stepping into the cab. As usual, he hadn't given me even a millisecond to say hello on my own.

"Hello, Mr. Yeung. How are you?"

"David, you're a smart boy! Gonna be a big boss, someday!" The two men laughed heartily. To my father, Mr. Yeung said, "Saved it," and shut off the videogame.

The only time I saw my father actively happy was when he was away from the restaurant and with Mr. Yeung. I guess it was a bit like me with my Chinese school friends.

Mr. Yeung pulled on the collar of his white snap-button shirt and sat up. The shirt and his spiky mostly-gray hair made Mr. Yeung look like a mad scientist. He grimaced as he reached for his seatbelt buckle and swung it across his chest with a flourish that would have impressed an ancient swordsman.

In fact, my father once told me that Mr. Yeung had played a number of swordsmen in Chinese films. He'd been a stunt double in his youth, jumping from one horse to another. He'd apparently even crashed out of a high-rise window in some *Die Hard* knockoff. A mishap had left Mr. Yeung with a bad limp, though. What hurt most of all was that he'd never been credited for any of his stunt work.

Dad had made it very clear before that I should never ask Mr. Yeung about his movie days. "It's too painful for him to talk about," my father had said. Painful indeed. The guy had gone from movie magic to hauling produce. No kid grows up dreaming of delivering supplies to Chinese restaurants in Jersey, but everyone has to pay bills, even Mr. Yeung. Besides, what other Chinatown gig could you get with a bum leg? He couldn't even sweep a floor. Just thinking about it made me appreciate the cleanliness of his truck, both inside and out. It couldn't be easy for him to maintain the condition of that vehicle.

We pulled out, headed west in slow traffic on Canal, and entered the tunnel back to Jersey. It sounded like the ocean.

When we got off at the Shark Beach exit of the Garden State Turnpike and drove into town, Mr. Yeung said what he always said. "Look at this place, it's so nice! So many trees! You live in a forest!"

After we parked at Tung's Garden, my mother charged out of the restaurant to greet us. Mr. Yeung must be giving us a really good rate, because my parents always go the extra mile to show their appreciation and friendship. As per usual, they went through the whole charade of trying to get Mr. Yeung to come in and eat, and Mr. Yeung played his part by saying he wasn't hungry or was too busy. These episodes always ended with him walking with his cane to the restaurant with my mother while my father and I brought in boxes of produce by hand truck through the service entrance. Everything always went directly into the cold storage, except for whatever Auntie Zhang told us to leave out.

When Dad and I were done unloading the vegetables, we joined Mr. Yeung and my mother at our employees' table. The adults gossiped in Mandarin, my mother asking Mr. Yeung how New Pavilion or any other perceived competitor was doing. I mostly tuned out, using the time when no one's attention was on me to try to read over some upcoming lessons while eating. This was a habit I'd learned from elementary school, when my mother used to push me to get at least two lessons ahead of the class. Sometimes, the strategy would backfire, though. For example, when the teacher would say, "And now we're going to skip the next two chapters!"

At some point, my father walked with Mr. Yeung back to the truck, my mother and Auntie Zhang resumed discussing soap operas in the dining room, and I went to the back and washed the dishes.

Standing over the hot sudsy water, I felt myself getting angry all over again. Studying the way my mom wanted me to, I'd ended up learning things my classmates never did, and yet they knew so many things I didn't. There were plenty of couples at Shark Beach High, even a few same-sex ones. Dating and relationships, what were they really like? I guess they offered the higher highs and lower lows that were a part of growing up. I think I was starting to feel some of that.

For so long, I'd only ever thought of Christina as a potential rival. Now I wanted to protect her from people like her ex, Tom Tsai. His stupid smug face kept popping into my head. When I thought of him, I wanted to push him into a wall. But why should I hate him? His only offense was dating Christina before me. I shook my head. My testosterone levels must be spiking.

Just chill, I told myself. I drained the sink and dried my hands. They felt soft, like a lover's not a fighter's.

I think my mother was so dismissive of the idea of dating because she and my father had never had a courtship themselves. At least that's what they said. They'd been introduced at a Chinese student group at Queens College in New York, and that was it. Then came the wedding, the kid, and the restaurant.

Come to think of it, maybe those Chinese soap operas were so popular with people like my mother because they finally gave them the chance to feel the mystery of falling in love.

I had to make sure the Christina thing wouldn't turn into a soap opera, though. What made for good TV would be awful to actually experience.

As the pace picked up at Tung's Garden, I tried to keep up. Time flew. The next thing I knew, we were headed home.

CHAPTER FIVE

I had a dream that I was chasing Christina Tau inside a moving train. Gravity was lighter than usual, so the pursuit had a dizzy hilarity to it. My feet only made contact every third step. Christina was wearing a long black skirt that slowly lifted until it covered her head. I was following a black flower whose stem wore lacy red panties.

Red, by the way, appeals to all Chinese regardless of political affiliation. It's the color of good fortune, and it can ward off evil spirits. Most kids know it as the color of the envelopes stuffed with gift money.

Would I succeed in getting my hands into Christina's red panties?

I could hear her laughing as she floated just out of reach.

"Hey, slow down!" I yelled at her.

The train entered a tunnel and everything went black. We tripped between cars and fell to the tracks.

Even though we were being run over by the train cars, we felt only ecstasy. When the coast was clear, I pulled her hands from her face only to find that I was staring into Betty Jung's eyes.

"See?" said Betty. "You're not a nice guy!"

I woke up tangled in the sheets, mounting my pillow.

I was freaked out by the dream, enough so that I needed to read over some more MCAT questions to calm myself. But my mind was still reeling from Betty's appearance in it. What was happening?

During all those years at Chinese school, I'd never thought much of Betty. She was that girl who kept to herself a bit. She'd worn braces for a while, long ago.

This past Saturday wasn't the first time we'd talked, and it also wasn't the first time she'd made some uncalled-for pronouncement about my character. But it was the first time I'd cared about what she thought about me.

My dream made no sense. Betty wasn't as sexy as Christina. She wasn't sexy at all, in fact, at least not in the traditional sense. Betty didn't wear the necessary clothes, jewelry, or beauty products to play that sort of game. She didn't play any games.

On Sunday mornings, my parents typically head into the restaurant by themselves and let me sleep in.

That morning, I left the house at around nine on my bike, pausing to check out our modest two-story brick house. Sundays are the only time I get to see it in the full morning light. Before World War II, Shark Beach had been famous for houses like ours, which had been built to lodge workers at the nearby brick factory. Now, after a decade of development, our home and the ones nearby were among the last of their kind still standing.

The neighborhood was empty as usual at that hour. I pedaled through some redeveloped blocks and coasted right past my bus stop. The streets were so dead, I felt as if I were haunting them.

I still miss the sleeping dragon, a derelict factory with discolored windows that looked like scales that used to be within biking distance. The entrance looked like a giant mouth with a few missing teeth. When I was in elementary school, big machines tore the dragon apart like pulled pork. Construction teams stomped the area flat and built blocks of mansions made of glass, metal, and brick reclaimed from the dragon.

These days, I can barely see those newly built houses as I ride past them; they're set back from the street and obscured by rows of evergreen trees.

It's all residential blocks with no traffic lights until I have to cross a two-lane highway near the end to reach Tung's Garden.

Sunday at the restaurant is the same sort of deal as Saturday, minus the Chinese school excursion for me. The first few hours, we trim stems from various vegetables, then we serve the lunch crowds. Our restaurant once got talked up on a vegan blog, and ever since then, all these white people have been coming in on Sundays. They only eat the vegetable entrees, so we need all the snow peas, string beans, green beans, and snap peas (when in season) that we can trim.

After 6 p.m., the dining room tends to quiet down. That's when pretty much all of our business changes to deliveries.

We have a team of four Chinese men who go out and deliver food on bikes for us. Most weeknights, we use only two or three of them—they split up the days amongst themselves—but we need all four of them from Thursday through Sunday. Nobody covers the town like they do. Ever since we hooked up with Bagged for online orders, they've been looking more buff than ever.

All four men are physics grad students at the state university in nearby Clairmont Township. They all teach undergrad classes as part of their fellowships, but they still find time to work our relatively crappy delivery jobs. I think with tips it comes out to $20 an hour, $30 during big nights. I used to think our delivery guys were just being greedy, moonlighting with us to hoard a little more money. It was only after Wang Yi, the funny one, told me that teaching paid "shit," that I realized their situtation.

"They force me to have office hours to help the American kids," said Wang, who always speaks to me in English. "The biggest problem is they don't want to spend time study. Want me do everything!"

The other deliverymen include Lee One, who is taller than Lee Two, and Bai Sheng, who rarely talks.

Despite everything, they have the best academic positions they could hope for as immigrant students without connections. Wang says that he was lucky to get into the U.S. at all, even if it was to attend a modest state university. The rich Chinese students—the kids of

Internet billionaires and generals—all go to name-brand U.S. schools. Wang's father is a coal miner.

Delivering food for Tung's Garden isn't the greatest job, but the four guys have stuck with us for years. Auntie Zhang always gets a little maternal with them, chiding them for not eating enough at meal breaks.

What our guys like most about their jobs, according to Wang Yi, is that our delivery range doesn't reach their university. Otherwise they might have to bear the indignity of delivering food to one of their students.

I spent most of Sunday evening prepping delivery bags by filling them with soy sauce, duck sauce, and fortune cookies. Even the Chinese American customers complain when they don't get their fortune cookies. That's how American they are.

A little after 9 p.m., I biked home and drank orange juice. We never have any at the restaurant, so it's something I crave at the end of a weekend at work.

Sundays are the only nights I'm released early from the restaurant, and the only time I have to myself in the empty house.

That night, I first finished all my homework. There weren't any tests scheduled for the coming week, so there wasn't anything pressing to study for.

I relaxed by thinking about Christina. Would it be worth it—in terms of money, time, and potential family discord—for me to go to this dance with her? What would she feel like in my arms?

I looked idly at our last messages.

Shit, I had forgotten to look into those tuxes that

Christina wanted me to wear!

I opened my old Asus laptop on my desk. COMME des GARÇONS was one of the brands mentioned in her photos. I knew it meant "like some boys" in French and that it was expensive. After some digging, I found out that the Nordstrom in our upscale mall apparently carried it. Then I nearly fainted when I saw how much the tuxes cost. Four digits! I had no idea they were priced at that level! There was no way I could afford that!

Armani, another brand among Christina's suggestions, was even worse. Nordstrom didn't have prices for renting tuxes, just links for booking an appointment. I rubbed my hands anxiously. How plausible was it that a store like that would entertain handing outfits like these to a kid with no credit card?

Everything was turning out to be a huge joke on me. Sneaking out to the dance with Christina would be tough, but at least that part would be free. How was I going to pay for the rest of it? She probably wanted flowers and a limo, too. I'd been so surprised that Christina had asked me out at all that I didn't know the vastness of the economic divide between us.

It made me think of a film I once saw in school where a retired baseball player said that although he'd grown up impoverished, he'd never thought of himself that way, because when you're a kid you don't think about money. Things are different here and now. In Shark Beach, the kids who don't think about money are the ones who are loaded.

CHAPTER SIX

The weather was getting a little warmer, so on Monday morning, Percy and Fred wore their Canada Goose parkas unzipped, strategically revealing the Polo logos on their shirts.

Jean's and Grace's ponytails lay on the deflated hoods of their Arc'teryx coats. As soon as Jean saw me, she walked over, rolling her shoulders back and getting ready to try to wind me up once again. Grace took out her AirPods so she could get a good listen.

I turned aside and acted as if I didn't see Jean approaching.

"Hey, David," Jean yelled out at me. "Hey, hey!"

Pretending not to hear, I yawned and closed my eyes, opening them again just as Jean reached in and began waving her hand in my face. One of her cold bracelets actually brushed the hairs of my left eyebrow.

I jumped back and pulled down my headphones.

"Now what?" I asked, genuinely annoyed.

"Sorry, didn't mean to hit you, David, dear," she said, drawing her painted nails across her right cheek. "It's so hard to get your attention. Maybe you're still in shock that Christina Tau asked you to go to the Dames Ball."

"A little bit," I admitted.

"I'm more shocked than you that my dearest and smartest friend stooped down to reach out to you instead of someone...normal."

I tilted my head. "And yet she did. I'll bet she thinks I'm interesting."

"She does think you're different, but I told Christina you were a nice, obedient Chinese boy. You probably don't even jerk off."

Predictably, the Fred, Grace, and Percy laugh track went off. All of them were Greater Shark Beach Chinese School pals, after all.

Before she could build up any further momentum, the bus arrived. Her crew made their way to get on board while I hung back.

"Hey," someone said. I turned and saw the white kid, who was now standing next to me. He hadn't said anything in months.

"Hey, there," I replied.

"David, I think you take too much shit from those guys." He probably knew my name from Jean's daily harassment.

"It's not a big deal," I said.

"Jean's the problem, you know."

"I'm aware of that."

"If you ever decide that you want it to stop, I know something about her that would shut her up." I looked him in the eyes. He wasn't kidding. What did this kid have? Pictures of Jean snorting drugs? Videos of her having sex? I tried to wipe the images from my mind.

"Maybe hold on to that for now," I told the kid.

"Whenever you want, just let me know. It's good."

He moved away to line up behind Jean and her friends. He was another guy on the outs, and he was trying to help me. I wanted to recognize that. I touched his arm.

"Sorry, man, I've, uh, forgotten your name."

"Alastair. But you can call me 'Al.'"

"Thank you, Al."

We ended up sitting together on the bus and chatting for a bit. It turns out Al and his mom had moved to Shark Beach from southern Jersey because our school district had the best coding classes in the state. They were actually living in one of the old-school brick houses like mine. His grandfather had just left for an assisted living facility.

Does Shark Beach High have the best coding classes because of the *actual* aptitude of the majority Asian population, or did the state allocate those resources to us because of the *perceived* aptitude of the majority Asian population? Hard to say. One thing is for sure, though. A lot of rich people live in Shark Beach. And rich people are always getting the best stuff out of the government. I'm just glad that Al and I got to benefit from it.

As both of us returned to looking at our phones, I wondered whether Jean would dare to attack me if I had my Chinese school crew with me. Andy alone was pretty intimidating if you didn't know him.

He, Chun, and YK probably had no idea how solitary I was during the week.

"Hey, man," said my locker mate Scott Sima. "I heard you're going with Christina Tau to the Dames Ball." He nodded his head as if impressed. I guess it wasn't that surprising that he knew. Word about me must be getting around!

"Yeah," I said. "Are you going, too, Scott?"

"I was asked, but you know, I'm sort of seeing this girl who's in Taipei now. She goes to the American school there. Our families know each other, and we kinda hooked up over the summer." He smiled stupidly and shrugged. "Not like that, you know. We're both Christian."

I nodded.

"You're going to have a lot of fun at the dance, David."

Scott closed his locker. This guy really could run for president someday. He was overflowing with charisma. He made me feel special by focusing on me. But it's not as if I could call him a friend.

"See ya soon, my studly friend," he said as he did a stutter step, cut around two people, and disappeared into the crowd.

OK. I totally claim him as a friend.

I craned my neck for a view of the bulletin board outside Mr. Wald's office. Still nothing next to "Harmony Health Systems."

Oh, shit, I had forgotten that he wanted me to make

an appointment to talk to him!

I looked up the online student-life calendar on my phone and saw that a number of days were already booked. A slot was open tomorrow during homeroom.

I got to my desk and tried to focus. Monday mornings are a good time to regroup and plot out the day and the week. I felt confident about my preparation for every class except for Honors English, the second-to-last period of the day. It was the only class I had with Christina. She'd be expecting to talk to me about my tux, and she probably wasn't going to like what I had to say. Judging from the morning's adventure at the bus stop, it was pretty clear that Jean must be giving Christina a lot of shit about having picked one of the most poorly dressed boys in school as her date to the Dames Ball. At this very moment, Jean was probably trying to exacerbate any doubts or second thoughts Christina might be having.

Christina couldn't have known that asking me to the dance would complicate both our lives to the extent that it had. Honestly, it was pretty brave of her to ask me out at all. Christina must genuinely like me.

Following her example, I should have the guts to tell my mother about the dance. That was the least I could do.

When I went back to my locker to swap out books before lunch, I was surprised to find Christina there waiting for me.

"David, did you have a chance to look over those outfits?"

"I did." I shifted my books to my left hand so my right arm would be free to hug her. She didn't indicate in any way that she wanted physical contact, though, so I shoved my right hand into my pocket.

"So what do you think?"

"They all look interesting."

"David! We have to match! I can't figure out what I'm going to wear until I know what you're wearing!"

"Maybe you should get your dress and then I'll get something that goes with it." She touched my right arm.

"You really don't know, do you? Okay, I'm going to assume that you don't already own an outfit like any of the pictures I sent you. Am I right?"

"You're right."

"So, it will probably take a week for you to get your tux after you go in for measurements. Then you can come over, and we'll evaluate in person what bowties and cummerbunds go with my dresses. We can't go by pictures." She closed her eyes and sighed. "You may not *need* a cummerbund, but I like the way they look."

"You want me to come over your house, Christina?"

"No, I want to meet you in the women's bathroom at Penn Station." She stomped her foot. "Of course I want you at my house! My mom definitely needs to see what you're going to wear in person."

So it wasn't just money that separated our families. It was also culture. The Taus seemed so typically American. Maybe having money granted a certain status quo.

"You know what?" I told Christina. "Can you pick something for me? I don't really care." Wrong move.

"If you don't care what you wear, it means you don't

care about me!" she snapped.

I knew from my mom that Chinese women could become enraged in half a second. I hadn't known Chinese girls could, too.

"Christina, I didn't mean 'I don't care,' as in 'who cares,' I meant that I don't mind. They all look great. I don't know how to choose just one."

"We're going to decide today," she said flatly. "I know you have lunch now. Let's go."

I thought the two of us were going to be alone. Instead, it turned out that I was meeting a committee, one formed and chaired by Christina, whose mission was to evaluate outfits for me. The other committee members were Cassie Bang and Shirley Wing.

Cassie is one of those girls who has enough money to dress simply and elegantly, and she always wears a cross on a chain. That's a detail I'd noticed because as she walks or talks it bounces off her pleasant chest. Everyone knows she's platonically seeing this guy who's a first year at Princeton. Cassie's father apparently once told the boyfriend that he couldn't marry (read, "have sex with") his daughter until he had successfully completed his medical internship and subsequent residencies.

Well, Cassie's boyfriend might not get to see very much of her, but he's already at an Ivy League college and has a girlfriend. Basically, he's living the dream.

Shirley is shorter than Cassie and Christina, but she makes up for it by wearing the most jewelry and talking the loudest. Shirley does whatever she can to ensure that she is never overlooked.

All three are members of the Chinese Council, an affinity group established at Shark Beach High years ago after a racist incident when Asians were still a minority in the school. The group's original mission had been to encourage cultural diversity by promoting Chinese culture and history. Once Asians became the majority six years or so ago, the group's main function shifted to organizing school dances and social events. The Chinese Council was promoting the Dames Ball, for example. Christina was this year's president. Cassie and Shirley were also officers in the group.

Christina tugged at the shoulder of her black turtleneck as she admired Cassie's long-sleeved black T-shirt. Shirley, wearing a black blouse, was hunched over her iPad. The three of them were the elite of Shark Beach High. I'd never thought I'd be sitting with them during lunch at one of the privileged tables in the back. Yet here I was.

"I think this is the one," said Shirley, pointing to a D&G outfit. "Something like this would go well with David's body type."

"He can wear anything," said Cassie, "but I wish his shoulders were wider."

"Cassie, don't shoulder-shame David," said Christina.

"Actually, I like D&G," said Shirley, "but this one is slightly better."

"Not bad," said Christina. "What do you think, David?"

Don't say that you don't care, I reminded myself.

Even if every single outfit looks almost the same.

"I agree with Christina," I said, playing it safe. "She has great taste." She smiled.

The one I actually liked was a textured jacket that a model was wearing with ripped jeans, an article that I already owned. It sure was cheaper than renting a full tux. I'd already mentioned this to them, but while the three of them thought it was a cool look, they decreed that since Christina was the president of the Chinese Council, I had to look fully formal. The biggest strike against my choice was that it wouldn't go with her favorite dresses.

"Anyway," said Cassie, "the Dames Ball is about women's empowerment. All women. You know that Steph Wang is bringing her girlfriend, right? They're *both* gonna wear tuxes. I think that's so cool."

"So cool," Shirley and Christina echoed.

The one notable absence from our group was Chinese Council VP Jean Chu, who was sitting two tables away with Percy and dutifully ignoring us.

"Jean's not happy," I said.

"Jean's secretly in love with Christina," said Shirley.

Cassie shook her head and said, "It's no secret."

"Jean's sweet when you get to know her, David," said Christina. "We can all chill together at the dance."

My biggest non-family-related struggles related to the dance had now doubled: figuring out how to pay for that tux, and being mentally prepared to spend a significant amount time with Jean and Percy. I'd probably need a long pull or two from Percy II's flask.

I glanced out the window. The skies were gray

and a light rain dabbed at the glass. Maybe this was what becoming mature was all about. Dressing up and learning to be cordial with terrible people.

"What about this, David?" Christina asked.

"That's great," I said. Wow, it was less than $500!

"Are you going to rent or buy?" asked Shirley. "If you're going to go to more events, it probably makes more sense to buy, David." She glanced meaningfully at Christina.

"I think David should rent for now," Christina said, smiling. "We'll see how he does." She seemed pleased with herself.

When lunch was over, we'd decided that I'd rent an outfit by Canali at Nordstrom. Christina was all set to book me for a fitting, but I told her I'd do it myself. The surprising ease with which the lunch meeting had gone down had given the whole dance situation a surprising feeling of normalcy. It wasn't so hard to fit in after all. How hard could it possibly be to talk to my mother about all of this?

My heart was pounding in fear when my mother picked me up as usual at the bus stop. I was full-on terrified to lay out all my plans in full, which I needed to do to even have a shot at her giving me the tux money.

"How was school?" she asked.

"Fine," I said. I saw her mouth twitch. She was suspicious when she didn't hear grades.

"No tests or quizzes?"

"No, nothing today."

"What about Harmony Health?"

"Still nothing." Whenever I didn't have a clear marker of success to report to her, she liked to go fishing for a deficiency.

"When are you going to hear?"

"Soon, I think."

We rode in silence a little bit. I couldn't tell if she was in a good or a bad mood, but figured I could go fishing, too.

"Mom?"

"Yes?"

"Do you think every Saturday night is going to be busy at Tung's Garden?" She actually laughed.

"Hope so! Don't you hope so, too, David?"

"Yeah, I guess."

I couldn't muster the courage to bring up the dance.

Once we got to the restaurant, I went into work mode. Every time I thought I was going to get a break for a few minutes, another task presented itself.

Soon the night was almost over. We were cleaning up. It was now or never. I'd already decided there was no way I was going to tell my mother about the dance once we got home. She'd said numerous times that when she gets home, she just wants to sleep. Plus, here at the restaurant, there was always the chance I could rally up some backup support from Auntie Zhang or my dad. At the very least, my mother would think twice before really lashing into me, if it came to that.

My newly found level of social acceptance—and the potential for a real-life girlfriend—was riding on being able to go to the dance. I could be as cool at

Shark Beach High as I was at the Chinese school in Chinatown! But in order for that to happen, I needed to go to Nordstrom. This week. There was no way to put it off any longer.

"Mom!" I said hoarsely. She was stapling receipts near the cash register.

"Yes?"

"Can you help me rent a tuxedo?"

"Tuxedo? What for?"

"I want to go to a school dance."

She put down the stapler and curled her hands into fists. "You want to go to a dance?"

My shoulders involuntarily shrugged out of fear.

"A girl asked me to go, and I said yes."

"A girl!" said my mother, like a TV detective announcing she'd found the murder weapon. I heard my father moving somewhere behind me, possibly taking shelter. "Who's this girl?"

"Christina Tau." My mother flared her nostrils.

"Is she your secret girlfriend, David?"

"No," I said. "I don't have a girlfriend much less a secret girlfriend."

"'Tau,' she said venomously, "It sounds like a Cantonese name." My mother sometimes expressed distaste for Cantonese people for no explicable reason. "How many times have I told you? You're not allowed to have a girlfriend until college! And you'd better get into an Ivy League school!" It was the end of yet another long day of work, but my mother didn't seem tired at all. She was as mad as I've ever seen her.

"You've said that enough times," I said. I looked

around for some silent show of support. Auntie Zhang's English wasn't great, but she could probably understand what was happening. Yet she was diligently wiping down a tabletop, her head bent. My father suddenly found that something in the kitchen required him.

After a brief pause, my mother was on me again.

"You're not even number one, are you?" She pointed at my nose. "All the way down at number eight! You spend too much time thinking about girls!"

That was a complete lie. It angered me into a fatal mistake: talking back to my mother while she was still fired up.

"I spend too much time working at this restaurant!" I protested.

"You know how long I work here? How long your father works here? You want to run around with girls while we're spending day and night here making money so we can live?"

Oh no! Don't let her start talking about money when she's this angry.

"Okay, look," I said, attempting to calm her down. "It's just one dance. It's not a big deal. Christina's parents are Chinese, too, and they think it's OK."

But there was no calm eye to this storm.

"They're not your parents! And that's not my child!"

"Why can't you understand?"

"No! You don't understand!"

Actually, I truly didn't.

"A lot of kids are going."

"Not you, David!" my mother thundered. "You tell this girl you don't want a girlfriend! And you don't want to talk to her anymore!"

"I already told her I would go," I said.

"Tell her you can't! You're in school, and school is for learning, not for girls!" She closed her lips and wiped her front teeth with her tongue, considering something.

"Give me your phone, David!"

"What!"

"Give me your phone! I don't want you talking and sexting with this girl!"

"I'm not sexting with her, Mom!"

"Who knows what you're doing!" I handed over my phone and half a second later it was zipped up in her purse. Nothing ever escaped from there. Not even light.

"How am I supposed to tell her I can't go if I don't have my phone?"

"You tell her tomorrow!" My mother threw on her coat. "And then you stop talking to her!" She had to yell for my father to come out of the kitchen where he had probably been cowering.

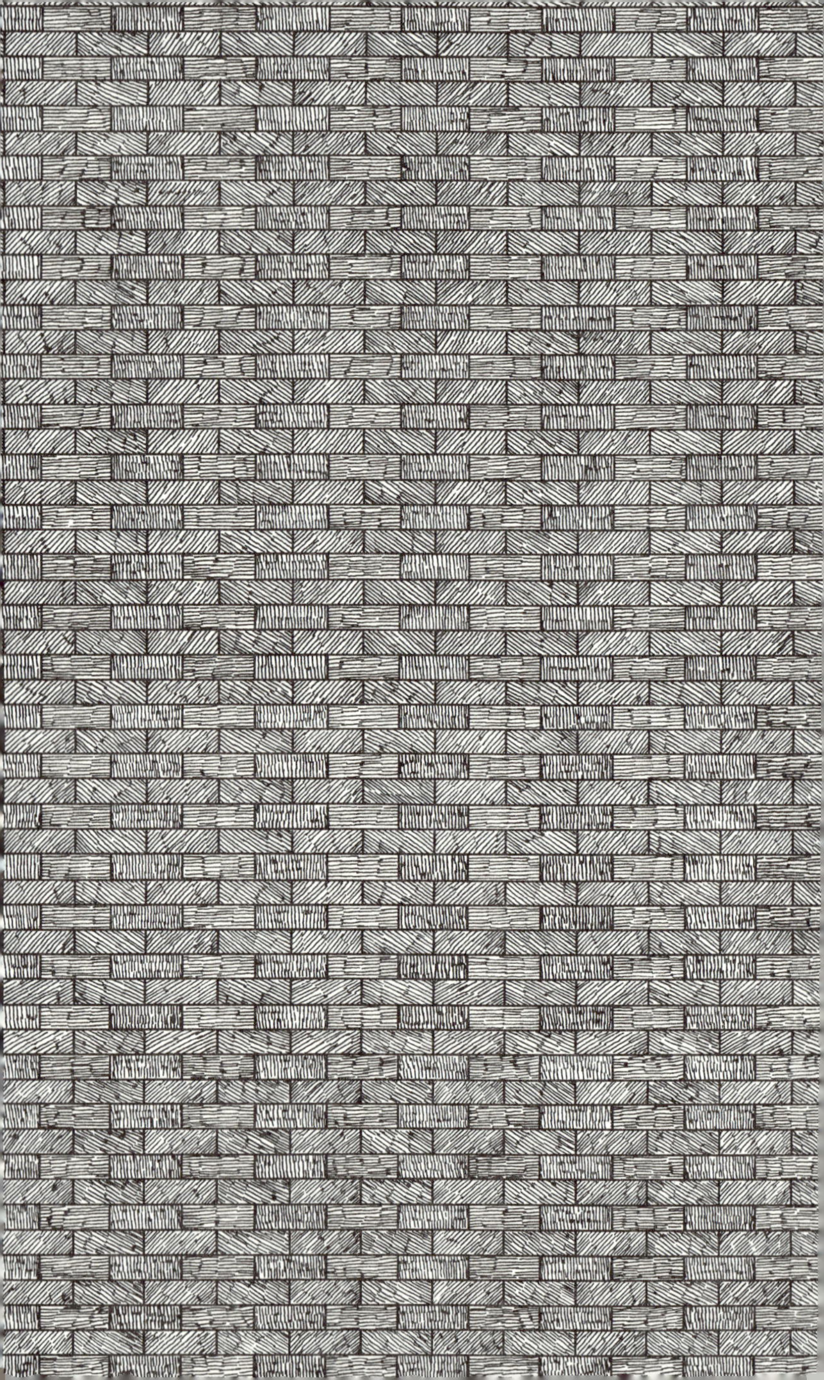

CHAPTER SEVEN

I was numb from the time I got into the car until I'd brushed and flossed my teeth. My father hadn't said a word the whole time. He'd been just another passenger on the ride home from the restaurant.

To be fair, there's almost nothing he could have said to change my mom's mind. Once she made a decision, that was that. The end. Eight years ago, she'd decided on a seeming whim that I would go to Chinese school in Chinatown, and I'd never once heard her express any regret.

A small part of me had no doubt known already that the confrontation between my mom and me about the dance would come down to this. That small part carried me across the room and into bed. I lay there like a fresh squid on ice, all tangled up with dilated eyes.

On top of everything else, I'd lost my crappy phone, an unexpected setback. If I ever dared bring up the dance with my mother again, I'd probably lose my crappy laptop, too.

What was I going to say to Christina? I hadn't given her even the faintest hint of a warning that my mother could conceivably bring an end to all this. Heck, we'd already settled on an outfit!

But maybe, just maybe, Christina could see the situation I was in. Maybe she would say that it was all right, that she understood, that we could go out another time. She must know what it was like to have Chinese parents. Right?

The next morning, I sacrificed my usual pre-homeroom rituals to go to talk to Christina at her locker. She looked up at me and smiled. This was going to be hard.

Right before I spoke, I licked my lips and held out my right hand in a conciliatory gesture. I thought about the guidelines I'd once read in the American Medical Association's newsletter for students about communicating effectively. Speak clearly and don't try to soften the blow, I reminded myself. Show empathy with your tone. That was how patients wanted to hear the worst news.

"Christina," I said, "I want to thank you for asking me to go the dance with you, but it turns out that I can't go. I'm not allowed to go on dates until I get into college." I didn't have to specify "Ivy League" because she was Chinese. She knew.

Her eyes went dull.

"What?" she asked.

"I can't go with you to the Dames Ball, Christina. My mom won't let me."

"But you said you could go," she said, her voice numb.

"Well, I was wrong," I said. "In all honesty, this was the first time I ever asked my mom if I could go on a date."

Christina faced me with her hands at her sides. "You lied to me, David! You're a liar!"

"I did lie," I admitted.

"Is your mother the real reason? Or are you lying about that, too? Are you seeing someone else?"

If I weren't so appalled at how badly this was going, I might have laughed at the last suggestion.

"Christina, I'm not lying about my mother, and I'm definitely not seeing anyone." My words were of no comfort.

"You screwed me over, David!" she screamed. "I took a major chance on you because I thought you just needed some polishing up. I didn't know you were a major project." She leaned against the wall and rested her right temple against the brick. "Oh, god," she moaned, "what are all my friends going to say? I told them that I believed in you. I'm so fucking embarrassed!"

I swallowed hard and took in her words. I can take it, I thought. Then Christina said the worst thing possible. "Jean was right! I never should have asked you out!" Hearing that awful name prodded me to respond.

"Jean," I said, "might not be a good person." People were coming down the hall to stare at us.

"She would never mortify me in public like this!"

"Honestly, Christina, you're the one raising your voice."

The next thing I knew, she'd pushed me. I nearly knocked someone over with my flailing left arm. As I regained my footing, I considered my options. Talking was only making her madder. Leaving quickly was the only reasonable thing I could do, so that's what I did.

My whole body was shaking. I felt like shit. And the day was just getting started.

The bell rang, and I began to head to homeroom. Oh, shit! My meeting with my guidance counselor, Mr. Wald, was now! If I still had my phone, it would have buzzed in my pocket to remind me.

I walked into a bathroom and washed my face with cold water. I patted my face with a paper towel and stared at myself in the mirror. *Hey, you're going to be all right*, I told myself. You have to put Christina aside for now. You need to absorb what Mr. Wald is about to tell you.

The inside of Mr. Wald's office looked like a miniature library focused on 378 in the Dewey Decimal System: college admissions. There had to be at least 500 books in there, many sprouting bookmarks through their top edges. *Beating the Admissions Game. Climbing the Ivy Wall. Unlock the Elite Colleges.*

"You're free to read any of those," said Mr. Wald as he watched me looking over his bookshelves. "As long as you don't take them out of this room."

"Do any of them work?" I asked.

"They all sort of do." He closed the door and walked around his desk. The wall behind him bore framed degrees from New York University and Hofstra—both good schools in their own right. But not Ivies. "You might read something that clicks with you but doesn't for someone else." Mr. Wald dropped into his chair and sighed as he opened up my folder. I sat down next to his desk.

"So. How are you doing, David?" he asked absentmindedly as he thumbed through some papers.

"I'm doing well, thank you. How are you?"

"I'm always good," he said without joy as he flipped through some papers. Mr. Wald looked up at me, his face suddenly serious. "Do you know why I wanted to meet with you specifically?"

"To help me plan for college?" He picked up a football that had been sitting on his desk in a kicking tee made of crystal. Mr. Wald rubbed both thumbs over the laces on the ball.

"David, you're one of only a few sophomores who have already taken the SATs. Why did you take the test this early in high school?"

"Well, I sort of had a dispute with my parents. My mother, really. She said I had to study for the SATs every day, and I said I already knew it pretty well, so I took the test to prove that I was right."

"And your score offered proof."

"Not really. I've gotten 1600 on some practice tests, but I couldn't pull it off for real."

"But you scored 1550!"

"Mr. Wald, I know you think that's a great score, but I should have gotten a perfect score. I know exactly what I did wrong." Mr. Wald slapped the football, which made a springy, questioning sound.

"David! Only three seniors got higher SAT scores than you! Are you upset you got one or two questions wrong?"

"It was probably more like six or seven," I replied.

He now grabbed the two ends of the football. "Did you tell anybody what you got?"

"Just my parents. No one else knows I took the test. Except you, I guess."

"Well, believe me, David, I've been doing this a long time, and I know a few things. One thing I'm certain of is that there isn't that much difference between 1550 and 1600. That just checks a box before an admissions officer looks around the rest of the application. I see you also did the summer coding camp. I'll bet you found it easy."

The coveted coding camp the summer before sophomore year was a good thing to have on your college application as well. A local software company ran it out of one of their conference rooms, I think for a tax break. They only took eight kids, the ones who scored highest on their test.

"I was good at it," I told Mr. Wald, "but it's not what I think of as my calling."

"What is?"

"Medicine. I want to be a doctor." Mr. Wald leaned back, and the springs in his chair laughed.

"Usually what I hear is, 'My parents want me to be a doctor.'"

"That's true for me, too."

"But what you're saying is that you genuinely want to be a doctor?"

I nodded.

It's such a stereotype, isn't it? The Asian American kid who "wants" to be a doctor. For me, though, my interest in medicine wasn't motivated by parental pressure or the lure of money and job security. My inspiration was cancer. Everything seemed to cause it yet there was still no definitive treatment. It all seemed so mysterious. I craved to know more.

I first became intrigued when I found out that Steve Jobs, inventor of the iPhone, had died of cancer. He'd been diagnosed many years before, and though he'd thought he'd had it beat, it had come back and claimed him. At a relatively young age, too. He'd had so many more years to look forward to and so many more things to invent. Maybe that's what made his death all the more tragic.

In my opinion, Jobs was one of the greatest Americans ever. Sure, he could be a dick. He openly humiliated people and screamed and lied to get his way. But that way also happened to be the right way. I've read that nobody dared to sit near him in the Apple cafeteria because he was always asking probing questions, and nothing anyone said would ever satisfy him. But because of that, he'd managed to put a smartphone in pretty much everyone's pocket. Even if your phone isn't an iPhone, it's been developed to compete with one.

Needless to say, Jobs and his fight with cancer was at the heart of my essay for the Harmony Health internship.

"Now, I see you don't have any sports due to a recent

injury." Mr. Wald was talking again.

"Shin splints."

"Yes, a minor annoyance in the long run. Pardon the pun."

I smiled to let him know I appreciated it.

"It's important to show colleges that you pursue your interests with determination. Have you been attending the meets this year?"

"Watching them? No, I haven't. No one watches us."

"You will. Go to the next meet. I saw on the calendar that there's one coming up against St. Rose. Say hi to all your teammates and the coach and root from the sidelines. It'll show that you're serious about your interests. Plus you'll get to know next year's competition. Make sure that you write in your college applications that you love track so much that while you were injured, you still went to the meets in a supportive role."

I nodded. "That's a really good idea, Mr. Wald." Since my college applications were at stake, I was pretty sure I wouldn't have any problem getting my mother on board with giving me time off to do this.

He lifted a hand to acknowledge the appreciation

"Here's another idea," said Mr. Wald. "When you're completely healed, join a running club through the summer and strengthen up for the school year. Okay? Now, what are your other plans for the summer?" I shifted in my seat and rubbed my left knee.

"Honestly, I'm still pinning my hopes on that Harmony Health internship." He let out a long whistle.

"Getting that internship is going to be harder than

getting into Harvard. You'll have to beat hundreds of other kids for the spot. Have a backup plan?"

I looked at him blankly. In the back of my mind, I thought, "Working at our restaurant."

Mr. Wald continued. "Other kids are going to have summer positions, very low-level ones, working at their parents' banks or law firms. Do you have any connections along those lines?"

"Not really," I said, trying not to feel too discouraged. "Well, I spend a lot of time working in our restaurant."

Mr. Wald nodded, in faint recognition. "Oh, right. I know the place. Are there some insights from that experience that you can reflect upon in a college essay?"

"Well, I used to resent being there. I remember this one time, I was complaining to my parents about how I had to work all these hours at the restaurant but still couldn't buy some stupid gadget that everybody else at school had. My father pulled me to the back of the restaurant and pushed me out the door. I thought I was in for a thrashing, but he held out his hands so I could see the scars and calluses in them. Then he said, 'This is all I have. I don't have anything else to give you.'" I paused to swallow. "And then we both cried."

"Oh my god, what a story," said Mr. Wald, his arms raised, one still holding the football aloft. "I love it. You have to write it just like that for your essay. Most kids in Shark Beach can't write from a place like that. I can see admissions officers lingering over it. Your parents really did give you a wonderful gift, David." I grimaced slightly and gave a slight shrug.

"Is there anything else you want to talk about, David? This is the time set aside for you, after all." Well, why shouldn't I bring up the dance with him? Mr. Wald had been pretty helpful so far. I placed both feet flat on the floor and looked at him directly.

"All right, here's something, Mr. Wald. I was asked to go to the Dames Ball. You know, that dance where the girls do the asking?"

"I know about it. I hope you have fun, David."

"Well, I can't go because my mother won't let me go on dates until I get into a good college." Mr. Wald exhaled slowly, faintly whistling the air through his lips. He placed his football back on the tee.

"David, you're not alone," he said. "I know you feel like you are, but you're not. A lot of others here are facing that same dilemma. It may seem like everybody's going to the dance, but a significant portion of the student body is subject to the same rules that you are."

"I know all that. But this was going to be my first time."

"It's a personal disappointment, David. No doubt," Mr. Wald stood up and put his hands on his desk. "But you can learn something from this."

I felt a little better after seeing Mr. Wald. Maybe Christina was feeling better, too. I didn't see her at lunch. Maybe she was laying low for a bit. Maybe she was getting ready to apologize for pushing me.

I was on my way to English class when I suddenly found myself stumbling backwards. My books went flying. Christina was shorter than me and had a lower center of gravity, giving her a lot of leverage. I didn't even realize that she'd shoved me—for the second time that day—until I slammed into our English teacher Mrs. Humbolt, another person with a low center of gravity.

Powers of concentration learned from practicing yoga must have been what gave Mrs. Humbolt the ability to take the hit without falling to the floor. She widened her stance quickly and almost instinctively, keeping both of us upright.

Any other teacher would have yelled at me or even shoved me back.

"David," said Mrs. Humbolt, breaking my name into two unstressed syllables as she looked me over first and then Christina.

"I am so sorry, Mrs. Humbolt," I squeaked.

Her eyes flashed. "Christina," she said evenly. "Why did you push David? Did he say something rude or push you first?" Mrs. Humbolt was slow to judge statements and events.

"David Tung is a coward!" said Christina, her voice cracking. She broke away and ran to the restroom. Mrs. Humbolt nodded.

"Hmmm," she said quietly. "You've broken her heart, David."

I certainly hadn't meant to. Now I felt terrible all over again.

I'd worried so much about how to tell Christina I couldn't go, but I'd never once thought how much pain it might cause her. It didn't seem fair that my mother's rules were harming someone other than me. Jean *was* right. Christina should have asked out someone who was normal.

Mrs. Humbolt followed Christina into the bathroom while I took my seat alongside the other students in the classroom.

The two of them entered the classroom shortly after the late bell rang. I was trying to make myself as inconspicuous as possible in my seat, four rows behind Christina's, but I couldn't help but look up guiltily as she stepped swiftly to her desk. Her face had hardened into a mask, and I saw the hint of a cynical smile.

"For this period," Mrs. Humbolt said, "I want you to write a letter to yourself. I'm not going to collect your papers or read them. I'm just going to walk around to make sure you've been writing."

After a false start, writing about meeting with Mr. Wald, I began a rambling apology letter to Christina. "I'm sorry that I'm not the person you thought I could be," I wrote. Then I looked up to see that Mrs. Humbolt was standing right over me, and, contrary to her earlier words, reading my paper. She moved on after a few seconds.

Right before the bell rang, she said, "Thank you, class." I collected my things.

"David," she said, looking at me intently. "Stay a second. I want to talk to you."

Shit. I glanced around and saw that Christina had already split. Early arrivals for the next class were coming in. They stood next to the bookshelves along the sides of the room as they waited for their desks to be vacated.

I went up to Mrs. Humbolt's desk, and she looked me straight in the eye. Speaking quietly so that the conversation remained between the two of us, she said with a touch of menace, "Do you know how hard it is in this society for a woman to ask a man out?"

"It must be pretty hard," I said. "I mean, it's not easy for anybody, I'm sure."

"A woman can be made to feel extremely insecure. You should remember that."

Given how terribly the day had gone, I was glad that at least Jean wouldn't be on the bus ride home. Since it was Tuesday, she and Christina both would be safely tucked away in the conference rooms, talking about Chinese Council stuff with the rest of the board. All of Christina's close friends were officers and would be in that meeting. Even if they spent the whole time talking shit about me, at least I wouldn't have to deal with it.

I boarded the bus and walked down the aisle past known Jean allies.

Did Percy just grin at me?

Well, to hell with him and all his stupid drinking friends.

I took a seat at the window two rows ahead of the wheel bump. I put my hands over my face and pressed my palms to my eyes. At least my classes went well. No biology quiz, good. Trig, French, history, all good. Gym/Health, stupid. English, kinda horrible, but no net change grade-wise. Dialectics, great.

Talking to Christina had been awful, but I was glad

that now it was over and done with.

Something glanced off my forehead. I took away my hands and quickly identified the object as a crumpled piece of paper. Turning around, I saw that the thrower was Jean. She was standing in the bus aisle, her face contorted.

"You're a goddamned loser, David!" she yelled as she tore another sheet out of her binder. I held up my left hand in a conciliatory gesture that could also block the next projectile.

"You're supposed to be at Chinese Council, Jean," I said.

"We called it off because our president had to go home! Because she felt sick!" Even though I was only about 10 feet away, her next toss missed badly, and the paper ball bounced off the back of a seat and out an open window.

"Do not throw things out the window!" warned the bus driver.

"If the president is incapacitated," I said to Jean, "isn't the vice president supposed to take charge? After all, that *is* the sole function of the office."

"I couldn't continue the meeting because Christina was so distraught that she went home with the key to the office!" She tried to rip out more pages, but she had grabbed too many, and the three-ring binder snapped open. Out of frustration, she hurled the entire thing at me. Papers, pencils, and erasers all went flying.

"Do not throw things on the bus!" warned the driver.

Percy bounded down the aisle past Jean and gathered the school-related detritus.

"Never mind that coolie, he's not worth it," he said to her. "Christina dodged a bullet."

"She thought David was going to be her date," said Jean as she gave me the death stare.

"Then things have changed for the better already," said Percy. "Now we don't have to be in photos with him and pretend to be friends." He gathered up all her things and tried to touch her elbow. She violently jerked her arm away.

"Eat shit!" she yelled at me before whirling around and stomping away to the back of the bus.

"Do not use profanity on the bus!" warned the driver.

When we reached our bus stop, I lingered to let Jean, Percy, Fred, and Grace exit and cross the street before I got out.

My mother was parked nearby as usual.

"How was school?" she asked as she always did. True to form, she gave no acknowledgement whatsoever of our fight the night before. I hadn't expected any. After all, she'd been victorious once again, and without having to make a single concession.

"There were no grades today," I said. Mom nodded.

"What about Hormone Health?" I had to cough to keep myself from cracking up at my mother's malapropism. The state of my hormones was the last thing she'd want to hear from me.

"You mean 'Harmony Health.' Still nothing."

"Yes, I meant 'Harmony Health.'" I hoped my mother wouldn't ask about Christina because I didn't feel like going there. "Did you see that Christina Tau today?" she asked, as if on cue.

"I see her every day," I said.

"Did you tell her you can't go to that dance?"

"Yes. She was very upset."

"*I'm* the one who's upset," my mother said. We rolled to a stop at a red light. This made me anxious. While waiting for the light to change, my mom would have a chance to focus on me instead of the road. "Do you flirt with girls in school, David?"

"No."

"Are you lying?"

With this accusation on top of everything else, my day had now officially hit a new low. I might embellish details from time to time, but I'd never outright lied to either of my parents. Sure, I had planned to lie to get to the dance, but that was a moot point now.

Putting my right knee against the door to brace myself, I said, my voice louder than I had expected: "Do you want to come to school with me tomorrow? I'd be happy to show you what my day is like, if you think I'm lying about any of it."

Her only reply was a dismissive wave of her right arm. The court didn't need to see any evidence to pronounce a guilty judgment.

It was quickly becoming obvious that this was going to be one of those days where I was so annoyed with my mom that it would be better for the both of us if I actively avoided talking to her. We drove the rest of the way to the restaurant in total silence. I didn't even bother to ask when I could have my phone back. I didn't want to show her that I needed it.

CHAPTER EIGHT

On Wednesday morning, Jean ignored me at the bus
stop, and Christina avoided me in school, and really
that was the best outcome I could have hoped for.
Well, not the very best. I mean, my name wasn't on the
bulletin board for Harmony Health. Also, Christina's
friend Cassie gave me the finger in the hallway. I was
like, "Really?"

Thursday was even better. I made it all the way
to gym class without encountering any real challenges.

The PE component of gym class could be enjoyable,
especially when it was full-court dodgeball. But
whenever we had a health module, our teacher
Mr. Scanlon struggled to convey the lessons to us
because he was the worst living public speaker in the
whole state.

Today, he was supposed to teach us about the
dangers of drinking and driving. Mr. Scanlon stood to
the side of the health classroom and put on a brave face

as he peered out at us.

"All right, guys," he called out. "How many of you people have learnin' permits?"

Most of the class, 20 out of 22 kids, raised their hands.

"Well guess what? When we come back from summer break, one or more of you won't be here. Because you'll be too busy bein' dead." He paused to take a nervous swig from his water bottle. "Who here wants their name on the memory plaque by the front office? The one for students who bit it?" No one said a word.

Mr. Scanlon was well on his way to frothing at the mouth, and as a result, most of us had immediately reverted to the standard operating procedure for surviving a Mr. Scanlon rant: 1) keep your eyes open but angled down toward the floor; and 2) never ever respond to any of his questions. Anyone who attracted his attention when he was in this state was sure to be picked out for a personalized hammering for the rest of the period. Mr. Scanlon was more comfortable when attacking than lecturing.

Our teacher hunched his shoulders and surveyed the room, daring anybody to meet his gaze.

"Anybody here ever drink and drive?" he asked to no response. "Anybody here drink?" Still nothing. "Anybody here...go to parties?"

Marshall Zhang raised his hand slowly. He was a nice, honest kid. Maybe too honest.

"Zhang." Scanlon savored the name. "So you're a party kinda guy?"

"Not all the time," Marshall said defensively.

"Do your parties have cake and ice cream on plates

with animal pictures?" They probably did, but Mr. Scanlon's question dripped with so much sarcasm, I couldn't help but snort.

"Tung!" Mr. Scanlon accused. I looked up and directly into his eyes. No avoiding him now. "You findin' somethin' funny?"

"No," I said. "Not really." That made some of the other students snicker.

Now that Mr. Scanlon had selected me as the day's sacrifice, the tension had gone out of the room. Everyone else was safe. He pointed the mouthpiece of his whistle at me.

"'Not really,' huh? Why were you laughin', Tung?"

"Honestly," I said slowly as I shucked off any effort to defend myself, "I laughed because Marshall probably does have cake and ice cream at the parties he goes to. He's a very innocent kid. That's obvious even to a casual observer."

Mr. Scanlon solemnly wiped his face with both hands. "Yes," he said as if in a trance. "I would agree that that's true about our good little friend Zhang. I wonder, though, about your inability to take the subject matter seriously, Tung. How can you laugh during my class about drunk drivin' when people are dyin'?"

"If we had settled into a serious tone, Mr. Scanlon, I wouldn't have laughed." Now that I'd been flushed out of my preferred stance of studied anonymity, I figured that not backing down was my only way forward. I'd seen too many kids meekly submit and still receive no mercy to even consider taking that approach.

I looked Mr. Scanlon in the eye and tried to read his

next move.

"Oh, I'll get real serious now, Tung. What kind of parties do *you* go to? I'll bet you don't go to too many. That's obvious to any casual observer. You don't really have any friends. You have this whole detached manner as if you don't care. Maybe you think girls find that cool. Maybe you're just scared to have feelin's."

I considered what he said and found that it didn't yet merit a response because there was no question attached to it. He continued.

"You think you're above this whole school and all the stupid little state-approved requirements and lessons we put you through. But do you think you're immune to the effects of drunk drivin'?"

"Yes," I said. He seemed stunned that I had spoken.

"So! You're immune, are you Tung? What an amazing power you have! You think you can drink a whole six-pack and then drive home fine?"

"I don't drink."

"Eighty percent of drunk drivers who were involved in fatalities didn't think they'd be drinkin', either! If you went to a party, and a halfway decent lookin' girl offered you a beer, are you gonna say no?"

"I don't go to parties."

"You don't party at all?"

"No. I'm either here, in school, or at our family restaurant."

Mr. Scanlon rubbed his hands together with enough intensity to start a fire.

"You know what, Tung? I am sick of your bullshit answers. Come down here and read today's module in front of the class." He headed to the back of the room and dropped on a forlorn chair whose desktop component had broken off. I stood up and sauntered to the front of the room.

"Go ahead, Tung," he yelled out from his busted chair. "The instructor's book is right there. You do 'Alcohol and Teens,' Lesson 2. Let's see you fall on your face!"

I opened the book and noted the first step.

"Mr. Scanlon, it says the students are supposed to turn their books to page 12. Where are our books?"

In mock panic, Mr. Scanlon threw his hands up.

"Oh, what are we going to do? We don't have books for the students! Well, guess what, Tung? A few years ago, some of the parents were so outraged by the section on 'Sexuality and Teens' that the books were removed! Gee, I guess you have to wing it, Tung! Make sure to hit all those bullet points and keep this class engaged!"

I looked over the class. Everyone seemed a little excited at the prospect of a showdown, but I knew from my own personal experience how easy it was to rapidly settle into a state barely above sleep mode. I cleared my throat.

"Well," I said, "these bullet points seem interesting enough for me to simply read them out. 'According to the 2013 National Survey on Drug Use and Health, 35.1% of 15-year-olds reported that they have had at least one drink in their lives.' Now, how many of you have already had at least one drink? Raise your hand."

Nobody budged. My gaze fell upon Percy II, the guy who'd offered me a flask in homeroom. He was now chewing gum like a cow. Maybe he was still trying to cover up his breath.

"So now it's not cool to say you drink?" I asked, looking directly at him.

He sighed, shrugged, and raised his hand. Two people followed, and then three more. After 10 kids had raised their hands, I looked over at Mr. Scanlon. He looked like a roof gargoyle, hunched over with his mouth open.

I managed to get through the first lesson, more or less with class participation, and at the end of the period a humbled Mr. Scanlon made it clear that he'd be taking the class back from here on out.

As I walked to my next class, I thought with satisfaction about how I seemed to have some affinity for teaching. Who knew? I had no problem speaking in front of the whole class, probably thanks to years of covering the front counter of our restaurant. I'd also found out I could adjust what I was saying and how I was saying it on the fly in order to keep students engaged. I could even tell who wasn't paying attention and pull them back into the flock.

That's what students were, after all: sheep being led from one lesson to another. Sometimes we rammed each other. Sometimes we didn't smell so good.

I didn't know if I had what it took to be a teacher, though. The effort of having to be on my guard every day would probably wear me down. I'd end up being just another jaded asshole in the teachers' lounge.

Public-speaking skills might help me in my medical career, though. I've watched videos of research talks at conferences, and the speakers are generally awful.

One medical doctor had the oratory skills of a motivational speaker, however: Harmony Health's Dr. Vivian Lee. She had an energetic, friendly way of talking, and she would nod solemnly when making more serious points. Anytime death came up, she would lower her head and fix her glasses.

It was sometimes hard to follow her actual words, however. She enunciated clearly enough, but the acronyms and jargon she tossed in sounded like Martian loan words. Apparently everyone else at the conference also vacationed regularly on Mars, judging by the murmurs of agreement from the audience.

Even trying to research the acronyms wasn't easy. Every time I looked one up, it would lead to two more. Most were related to science or medicine, but some were just euphemisms. "SAE" stood for "serious adverse event," "SR" for "survival rate."

I rubbed my hands together as I walked the school hallways. Being a doctor wouldn't be easy. I knew I could walk the walk, but talking the talk could be a problem. I mean, I'd badly miscalculated my discussions with my mother and Christina, and look where that had gotten me. I was still feeling negative vibes from both.

Dr. Lee herself had said that it was an issue when a doctor had trouble being honest with her patient that the end was certain and near. How would I handle such an eventuality? Would I have had the balls to tell someone like Steve Jobs that he was probably going to die? Or would I have resorted instead to mealy-mouthed mouse squeaks about how his treatment had a 50% SAE and a 20% SR?

I wanted to heal important people who suffered from cancers that were nearly untreatable, but it was far more likely that I'd probably be watching them die. Some more quickly than others.

I'd read that oncologists suffer high rates of depression, anxiety, and burnout.

But Dr. Lee seemed to be doing well. Maybe she had a mild case of dissociation. Maybe that made it possible for her to do her job without feeling too much.

I hoped to do the same. The pressure to get high grades while working at a restaurant was probably just prepping me for a mental disorder that would be helpful for my chosen occupation.

I would thank my mother for putting me on that track, but our people don't discuss mental health.

CHAPTER NINE

Later that week, I sat on the outdoor bleachers and shivered from the cold and excitement of being near the track again. My mother had as expected given me the time off from work to attend the meets, especially after I told her my guidance counselor had recommended I do so.

My fellow spectators were a first-year student who was keeping time and Bessa Norton, Mr. Norton's wife. My dialectics teacher had just started coaching track and field.

The visiting team was St. Rose, a small Catholic school that was as white as we were Asian. We had a way bigger student body, though, so it wasn't really a fair meet. I looked over at Bessa's scoresheet, and it was ugly. For the most part, my team was getting killed by the other big public schools, so getting this one easy win felt good.

Someone grabbed my shoulder. It was my friend

Yaro. His first name is also David, but I never called him that. No one did.

"Couldn't stay away, huh?" He had already changed back into jeans because his races were over. Lanky and with legs that are longer than mine, Yaro rules the dashes, though I had him beat for long distances. His light brown skin blends in with many of the Asians, but he has way more freckles. He generally keeps his hair short, though one summer he'd come back with cornrows.

"How could I? Someone's gotta be a witness to the way you're destroying the competition!"

He shook his head slowly. "St. Rose isn't competition. This is just light work."

"Think about this, Yaro. If you'd stayed in Catholic school, you'd be on their team."

He shuddered.

"Anyway, it's good to see you here," he said. "No one comes to these meets."

"Speaking as an observer," I said, "it is kinda boring watching people go round and round."

"Here's something not boring." Yaro held up a rumpled notice and shook it at me. "Look what I found in my gym locker today."

I snatched it from him in a rude way that you could only do with people close to you. Student athletes were being informed that the weight room would be closed for asbestos removal.

"Yeah, they've known for years about the asbestos," I said. "We're probably immune to it by now." Yaro twisted his mouth.

"This is no joke, son. I got asthma. My parents are gonna sue this district so fast!"

I'd read up a bit about asbestos, about the facts versus the myths. "As long as it isn't flaking off, it's not a danger," I said. "Sometimes it's safer to leave it in the walls rather than remove it."

"What about the vents? Aren't asbestos fibers coming through them?"

"In this particular case, I wouldn't know." I handed the notice back to him. He curled it into a cone.

"If this isn't a big clusterfuck, then why do we have to sign a liability waiver?"

"Ask your dad. Isn't he a lawyer?"

"Aw, he's gonna hit the roof when I show him this!" Yaro chuckled at the image.

"Yaro, you have a 20 Questions for me?"

"You never responded to my comment on the last one!"

I scratched my elbows. "Oh. My phone is in the repair shop."

"David, you gotta get a new phone, already! Okay, well, how about this. There's this hot girl who asks a guy out to a dance. The guy says yes at first, then says no because his mother won't let him."

Coming from Yaro, an old friend, this was actually very funny to me.

"Hmmm, who could you possibly be talking about."

"Hey, David, too bad you're not coming to the Dames Ball. We could've hung out."

Yaro and I rarely hung out outside of school anymore, due to my restaurant duties.

"I have to work that night, anyway," I said.

He sniffed and leaned in to me. "I heard that you're not allowed to date girls until college."

"Yeah, it's true," I said.

"Aw, man, I'm sorry, David."

I glanced at my feet. "Hey, I lied to you, Yaro. My phone isn't broken. My mother took it away."

"What! How come?"

"She was angry that I wanted to go to the Dames Ball."

"Man, that is seriously...Asian. Thank you for telling me the truth, man. You know I can handle it."

"So who are you going with, Yaro?" I asked. He shrugged with embarrassment.

"I'm going with Christina! I thought you knew! She told me all about how you couldn't go." There was no guile in his eyes, and his face became twice as friendly as he continued talking. "You're crazy. I totally would have figured out some way to sneak out to see Christina. She's cute."

"Easier said than done. Plus, your mom isn't as good with knives as mine." Yaro cracked up because we both remembered how my mother had once shown him how to hack a big beef bone to get the marrow out.

"I hope you and Christina have fun," I heard myself say.

"Well, I hope your restaurant kicks ass in the receipts department that night. Laters!"

"Yeah. See ya." We did a one-arm hug, and Yaro jumped off the bleachers and left.

Christina. She and her crew probably didn't give two shits about Yaro, even though he was popular. She'd only asked him because she knew we were old friends, and she'd figured it would upset me.

Yes, I was annoyed she was going with someone I knew and actually liked. If she'd gone with some copy of Percy I or II, I wouldn't have cared at all.

Christina's closest friends silent-hated me all week. But on Friday morning at the bus stop, Jean couldn't help but dig in.

"David, I want to let you know that Christina has followed my advice and found another boy to go with her to the Dames Ball." Her eyes gleamed with evil power.

"That's great," I said.

"Don't you want to know who?"

"You mean 'whom.'"

"'Who' works!"

"No, it doesn't. Your question in full would be, 'Don't you want to know with whom she is going?'" She straightened up and twisted her right leather flat into the ground.

"That's wrong," said Jean. "My question is actually, 'Don't you want to know who's taking her to the dance?'"

"That's grammatically correct, but it's the Dames Ball, so she's actually the one taking him to the dance. 'Don't you want to know who she's taking to the dance?'"

"You're an asshole, David!" Jean hissed.

"And yes, I did hear the good news." She looked taken aback by the mildness of my reaction. "Yaro's a good guy." I continued. "And if I can't go, I'm happy that someone else can show Christina a good time. She deserves it."

Jean didn't know what to do with my well wishes.

"I'm only sorry that she had to experience those horrible few days with you first, David," she spat out before retreating back to her pack.

I was reaching to put my headphones on when Al, the white kid, came up to me. He was smiling in a funny way. He looked way too young for high school.

"Hey, David. Do you have a sec? I wanna ask you something."

"Sure," I said, unsure of what was coming next.

He looked nervous. "I'm having a hard time, David."

I blinked. "What do you mean?" I asked.

"Sometimes I wonder if it's because I'm new here or if there's a reverse-racism thing going on. Most of the other kids, the Asian ones, won't talk to me. Except for you."

I nodded. Shark Beach High's student body wasn't always that welcoming, even to Asian kids.

"Al, I'm sort of the black sheep at school, you know. I guess you're a white sheep."

He tilted his head at Jean and her friends. "How come they don't like you? Did you do something to them?"

"Nah, they're just idiots. I guess running a restaurant—one like ours—is considered manual labor, not a professional occupation. That makes me an outsider here in Shark Beach. Plus I don't go to the same Chinese school that everyone else goes to on Saturdays. I go to a Chinese school in the city. So that's another strike against me."

"Tung's Garden—that's you, right?" Al asked. I nodded. "My mom goes there for the weekday buffet sometimes." He crossed his arms. "Why do you go to a different Chinese school?"

"Let's just say it's a community dispute."

He glanced sideways at Jean, Percy, Grace, and Fred.

"Those guys," I said, "have been building up camaraderie for years. They're a little insular."

I was proud to have used "insular" in a conversation. I also thought about my pals in Chinese school. We were tight, too. If we attended the same public school, we'd probably also push people around or ignore them.

"It's not right, though," said Al. He glanced at Jean and turned his entire body to face me full on. "I told you before I had some dirt on her."

"Yeah, you did."

"It's some damaging material. Do you wanna know what it is?"

There was no hiding the fact that I was curious and annoyed enough to indulge that curiosity, even against my better instincts, which were telling me not to involve myself in something that could be illicit. I shifted my feet in anticipation. "Sure."

"Well, my mom's boyfriend does network security for the mall. He maintains the devices the mall cops use." Al brought his face in close to mine and dropped his voice. "They busted Jean for shoplifting some makeup over the holidays."

"What? Her family's loaded! Why would she need to shoplift? Are you sure it was her?" We were practically whispering at this point.

"Yeah. A hundred percent sure. If you get pinched at the mall and you're a minor, they take a picture of you and make your parents pick you up. They're supposed to delete all the photos after a few months, but my mom's boyfriend uses some of them for a slideshow screensaver on his personal laptop. I saw all the girls he's gotten, but Jean's the only one I don't like."

"Al, honestly, I'm having a hard time believing you."

Al frowned, played with his phone a bit, and then showed me a picture. Her eyes were pink and puffy, but that was Jean in the mug shot all right. She was holding a sign that spelled out in handwritten block letters, "JEAN CHU STOLE $20.75 IN MAKEUP FROM SEPHORA." She was clearly scared out of her wits in the photo. It was the first time I saw her looking like a kid.

I couldn't help but feel bad for Jean, despite how unlikeable she was. Being picked up for stealing could destroy her college applications. She must have seen her life flash before her eyes when she was in front of the camera. I wondered if Percy knew about it.

Al pulled back his phone and typed on it.

"I'm sending this to you," he said.

"OK, thanks," I said.

"Ah, what's your number?"

"Actually, please send it to my gmail," I said, "I don't have a phone." I typed it in for him and I saw him press send. Now that photo could live in the cloud forever.

"You used to have a phone, right?" he asked.

"My mother confiscated it to keep me out of trouble," I said. He looked confused. "It's an Asian thing."

Weirdly enough, that brief exchange with Al shifted something for me at school. As I walked the hallways,

I felt a new confidence. I was at ease as I made my way through the crowds. I had the power to destroy somebody's social life, somebody I didn't like.

Let's take a look at the internship board. Whoa! There was now a "TBA" by the Harmony Health name.

I ran into Mr. Wald's office. He was sitting at his desk, reading papers in a folder.

"Hey, Mr. Wald," I said, feeling myself running out of oxygen. He looked up at me and smiled. He knew what I was going to ask. "What does 'TBA' mean?"

"David, it means that Harmony Health has narrowed down the applicant pool." He shrugged. "That's all I know."

"Am I still in the running?" Mr. Wald's smile grew a degree sadder.

"I hope so." I went to my locker, hope at a low ebb.

Scott Sima, my locker neighbor, turned to me and said, "David, I heard about your problem with the dance, and all. Your mother won't let you go, right?"

"Yeah," I said. "It's okay, Scott, don't worry about it."

"Look, I just want to say, stay focused on the things you can change, and stay positive." I thought about Jean's picture and the terrible power I now had.

"Positive?" As in, try not toy with someone else's life?

"Yeah. Make the best of everything you got." He bumped shoulders with me as if I were a teammate. "You got this, papi!"

I heard what Scott was saying, but I wasn't willing to abandon all my weapons just yet. Being a nice guy had gotten me nowhere.

I couldn't stop thinking about different ways I could destroy Jean's reputation. Maybe I could even find out where her mother and father worked and email the mug shot to all their colleagues.

Or I could post the picture online and tag her. Oh, we weren't connected on Facebook, so maybe I couldn't tag her. But if I requested her friendship, then I could tag her picture until she actually rejected my request. Or maybe her settings wouldn't allow me to. The permissions rules kept changing—how annoying!

I was overthinking again, but the thoughts were delicious. Yet a part of me also knew I could never actually do any of it. Not even Jean had done anything horrible enough to deserve the kinds of revenge I was contemplating.

Soon enough it was Saturday morning again, and as usual, my parents, Auntie Zhang, and I were preparing snap peas, tossing the trimmed pods into a big metal bowl. Each landed with a little ring that sounded like a soft strike against a zen bowl gong.

Things were anything but zen underneath the surface, though.

I was still quietly resentful that my mother had stopped me from going to the dance. I had been channeling that frustration physically into my work, and had ended each night with sore arms. What else could I do? Go on strike?

That was the nuclear option because it would destroy everything.

Only time could wear down my mother's anger at me

for daring to challenge her anti-girlfriend law. Bringing it up again would only result in me getting another earful. In fact, we hadn't spoken much about anything since she took my phone.

Bong, pealed the bowl.

"Did you see the actor they got to play the prime minister for the flashback scenes?" my mother asked Auntie Zhang.

"Yes, I like him a lot," said Auntie Zhang.

My father and I boarded the train to New York City. I no longer had a phone, so I brought printouts of some questions from a genuine MCAT quiz given a few years ago.

I lay the printouts against my chest and imagined my Chinatown friends making fun of me for losing my phone. Chun would laugh at me, I'm sure. Maybe Betty would, too.

As I thought about my friends, it struck me once again how my father and I were able to loosen up and be ourselves on these trips. Meanwhile, my mother and Auntie Zhang would be watching Chinese soap operas on the big TV back at Tung's Garden. Saturday mornings were an escape for all of us.

I met Chun and Andy in the Chinese school lobby, and we lumbered up the stairs together.

"Did you know there's going to be a big meteor shower in two weeks?" Chun asked us. Two weeks? The Dames Ball was in two weeks.

"You get that from following Neil deGrasse Tyson?"

I asked. His face fell slightly.

"Him and other people," Chun said. "There are going to be fireballs, too. And this is no bullshit, right here: In ancient China, people believed that bad things were going to happen to the emperor whenever there were comets and stuff in the sky because it meant that heaven was displeased."

"It was bullshit then, and it's bullshit now," said Andy. He never said too much, but he liked to call BS on Chinese superstitions.

YK was selling cards to kids on the second-floor landing, again. From the looks of it, he'd managed to squeeze another $30 from little Carl Ching. Transaction completed, YK joined us as we continued our upward march.

The four of us walked into performance class together, drawing a suspicious look from Mr. Chen. Betty was walking away from him, as if they had just been chatting.

"Listen, everybody," Mr. Chen announced. "Believe it or not, in three weeks, we're going to be on that stage, so let's finalize those seven-minute scripts. Any groups that haven't yet integrated have to get that done today." He looked at me meaningfully before continuing. "Next week, we're going to practice the movement, so the words need to be written today or at some point before we meet again."

YK, Andy, Chun, and I noisily pushed our desks together into a plus sign. We all looked at each other.

"You guys," I said. "I think Betty just told on us to Mr. Chen."

"Who does she think she is?" asked Chun.

"She is right, though," Andy said lazily, looking at his fingernails.

"What do you mean?" Chun was getting agitated.

"He means, we don't have any girls in our group," YK chimed in.

I shoved my fists into my elbows and leaned my face into the middle of our desks.

"Well, how about this," I said. "Let Betty's punishment be that she has to join our group."

"Yeah!" said Chun. "She's gonna run away screaming."

In all honesty, I actually wanted Betty to join us. She was definitely annoying, but I had the feeling that she could get stuff done.

"Why don't you ask her to marry you, already?" grunted Chun. "We've seen you two looking at each other longingly."

I frowned at him. "I mean, I do have to ask her to join us," I said.

"I'm just messing with you, Dave. Ask her already."

"She'd be good," Andy offered.

"Go get her, David," YK said amiably.

I stood up, took one step toward her, and felt the fear of rejection spear my stomach and heart.

What the hell? I shouldn't feel this way. I wasn't asking her for a date. Or even to go to a dance! And I'd talked to her plenty of times already, though we'd never shared super-long conversations. Or even an average-length conversation, really. Last week, I'd even had to defend my honor against a barrage of accusations by her.

I took a few steps and paused again.

Asking her to join our group would be a pretty brief exchange. Man, why was it so hot at school today? Take a breath. Just act as if you want to borrow a pen. It's a no-stress situation. I resumed walking. Yeah, that's it. There we go.

When I got closer to Betty, I nonchalantly sidled up to her. I'm sure she noticed, but she pretended to be engrossed in the songbook.

"Excuse me, Betty, can I borrow a pen?" Oh, no, why did I say that?

She smiled, and her eyes had an expectant quality to them.

"So the Jersey boy who comes to class late all the time wants to borrow my pen?" asked Betty. "You've got one right in your pocket, David." My right hand shot to my shirt pocket and pressed the Tung's Garden ballpoint pen against my nipple.

"Now that I've got the pen, I actually want to borrow you." I crossed my arms and basked in my wit for two seconds. "YK and Andy and Chun and I all want you to join our group."

She opened her eyes wide. "What! The four kings are requesting my presence? Oh my!" she squealed. She let her voice drop back to its normal register before adding, "Why should I join your group?"

Kathy Wong, whose Mandarin name was Keqing, grabbed Betty's arm with a quickness she'd probably learned from her mother. Kathy's hair featured some purple highlights, and she usually wore peace-punk band shirts from the 1990s. Betty never seemed terribly enamored of Kathy, but Kathy sat next to Betty whenever she could.

"Chun is a jerk," Kathy spat. "You don't have to join up with those guys, Betty. We can put our own group together."

"We would still need a boy," said Betty.

"We can get Warren to join!" The three of us looked at skinny Warren who was haplessly tangled in his seat. From his neck up he looked like a baby owl. Below that he was a giraffe that had never learned to stand.

Betty turned to me. "Can Kathy join, too?"

"I don't want to join them," Kathy snapped. "And I don't want you to join them, either, Betty."

Betty shrugged. "They need help," she said.

"Then go!" said Kathy. Betty stood up and dragged over her desk next to mine. "But know that I am questioning our friendship!" Kathy called out.

"We live in the same building," Betty said by way of explanation to me. Over her shoulder, she called out: "Let's make seitan musubi tonight." That seemed to appease Kathy, who turned to Warren and tried to look busy.

"You're Chinese," I said. "Why do you want to make Japanese food?"

Betty gave me a cute little smile as she sat down.

"Why do you speak English, David?" she asked.

Damn. Her snappy reply gave her instant authority in our group.

We—the boys, that is—opened our books up and pretended to treat the assignment seriously.

It was simple, really. We had to write a little skit

based on the Chinese classics and work in a few one-minute songs. The whole shebang was supposed to be seven minutes or less.

Betty surveyed all of our faces. "Let me guess. You're going with *Romance of the Three Kingdoms*, right?"

"Yeah, it's got a lot of potential," Chun said in a tone that was intended to mock her drive to be productive. In truth, he'd never read a single page of the novel. None of us had. But we all knew the stories from the cartoons, TV shows, and videogames. The plot line, we figured, was sort of like Robin Hood if he had a whole army and was fighting to win all of China from corrupt officials.

"That's good," Betty continued. "I've been planning ahead, and I think we should go with mashing three scenes from the book into one skit: the oath taken by the three sworn brothers in the peach orchard; Cao Cao's encounter with the Daoist magician; and then Liu Bei trying to convince the strategist Kongming to join his cause." We boys nodded. Yeah, those names sounded familiar.

She opened her notebook and pulled out a crisp sheet of paper with printed summaries and handwritten notes all over it.

"So, Chun, Andy, and YK will alternately play two of the three brothers," Betty continued in a perfunctory voice, consulting her sheet. Apparently, everything was already settled in her mind. "I don't care which one of you is Zhang Fei or Lord Guan. Just pick your favorite. I'm going to be the Taoist magician and Kongming. David is going to be Cao Cao and the third brother, Liu Bei."

Damn, she had everything all planned out! I craned my neck to get a better view of her paper. She had written out cast lists for the scenes between blank spaces for the songs we would be responsible for working on.

"Betty," asked Chun with suspicion, "have you been working on this your entire life?"

"It doesn't take that long to outline the basics," she said. "There's still a lot of work to do."

"How did you know you were going to be working with us?" I asked. Betty rolled her pencil between her hands.

"If you hadn't asked me first, David, I was going to ask to join myself. Anyway, I don't know any other girls in this class willing to work with you guys. After all, Chun is in your group. So it's not as though I had to worry about competition." She tapped the eraser end of the pencil on the desk.

"You have a problem with me?" asked Chun. She ignored the question. "Is there something wrong with me?" he persisted.

"You're not nice," said Andy. Chun seemed hurt by the remark, but nobody spoke up to challenge it. Well, Chun would get over it.

YK ran his index fingers down the cast list. "How come you and David are the stars of two scenes and the rest of us only get one?"

"Everyone is in every scene, and besides, the three brothers are the overall stars," said Betty. "You all know this from reading the book like I did, right?"

YK's face faltered. "Um, yeah."

"Everyone's going to have lines in every scene. It's just that David and I are going to have two songs and you three will each have one."

"I have a good voice," said Andy.

"Sing the national anthem for us," Betty challenged.

"Not in front of you!"

"Then how are you going to do it in front of the whole school?" Andy sucked in his lips.

"I liked our group better before this one joined," said Chun as he glared at Betty, who responded by narrowing her eyes.

"Maybe you'd rather have Kathy join instead, Chun." Betty turned in her seat. "Hey, Kath! Kath! Chun says he likes you!" Kathy, who had been showing Warren what to read, looked over.

Chun stood up and waved his arms. "No I don't! I never said anything!"

Kathy shot him with a near-lethal dose of Death Glare before noisily turning her back on him.

"Do you want her in the group or me?" Betty asked Chun quietly.

"You! Okay?"

"Then sit down and listen. We've got so much to do." She turned to me. "David."

"Yes," I said.

"Find a song that two strategists would sing to test each other. Like a "you're terrible because you used me" song. You guys, find one song each about eternal friendship and brotherhood. I'll find one about magic and enchantments."

Chun, Andy, and YK sullenly paddled through the pages of the songbook. The song lyrics, which were written in Chinese characters, were meant to be sung in Mandarin. None of it had been translated into English. Neither Chun nor Andy could read Chinese characters well, so the exercise was pointless for them. YK, who had gone to school in Hong Kong, could read characters almost as well as the teachers, so he'd be able to explain them to Andy in Mandarin. We could only presume that Chun would eventually catch on at some point. Or not.

I was able to read characters a little bit because I'm too diligent a student to not learn anything, even when kicking back in Chinese school. Betty could read a whole bunch, though, and I watched her lips move as she silently pronounced song lyrics.

Having Betty on board literally brought organization to the table for the first time. On the other hand, I hadn't expected her to instantly assume leadership without even waiting for a consensus decision. Our M.O. had always been to do things with no particular person in charge, even if working like that always led to us flaunting our obvious lack of preparation. It was a little embarrassing, sure, but the stakes were so low— no parents attended, and no college was going to look at my Chinese school records—that I never particularly cared about how we came off. Fumbling about for 11 minutes on a stage didn't faze me at all. It didn't seem to affect YK or Andy that much, either. That's probably why none of us could be bothered to put much effort into these skits in the first place.

For Chun, though, the whole experience was

agonizing. As much as Chun loved being the center of attention in a class situation or talking back to teachers, he became seized with stage fright when in front of an actual audience. As a result, he would forget all his lines and even lose track of basic coordination skills, tripping all over the place.

Betty probably couldn't improve Chun's performances, but her mere presence was still a game changer. She was pushing us to reach our "true potential," as some SAT-prep academies promise. Maybe we would even find ourselves able to come up with something that would get us a standing ovation.

Then again, maybe not. We were just a few minutes into the reign of Betty, and already Chun was texting, Andy's head was propped up with his hand, fingers over his mouth, eyes closed, and YK was doodling.

Betty was now steering the ship on this project, but she had also divided our group, disrupting a collective sense of being, and each of my friends were rebelling against her in his own way. Betty and I singing two duets? Why did she have to go and plan something like that? She either knew something about my singing voice that I'd never discovered, or maybe she just presumed I was the most competent of the bunch.

I shifted in my seat and glanced over. Betty was in battle mode. Her face wore an expression I recognized from myself at Shark Beach High. As her eyes raced through Chinese characters, assessing and dismissing songs loved by generations of Chinese parents, she flipped pages with an efficiency that my mother would have admired.

It was when she brushed her hair back over her right ear that it hit me. Betty was cute.

That's a stupid word, isn't it? "Cute" is something people use to describe Hello Kitty or an embroidered pillow. Despite having an above-average vocabulary, I couldn't come up with a better way to describe Betty. She was someone you had to see up close and in action to really appreciate. And I wanted to get up close to her.

Betty was a girl I could talk and share a laugh with.

Christina Tau, on the other hand, played up her sexiness. Ultimately, that put her in a position of seeking approval from boys, certainly, and her friends as well. Of course, she also had her own demands.

Betty Jung didn't care what I or anyone else thought about her. She had her own standards about whom she would chill with. Chun didn't make the cut, but Kathy the punk did. And so did I, apparently.

I wished we were planning something more fun than a throwaway musical number.

I wished it were just Betty and me planning something.

If we were a couple, would she expect me to execute her endless flow of orders? That was pretty much what had become of my dad's life, as far as I could tell.

Betty brushed her hair back again, and I stared at the profile of her face. Yes, she was indeed cute.

As if reading my thoughts, Betty looked up at me and glowered. "Find a song," her raised eyebrow said.

I nodded and heeded the unspoken command.

She then turned to YK and said, "jia you." This literally meant, "add oil," but figuratively it meant, "let's go." Without a word, he, too, stopped doodling and opened a songbook.

By the end of the period, we had managed to select three songs, and had even started writing parts of the skit.

"Guys," Betty said, "Let's meet up at snack time and finish at least one scene."

"Betty," I said, "we're usually a little busy at snack time." Betty rapped my left pinky knuckle with her pen. "Oh, shit, that hurt!" I squealed. She made fists and cracked her knuckles one-handed.

"Where did you learn that from? You got brothers, or something?"

She tilted her head and narrowed her eyes menacingly.

"We're going to work on this at snack time, David!"

"I completely agree with you," I said, trying out a little technique I'd learned just recently from being around Christina and her friends.

Betty saw right through this lip service.

"I'm serious," she said as she slapped my shoulder. "We're already way behind!"

When it was time for the boys to head off for Confucian philosophy and the girls to go to dance, a part of me didn't want to say goodbye to Betty. Another part of me was relieved that I could stop being so on my toes.

Dr. Wu, our ghost-eyed teacher, was annoyed that the boys weren't completely silent as we entered his class, and he singled me out for special treatment once the handouts were distributed.

"David," said Dr. Wu. "Stand up and read the first sentence out loud."

Dutifully, I stood and read, "The Master said, 'Fine words and an insinuating appearance are seldom associated with true virtue.'"

"What does that mean, David?" he asked. I cleared my throat.

"Basically, appearances are deceiving," I said, determined to defend myself. You see, in Chinese school, teachers were fond of punishing wayward students by making them stand up, an act meant to humiliate. It wouldn't work with me, though. I was a top student in Honors Dialectics, and I could argue against anything.

"So what's the lesson, David?"

"Don't always trust other people." I rubbed my palms. Bring it, Dr. Wu.

"It's deeper than that, David. The lesson is, don't trust your own eyes."

I couldn't help but stare at the ghost in his left eye socket. I heard Carl Ching snicker, but Dr. Wu remained focused on reforming me.

"Or even more broadly," he added, "don't trust only in your senses because they can be fooled. Don't you agree, David?"

I was about to answer in the negative when Chun spoke up, trying to take some heat off of me. "But isn't that a Daoist idea, Dr. Wu?" Our teacher's neck turned red as if freshly slapped.

YK and Andy covered their mouths. Chun was baiting Dr. Wu, who had nothing but contempt for

Daoism, deriding it as a "sham religion of the idle" when pressed. Never mind that it has a billion or more followers.

Dr. Wu is easy to wind up, and Chun, as usual, was the best at it. Any other teacher would have just shut Chun down or ignored him, but Dr. Wu always made the mistake of engaging. That was a fatal error, because Chun wasn't invested in any particular position. His only purpose was to provoke and irritate. If he was able to get things just right, though, there was a chance that Dr. Wu might become annoyed enough to leave the room for the day, leaving us to our own devices before snack time.

"It's not a Daoist idea," Dr. Wu declared. "It's a good Confucian lesson. For example, let's say you meet with someone who says he is an excellent personal financial advisor. He seems like someone who knows what he's doing. Has a nice suit. Seems educated. You trust this image that you have of him, so you decide to sign over all your savings for him to manage." Mr. Wu held up his right hand as if taking a pledge. "After a few months, the man disappears, the office is vacant, his phone number and email are no longer in service. What do you do then?"

"You should sue him," said YK. Dr. Wu smiled weakly.

"You can't sue someone when you don't know where they are or what their real name is."

"Call the cops," said Andy.

"They don't handle this sort of thing."

"Did you try to contact other people who got scammed like you?" asked Chun.

"I tried to but…" was all Dr. Wu managed to get out before stifled laughter popped around the room. He crossed his arms and said, "So you think it's funny that I was ripped off? Yes, I will admit that I was a fool. I also think, however, that all of you can learn from my mistake. If only I had cherished the lessons in the *Analects* and taken them to heart, I would not have been fooled so easily. Neither should you."

"How do we know *you're* not another man trying to bamboozle us with your pleasant talk and nice clothes?" asked Chun. Mr. Wu's mouth shut tight and his cheeks puffed out.

"You think this is a good shirt? You think these pants are fancy? Everything I'm wearing cost less than $20!" That caused the dam to break, and the entire class unleashed a torrent of mean-spirited laughter. Mr. Wu nodded to acknowledge that today's class was a lost cause. He bowed and gave a grand wave. "Keep your handouts! Treasure them!" were Dr. Wu's parting words as he picked up his bag and charged out the door.

"Thank you, Chun," I said. "He was gonna ride me hard today." Chun gave a devious smile.

"Aw, it was my pleasure."

"That's got to be a new record," I said. "Five minutes, tops."

"Are you sure he's gone?" asked YK.

"He never comes back after he leaves," I said. "Never."

Just in case, everyone sat quietly for about two minutes before taking out our phones and plugging up our ears with buds or Beats. Strangely enough, now that the teacher was gone, all the boys were quieter and better behaved.

Oh man, how I wished I still had my phone. Well, nothing to do but pull out the MCAT printouts I'd brought for just such an occasion. I read a new question and chewed slowly on what the answer might be. I read the question again and again, slower each time, until the questioner's intent began to reveal itself. This method doesn't work with Confucius's words, by the way.

I looked over Dr. Wu's handout for a few seconds and folded it in half without a thought. Several of the boys crumpled theirs up and chucked them into the wastebasket. Other copies carelessly slipped to the floor.

If only Dr. Wu had found a way to make his lessons more accessible to us. It would actually have been interesting to hear how he had been swindled, and how Confucius had warned of such deception.

But maybe the Master's material didn't lend itself to boys growing up in modern American society. For example, Confucius had nothing at all to say about love—romantic love. The few times he used the word "love," it was to express diligence to duty, one's "love" of state and elders.

Other Chinese things were similarly flawed. *Romance of the Three Kingdoms* had no romance in it at all. Maybe the problem was that so many seminal works of Chinese culture were written by men during periods of continuous warfare and conflict, a time when refining battle strategies and maintaining the loyalty of citizens in each warring state was paramount. Falling in love had to take a backseat in the war chariot.

Or maybe the problem was that Chinese culture primes its people to endure hardships such as immigrating to a new country and giving birth to kids who then had to endure their own challenges. In the midst of all that, love was little more than an afterthought. Work itself was the only ideal that immigrant couples could hold on to.

That seemed to be what had happened to my parents at least. They came to this country, respectfully married each other, and had a kid whom they expected to continue contributing to the family, following the heavenly ordained sequence of life events: get a good education, have children, and work as much and as long as possible so the next generation could be better off. What was romantic and beautiful about that?

The Chinese phrase for "cute," as in, "I think so-and-so is cute," is ke ai, literally "can love." Did my parents ever think they could love each other? Now that they were fully engaged with the work portion of their mortal duties, I couldn't imagine them going on a date together. My mother couldn't even bear the faintest whiff of a possibility of me dating.

My mother. She had grown up in a hard-line Shanghainese family that had fled from the Communists to Taiwan during the Chinese civil war. They had been rich in China and would have suffered greatly during the Cultural Revolution there if they had stayed.

My mother's childhood in Taipei had been a bitter one, filled with beatings and exhortations to study harder. After all, although her family had lost its fortune, they were still Shanghainese, which meant they were smarter than the other people who had washed up in Taiwan, most of whom came from lesser stock.

She must have seen my desire to go on a date as something one of those unworthy, unchaste, and chased-away boys of her youth would have wanted to do.

My mother needed to see teen dating through the eyes of another, younger version of herself. As a girl, she had snuck movie magazines into her locked, windowless room. My mom still had those magazines. They symbolized the only escape she had had as a girl. She never got to see the films featured in them, but at least now she was able to watch TV dramas with Auntie Zhang.

Those soap operas are ridiculous, by the way. People fall in and out of love all the time, seemingly without jobs or other duties. Viewers like my mom and Auntie Zhang pine for lives like that.

I probably looked as if I were asleep, because something landed in my slightly opened mouth. I spat out a crumpled piece of paper. Chun and YK were laughing uproariously, slumped over their desks, hands over their mouths. Andy looked mildly amused.

When he caught his breath again, Chun said, "Damn, son, that ought to teach you to breathe through your nose. You're going to have to stop these annoying personal habits of yours when you're around Betty. White people don't tolerate bad manners."

How dare he talk about Betty like that. She'd been busting her ass so that we wouldn't have to flail about through another show! On top of that, Betty's Mandarin was so much better than his! A response was obviously in order.

Casually leaning back, I raised my right arm, turned my hand palm-up, and rolled up my fingers, readying my not-so-secret weapon. Chun straightened up at his desk and tried to prepare for my attack without looking too cowardly. He couldn't defend himself, though, because he had no idea where I would strike.

He sprang out of his chair and backed away to the front of the room. I followed him, my right arm held out and primed.

"Hey, I'm really sorry," he started to say. "I was just joking."

Too late! My arm lashed out and a finger sprung out to deliver a flick to his left ear and another to his left eyebrow.

"Ooh, sheesh!" he cried.

"Get him," said Andy.

"David's got the cobra!" said YK.

All I had to do was focus on a patch of exposed skin and the nail side of my middle finger could thwack it. This was an old playground skill that had never left me.

Left nostril. Pinky knuckle.

Chun jumped up and hopped over to the vacant teacher's desk. I stood up and approached him.

As I drew closer to Chun, all the boys in the class hooted.

"Truce, Dave!" Chun offered. I shook my head and raised my arm to deliver another strike.

"Hey! What's going on here!" someone yelled from the door. It was Principal Ho. "Where is Dr. Wu?"

Nobody said anything.

"You two, sit down right now!" We slunk back to our desks. Our big mistake had been leaving the door to the classroom open.

"You boys think this is a class for monkey-style fighting?" Principal Ho skated to the teacher's desk and looked over its bareness before turning to Chun and me to chide us in Mandarin. "You two, I'm disappointed. Extremely disappointed."

"Extremely" doesn't sound so bad in English, but in Mandarin, "fei chang," it elevates a simple misbehavior to a major crime. I lowered my head.

"Principal Ho," said Chun in English.

"Yes?"

"Before Dr. Wu left, he got a phone call. I think he had to run out for an emergency."

"What sort of emergency?"

"He didn't say. He only mumbled something about us staying in class. I'm sorry that David and I were goofing off a little. It was wrong for us to take advantage of the situation." The principal coughed and looked at his watch.

"Well," the principal said. "I have to go check on the other classes, and I'm sure Dr. Wu had a good reason to leave. All of you, just read your handouts, and if you have to talk, then talk quietly." Principal Ho brushed off his arms, nodded, and left. This time, we made sure to shut the door.

CHAPTER TEN

The four of us loaded up our plates and took our customary table near the exit. As we were getting settled, Betty pulled up a seat and dropped her paper plate down next to mine.

"Hi guys," she said. "I figure we should eat for 15 minutes tops and then work on the skits for the remaining 15 minutes." Her right knee bumped against my left thigh, almost causing me to gasp out loud.

As thrilling as that small collision was, I wasn't thrilled by her work ethic.

"Betty," I said, "I think we should just skip the work. We're not going to get that much done in 15 freaking minutes, anyway."

"We're already too far behind, David," she countered, shaking her head. "Even if we can only get a tiny bit done, that's still something. We're all together now, anyway. Let's just talk it out and type what we say. It'll be fun and easy."

Andy looked down and said, "I don't want to write. Just tell me what to say."

"I don't want to write, either," Chun said, his mouth full of lo mein.

"You guys sure as hell don't want me to write," YK sighed.

Betty pulled out the disposable chopsticks from their paper sleeve and rubbed them against each other to get rid of the splinters. She then proceeded to wield them expertly, sorting intently through tangles of lo mein.

"Did you lose something in there, Betty?" I asked.

"Sometimes there are small pieces of pork or chicken," she said. "I don't like to eat meat." Chun pounced on the opportunity.

"That's not what I heard about you and meat, Ms. Jung."

"I heard you were a virgin, Chun," said Betty. "When do think you'll finally have sex?" This girl wasn't afraid of anything. My heart was in my throat.

Chun made a face as if his molar had cracked. Betty was young and only half-Chinese, but she was clearly already practiced in the use of that Small Personal Triumph face that my mother had perfected.

She elegantly tucked a steaming wad of noodles into her mouth and slurped it up. Meanwhile, Chun glumly gnawed at a spare rib that looked like a saucy, burned trapezoid. YK ate chunks of barbecued pork over white rice with a fork. Andy sipped chrysanthemum tea from a drink box and straightened a stack of three almond cookies on his tray without eating them.

I picked at my rice, but with Betty sitting there,

suddenly felt reluctant to eat the pork on my plate.

"Are you a vegetarian?" I asked her. She snorted.

"Not at all," she said. "I just don't trust the meat in Chinatown, especially the stuff they sell to institutions."

"It tastes all right," said YK.

"You can't see the lesions in the pork through the food dye and glaze," said Betty.

YK put down his fork and wiped his mouth. Chun pushed his chair back and crossed his right leg over his left knee. "Why do you have to sit with us, Betty? You're a constant freaking bummer."

"She's funny," said Andy.

"Thank you, Andy," she said, wiping her face with a napkin and taking out her phone. "Well, I'm probably the fastest typist here, so I can do the typing if you guys talk."

"Just one second," said Chun. "David is a pretty fast typer, too. I think he should take notes." My face heated up. Time for a confession.

"I don't have a phone anymore, guys," I said. "My parents took it away."

"Why?" asked Chun. "Was it too expensive?"

"No," I said. "It's because I wanted to go to a dance with a girl. I was going to sneak out, but I needed to rent an expensive outfit, and I couldn't do that on my own. So I asked my mother for help, and she took away my phone."

"Holy shit, that sucks," said Chun. "All these Chinese parents don't let their kids date, but that hasn't stopped the propagation of our people. There are more of us every year, right?" He looked at Andy. "Are you allowed to ask a girl out?"

"No," said Andy.

"YK, do you ask girls out?" YK closed his eyelids and raised his eyebrows.

"I work, I don't have time."

"What about you, Betty?" asked Chun. "Do you go on dates?" She tugged at the ends of her sleeves.

"I can do whatever I want," she said. "What about you, Chun? I never see you with girls at school." He gave Betty a pained smile.

"I haven't found a girl that I'm into. Yet." He looked at her meaningfully. "The current crop isn't so hot."

Just then, Principal Ho came into the eating area, ambled over to the black-tea dispenser, and filled up his doubled paper cup.

"Looks like the coast is clear, guys," said Chun. The other guys immediately got up and began walking away. I turned to Betty. I felt I owed her some sort of explanation.

"I'm gonna go out with these guys for a few."

"David," said Betty as she furiously wiped her hands with a napkin so thin it feathered apart. "We have work to do, David." Wow. She must really be mad. She used my name twice.

"I have to go," I said as I stood up.

"It's not cool leaving me at a table by myself." Thinking quickly, I handed her my book bag to show her that I trusted her with my key personal possessions. I also wanted her to see that I liked her enough to have that trust.

"What am I supposed to do with this?" she asked.

"Hold on to it," I said. The other three guys had already left the hall. "If you feel like reading MCAT questions, I printed some out!"

"Why, David?"

But I was already too far away. I still had to almost break into a jog to catch up with the others.

I was the last one out on the third-floor fire escape.

"Thanks for waiting up, guys," I said sarcastically as I eased the door closed behind me.

"You've changed, Dave," said Chun as he flipped his lighter to Andy. "In just a few hours. Looks like you're ready to ditch us to get some kissy face."

YK laughed so hard he coughed, and he coughed so hard the cigarette fell from his lips to the ground below. Andy lit up a new cigarette and handed it to me.

"She's cute," Andy offered.

"You're only saying that because she's white," said Chun.

"I'll bet white people don't treat her like she's white," said YK. "I'll bet they're just as racist to her as they are to us."

I blew out some smoke.

"As you are to her, you mean," I said, handing the cigarette to Chun. "Chinese people can be racist, too. People in Chinatown probably treat her like shit. The folks at school certainly do."

"Are you kidding me?" said Chun. "Chinese love white people because they leave decent tips! You ever wonder why the wait staff always goes out of their way to serve white people and make sure they're comfortable? Because their tips make it worthwhile. Isn't that right, Dave?" He took a big drag before passing the cigarette to YK.

"Well, most of our in-restaurant business is the buffet, so the diners get their own plates and serve themselves," I said. "They even bus their own plates. Almost nobody leaves a tip. Not unless someone's baby throws up or throws food or something like that.

"I'll bet your food's so bad, people are puking there all the time," said Chun.

"David," asked YK as he took a hit from the cigarette, "did your mother really take away your phone just because you wanted to go on a date?"

"Yup," I said. "I can't date until I go to college. Or maybe until I get admitted to one. Honestly, I'm not sure about the timing."

"I got something else to say about that," said Chun. "You know, you got so many smart Chinese people who are always studying, worried about their grades. Then when they hit 27, they have all these degrees, but they're lonely because they're so smart they never did anything stupid like fall in love. And let's face it. Falling in love is one of the dumbest things in the world you can do. It's completely irrational. It makes you do stupid things."

Chun had never seemed more sincere. We didn't know where it came from, but he still had more to say.

"There's only one reason to fall in love," said Chun, his voice breaking a little bit. "Because you can't live without them. You want to be with them for the rest of your life. I mean, my parents..." He couldn't continue.

Chun turned his back to us and pretended he was stretching his arms, but we could tell he was wiping away tears.

"That's the truth right there," I said.

YK opened his mouth and tapped his left cheek, creating a chain of identical smoke circles. 10, 15...20? I watched one follow the next, each one in its turn floating away and fading.

"You should do that for the talent show," I told him. Chun turned around, sniffing. He watched YK's feat with reddened eyes.

"That's easy," said Chun. He gave it a shot and blooped out pathetic puffs that disappeared immediately. Chun passed the cigarette.

"Sometime soon," Andy said to the sky as he took a long drag, "I'll need you guys to help me in something." As he leaned back, a ribbon of smoke unfurled sleepily from his nose and vanished.

"I think you mean 'help me with something,'" I said. He narrowed an eye at me.

"What are you gonna need help with, Andy?" asked YK.

"Yeah, what is it?" asked Chun.

"We'll see," was all he would say.

"Just say it, Andy," said a voice by the door. We all turned in unison to see the now open door framing a scowling Betty. She looked like defiance personified.

"Close the door, dumbass," said Chun. "You want us all to get caught?" She stepped onto the fire escape and swung the door shut.

"If you guys had any brains," she spat out, "you'd

be lifting each other up instead of indulging in these destructive habits. Also, you're helping Big Tobacco. Those corporations don't give a shit about you and your health."

"Ha," said Chun. "We're smoking Chinese cigarettes. We're supporting Chinese people."

"All the way from the Middle Kingdom," said Andy as he held out the open, puckering end of the pack to Betty.

"Jesus, get them away from me, Andy," she said. He looked embarrassed and tried to put the cigarettes back, missing his shirt pocket the first time.

"I'd prefer it if you didn't say, 'Jesus,' Betty," said YK. "It's not right to take that name in vain."

Betty opened her mouth to apologize.

"Jesus, YK!" Chun interjected before Betty could speak. "Jesus, Jesus, Ja-hee-susss!"

"Everything's a joke to you, huh, Chun?" asked YK.

Chun held up his hand in defense. "At least I'm not a hypocrite. You think Jesus is cool with you smoking?"

"I didn't say I wasn't a sinner, but I've accepted the fact that Christ died for my sins," said YK. I stepped in.

"YK, we agreed before not to talk about religion. Don't let Chun bait you." I noticed that Betty was biting her upper lip. "Also, I think Betty wants to apologize."

"I'm sorry, YK," she said, shooting me a grateful look. Betty's fingers were on my elbow. After a small squeeze, she withdrew her hand. It was a small gesture. So small that none of the other guys even noticed.

But her touch charged me more than being with Christina ever had. My whole circulatory system went into overdrive. Of course through my crotch, but also through my right ear, which seemed to go deaf for a few seconds. I knew from my studies that this temporary hearing loss was due to a lack of blood flow in my inner ear.

"Don't worry about it, Betty," said YK. He dragged the lit end of his cigarette along the building wall, sending a spray of sparks at Chun.

"Jesus!" said Chun.

The bell rang signaling the end of snack time, and the five of us left the fire escape soon thereafter. Betty and I went through the door last. As we walked through a dim area near the stairwell, she touched me again on the arm. "You're the best one out of all of them," she said quietly as she gave me back my bag, sort of brushing my left hand and arm in the process. I put my hand tentatively on her back for a few seconds, and we glanced at each other to acknowledge there was something there.

That was our only real connection the whole day, though. Calligraphy and tradition classes provided no opportunities for socializing, and, as always, she was one of the first people out the door as Chinese school came to a close. I casually looked for Betty on the street as I left the school myself but saw no hint of her.

Locating Mr. Yeung's truck, I jumped into the cab and snapped on my seatbelt. Meanwhile my father, sitting in the middle seat as always, struggled with his belt for more slack.

"Every week, I have to adjust this thing," my father

said to Mr. Yeung in English. For some reason, the two only ever spoke English to each other when in the truck. Maybe my father didn't want to make Mr. Yeung, who was Cantonese, speak Mandarin. Or maybe the two of them were making an effort to make me feel included. When we were at the restaurant with my mom, though, they only spoke in Mandarin.

"Do you have a teddy bear that you usually strap in here?" my father asked.

Mr. Yeung chuckled. "I usually strap a ghost in there. Who else would keep me company while I'm out making deliveries at all hours of the day or night?"

My father wet his lips and tried to smile. I knew that he was afraid of spooky things. He couldn't watch scary films for shit. I once showed him *Paranormal Activity* on my phone, and he tore out of the room like the restaurant was on fire. That was when I still had a phone, of course.

In any case, nothing was scarier than riding with Mr. Yeung at the wheel. The guy drove like the border was about to close. But he always seemed to have magic on his side. Somehow the front end of the cab would shrink just enough to let him switch lanes without scraping off the rear bumper of the car just in front of him. And whenever we headed west through the notoriously heavy traffic of Canal Street, he always somehow managed to pick the fastest lane.

Mr. Yeung's truck never met a yellow light it couldn't beat. Maybe stunt driving was his true calling, not being a stunt double.

Suddenly, it began to rain. Not heavily, but enough

to be annoying. Scratchy clouds began to slide across the sky, replacing the earlier sunshine.

"Ey, David!" called Mr. Yeung. "I'm having a problem with my wipers. Can you press the dashboard?"

"Where?" I asked. "I don't see a button."

"Push anywhere. Use your whole hand. I think there's a wire loose." I had no idea where this was going. I reached out my right hand and pressed the palm against the dashboard.

"Like this?" I asked.

"Harder." I slapped the dashboard. The wipers shrieked across the windshield, and I jumped. Both men laughed at me.

"You think I'm the scaredy one," my father said, slapping my knee.

"I thought he was going to jump through the roof," said Mr. Yeung.

"Pretty hard to do while I've got a seatbelt on," I pointed out.

"Oh, yeah," said Mr. Yeung, ignoring me. "Right through the roof!"

I don't think Cantonese people are any better or worse than anyone else, but I will say this. They laugh way too long about things that aren't really that funny.

"Ah, ah, ah," continued Mr. Yeung, gasping. "Like an ejector seat, David. Going right up to the moon, ah, ah, ah!"

His mirth finally dissipated when we got to the tunnel to Jersey, where ongoing construction made it necessary for two lanes to merge into one, forcing even Mr. Yeung to put both hands on the wheel and focus on driving to Tung's Garden.

That night, deliveryman Lee One spent a good half hour trying to convince my parents to require phone orders to prepay by credit card. He was taller than Lee Two and sat diagonally in his chair at the employees' table, leaning the right side of his rib cage against the battered backrest as he went off.

Lee One was mad, and I've learned over time that angry Chinese people always tell the best stories because they drop all pretense of being tactfully hesitant. Earlier that evening, he'd delivered a $50 order to a house, and the woman who'd answered the door had been short on cash.

Wang Yi, the funny grad student, told me in English, "He's saying she didn't have money for the tip. And he said, 'No problem.' But she couldn't even pay for all the food. So she gave him half the money and a necklace."

My mother found the story hilarious and asked to see the necklace. Lee One put it on the lazy Susan and spun it over. My mother stopped it short with her fingers and some sauce from the pea shoots spilled over the side of the dish.

"Looks cheap," she said in English.

"This is her," said Lee One in Mandarin, holding up a business card. I didn't need Wang to translate simple phrases like that.

"Let me see," said Lee Two. Lee One handed it over to him past my face. I froze when I saw the name. "Janet Muntz." It was my Algebra 2/Trig teacher. She'd bought me a Payday bar from the vending machine in the faculty lounge. Now she was broke ahead of her own payday.

"Was she good-looking?" asked Lee Two.

"You know white people," said Lee One. "Nice face, bad body."

Auntie Zhang and my father laughed. Even Bai Sheng, the silent one, broke out into an open-mouthed smile.

"Hey," my mother chided the whole table, "don't talk like that in front of the children."

"I understand that," I said, sending everyone into a wave of laughter.

"Are you learning anything in Chinese school?" Wang asked me in English. "Stay with me instead. I'll teach you better Chinese!"

"He can eat Chinese food no problem," said my mother nodding dismissively in my direction, "but he can't speak Chinese."

"If don't live in China, you can't learn Chinese," Wang pronounced. He piled meat and vegetables into his bowl, lifted it up, and shoveled food in his mouth.

I wondered for a second if Wang or any of the other three grad students were going out on dates, then realized almost immediately how unlikely that was. They spent their weekend nights with us.

I ate some dinner, but as Saturday night went on, I found myself getting a little hungry. When there was another hour to go before closing, I did a solo raid of the walk-in fridge for leftovers of Auntie Zhang's superior peppercorn beef. New Pavilion didn't stand a chance against her.

I was about to open the microwave when Auntie Zhang charged over from the gas range, wrenched the plate from my hand, and tossed the cold peppercorn beef into a hot wok.

"This is the right way," she said in Mandarin. "The microwave makes everything taste like American cheese."

In our culture, you have to grab things and force your will on people to show how much you care. The more energy you put into it, the more love you are expressing.

If I had tried to fight Auntie Zhang by grabbing my plate back, she would have been devastated. The deed and the person are the same. Even if my only intention was to save her some trouble, she would have taken it as a rejection of her.

I watched Auntie Zhang as she slammed the end of the sweep knife—something close to a spatula—against the wok, playing a tune with metallic scrapes. When it was thoroughly heated up, she scraped every last bit of the peppercorn beef out of the wok and into a bowl for me.

I wondered about Auntie Zhang, who was always in her own way looking out for me. Had she ever been married or in love? Was she pouring all her heartbreak into her incredible cooking? My parents never told me anything about her, and it would certainly be impertinent for me to ask her about her life. If I ever did, she'd probably just say something like, "Doesn't matter."

She handed me the bowl. It smelled incredible. I thanked her and was about to go when she clutched my wrist and dropped a glob of stewed bell peppers onto the beef for good measure. They were freshly cooked, and I hadn't even noticed her doing it.

"You study hard, David," she said in Mandarin. "You have to go to a good school and get a good job. Otherwise you'll end up being my assistant here, rolling dumpling skins forever! Ha ha ha!" She was laughing so hard, I saw a single gold molar flash in the dark of her mouth.

"Auntie Zhang," I said, "you would fire me on the first day!"

I wandered out of the kitchen to the employees' table, in a better mood than when I'd gone in. The food was so good I practically inhaled it. I even put some extra rice into the empty bowl to sop up all the sauce and slurped that up, too.

I wasn't able to read all the messages I had missed by not having a phone until I finally got home and opened up my laptop.

Betty had sent an email! Judging from the time stamp, she'd sent it late in the afternoon.

"David," it read, "I'm sorry your mom took away your phone. But you may still have a computer. You need that for school, right? Anyway, there's no reason why we can't work on the skit this way. Oh, by the way, I got your email address from your MCAT printouts. Why are you studying for the MCATs? Don't you have to get into college first?"

Wow, that girl was resourceful, and also kinda relentless about this skit thing. I was both intrigued and slightly repulsed at the same time.

"Thanks, Betty," I wrote back. "Give me a day or two to think about the skit first. Yeah, studying MCATs now

is part of my long-term strategy for becoming a doctor."
Should I write a little more? Like, we absolutely shared
a moment today, didn't we? I shuddered. Hadn't I
already gotten in enough trouble already with my
mother over girls? I hit send and moved on to the next
browser tab.

I went to my RSS feed and read a little bit about a
drug that was dissolving tumors in clinical trials. Earlier,
during one of my regular searches for news about Dr.
Lee and Harmony Health, I'd seen that she was now a
confirmed speaker for the American Society of Clinical
Oncology (ASCO) meeting in June. That conference was
a big deal, where data from high-profile drug trials would
be announced. If I read up on her latest research, I might
understand the Martian loan words that she would no
doubt use in her ASCO talk, the video of which would be
posted online after the conference.

Would I be her intern by the time it posted?

I was wading through medical acronyms in one
of her papers from last year when I saw an email
notification pop up. It was from Betty.

"If you're still up, maybe we can write a little bit
now. Also, wow, your parents are forcing you to be a
doctor? Isn't that a bit old school of them?"

Did she not comprehend that I was trying to avoid
working on the skit? Or maybe she didn't care?

On the other hand, Betty seemed curious about me.
It was weird to be the focus of someone else's attention,
but it also felt surprisingly good. No one had ever
emailed me personal questions before. I found myself
opening up a bit, telling her how arrived at my decision

to become a doctor. I told her how reading about the life of Steve Jobs had convinced me to go into cancer research because the loss of a great man like him was a loss to the world. I even told her how I'd written about Jobs in an essay for an internship I wanted.

I ended with a question of my own: Why was she up so late on her computer? She wrote back almost immediately. "I'm finishing a school project due Monday. I hope you get the internship!"

Seeing her reply pop into my email box as soon as I'd written back to her was kind of exciting. A bit like texting, but more serious and with full sentences, which made it feel more sincere. I wanted to keep the exchange going, so I made sure to write back quickly as well. "Thanks. It's pretty competitive, but at least I haven't been rejected yet. What about you? What do you want to do?"

As it turned out, she'd been thinking about going into international finance, though that was just a means to an end. What she really wanted to do was to come back to Chinatown to start a nonprofit with what she learned.

I told her that if she went into international finance, she'd probably end up living in a place like Shark Beach someday. Then I told her that Shark Beach was actually landlocked, no beach anywhere, and that the only sharks around were the other students.

She found that funny, which put me in a good enough mood that when she said that we should probably make an effort to work on a script, since we were already typing, I agreed. We wrote back and forth some lines in character, me as Liu Bei, the poor-but-ambitious warrior trying to restore the Han Dynasty, and she as Kongming, a brilliant strategist reluctant to join Liu's band. It was all relaxed and turned out to be quite fun. She called me Jiffy Liu Bei, and I called her Donkey Kongming. Stupid stuff. I didn't know that a girl could like dumb jokes, especially one as smart as Betty.

At one point, I glanced at the time. 2:29 a.m. Whoa! It was a good thing I could sorta sleep in on Sunday mornings.

"I gotta sleep," I wrote to her. "Good night."

"Good night, David. Let's write more tomorrow."

"Yeah, but let's start earlier!"

I felt fine the next morning while pedaling to the restaurant, but as the day wore on, I started to flag. I struggled to keep the restaurant's buffet fully stocked. Everything seemed to be moving a little slow, or maybe I was just too sleepy to register things in real time. My mom wasn't too pleased that I rolled in a bit later than usual for a Sunday, and a few times I caught her looking at me with her face contorted with suspicion and menace. I think she was wondering why I wasn't more morose about losing my phone. But I couldn't even get annoyed. In fact, I was feeling inexplicably cheerful. Well, not inexplicably. I returned home around nine that night and immediately jumped onto my laptop to get in touch with Betty again.

This time, I emailed her first. We actually wrote almost a page of dialogue before we ended up talking about ourselves some more. We both ran track, as it turned out. She had tested into a school for gifted kids that took up certain floors within the same public high school that Chun went to. They had so little space in New York schools, they couldn't even keep the smart kids like Betty away from the dumb kids like Chun.

"Chun says he's popular," I wrote. "Do you see him a lot?"

"Yeah, I guess Chun and his hoodlum buddies could be described as popular. When they're not suspended." I felt my eyebrows rise. I could imagine him getting ejected from a class for horsing around, especially in a real high school setting. I was always surprised by how much he managed to get away with in Chinese school. But suspension meant that he was getting in much deeper trouble than I'd ever suspected.

"It's not like he's in a gang, Betty."

"Not yet."

"What does he get suspended for doing?"

"Okay, I only know of one actual time when he got suspended. You'd have to ask him about it. Anyway, I haven't been to school much this semester, either. I'm on an independent-study track this semester, studying for an IB. I only have to come in three days a week, and for track meets or tests."

"What's an 'IB', Betty? 'Intestinal blockage'? Never heard of that before."

"It stands for International Baccalaureate. It's like a globally accepted standard for advanced classes."

"What do you do with an IB?"

"You can study abroad. And it shows you're an independent thinker."

I could have told her that last bit. Man, high school

in the city sounded like a mess. A school within a school? Like nesting dolls? An IB?

We returned to talking about track and running shoes. Then I realized that it was almost 10:30 p.m. My parents would be coming home any second, and I still had some homework to do. We managed to add a couple more lines to the skit—the supposed reason why we were emailing in the first place—before saying good night again.

CHAPTER ELEVEN

On Monday morning I woke up from a dream about Betty where we were trying to give each other static shocks. I got to touch her all over, and the bits I could remember made me smile all the way to my bus stop.

When I got there, Al raised an eyebrow at me.

"What's going on, David?" he asked slyly.

"Not too much," I said. "I'm glad it's Friday. I mean, Monday. Actually, I'm not too happy it's Monday." Man, that dream had me confused about what day it was!

Al came in close and asked, "Dude, are you gonna use that picture or what?"

"What do you mean, 'use'? Like post it on the Internet?"

"Just show it to Jean! She'll freaking freak! Today's a good day!"

"Why?"

"It's April Fool's day!"

"This isn't just a harmless prank, Al. I don't need

to hit her over the head with something as bad as this. Not yet, anyway." I figured there was no need to let him know that even had I wanted to, I didn't have a phone with which to enact the big reveal.

Al's eyes bugged a little in disappointment. "C'mon, David. Just do it!"

"If you're dying to throw it in her face, why don't *you* show it to her?"

"She doesn't even know me. You're the one she's been a bitch to, not me."

I shrugged. At the moment, I was in a happy-ish place. Not even Jean could take that away from me.

"I don't like Jean, but the most she does is try to get a rise out of me or call me names. I pull this out and her life is like, done!"

Al's eyes lit up.

"Yeah!" he said. "She'll have to move away!"

"So what you're telling me is that you basically want Jean to go through what you've been going through. I'm sure it sucks being the new kid—you of all people should know that. Why wish it on someone else?"

"Because some people deserve it. I sure didn't."

Just then, a familiar voice called out. "Oh, David?"

"Yes?" I asked, turning around languidly.

"I hope I'm not disturbing your little losers' summit over there," Jean said. "I imagine you have an agenda to stick to."

Just a few moments ago, I'd been thinking about Betty and talking with Al about finding a moral high ground. Now I was pissed off, which was probably exactly what Jean was hoping for. Bad move on her part.

"Jean," I said, "you wouldn't be calling Al a loser because he's white, would you?" She rolled her right shoulder dismissively.

"No. I'm calling him a loser because he's talking to you."

"You know, it would be racist of you to call a kid a loser because of the color of his skin," I continued. "If Al and I reported this incident to the office, you sure wouldn't come off too well, Jean."

"Yeah, sure, like anything about Al even matters," she said.

"What!" I said. "Don't call Al a 'cracker'!"

Jean pointed at my face. "I never called Al a 'cracker'!"

"Al, did you record that?" I called over to him. Al held up his phone in victory.

Jean held up both hands, palms out.

"What the hell!" she shouted, "I never even said that!"

"It's all here on my phone," Al said. "Jean called me a 'cracker'!"

Jean was beginning to panic. She turned red and grabbed for Al's phone. But by then, Percy had come to Jean's side. He tilted down his face so she was looking directly at him and said, "Give it a rest, Jean. Don't give them the satisfaction."

"I am not a racist!" she called out, unable to keep herself from re-engaging.

"Jean's a racist," I replied, nodding to an imaginary crowd for confirmation.

"She's a racist," Al agreed.

At this, something inside her seemed to break. She

covered her face with both hands and leaned into Percy. She might even have been crying.

"Are you assholes happy now?" he yelled at us.

"Yes," I said.

"Very," said Al.

Giddy as I was from the morning's showdown with Jean, I sobered up when I saw the "TBA" still there next to Harmony Health on the internship board

Continuing past it to homeroom, I jingled the pennies in my pocket. Now that I no longer had a phone, I had to figure out some other way to get a look at Mr. del Pino's socks, and this is what I'd come up with.

As soon as he approached, I'd drop my change on the floor and kneel down, presumably to pick up the coins. This, in turn, would give me a direct view of his socks.

The only problem is, the plan almost didn't work. When I knelt down to pick up the coins, Mr. del Pino got on the ground himself, his legs pointing away from me, in an effort to help!

"Excuse me, Mr. del Pino," I called out, thinking quickly. "I think I saw a coin roll under your foot."

"Which one?" he asked.

"I'm not sure." He stood up and peered under his legs one at a time, revealing his socks in the process. One was black. The other was dark red!

That day in class, as expected, Mr. del Pino dropped a short quiz on us in the last seven minutes of class, just when people were beginning to breathe easy. There was something slightly sadistic about how tricky he could be. That said, and I hate to brag, but I nailed it. Wait, scratch that. I actually do like to brag, but I get so few opportunities to feel good about myself in this highly competitive school, I forget how wonderful it can be.

I was on my way to French class when Christina came down the hallway toward me. She waved a hand in my face.

"Earth to David!" she called. I managed a smile.

"I can see and hear you, Christina."

"I wanted you to know that I'm taking someone else to the dance."

"Yes, Yaro told me," I said, giving a fake smile. I didn't want her to think she'd been able to cause a rift between my old friend and me. I shifted my books to my other arm. "Well, I hope you guys have fun," I said, nodding stupidly to indicate that I was about to go.

"He's a really great guy," she persisted. "At least he's normal!" She was obviously trying to get a rise out of me, and she didn't want me to leave quietly. Speak clearly, I thought to myself, and don't escalate the situation.

"Look, Christina," I said. "All of that's true. Yaro really is a great guy, definitely more normal than me. And I really am glad you found someone else to go with you. I just hope you're not using him only to get back at me, because he doesn't deserve that. Yeah, you didn't deserve me flaking out on you, either. I know that you're probably really embarrassed by that. I mean, I'm embarrassed by it, too. But my mother pulled a power move, and there's nothing I can do about it. So in reality, your beef is with my mother, not me, because I was ready and willing to go with you. And, honestly, I guess before I asked my mother for the money to get a tux, I could have snuck out to meet you in my school clothes, but there's no way you would have gone for that."

It felt good to say those things because they were all true.

"You're right, David," said Christina. "I wouldn't have gone for that. Not just because it's a little too Cinderella for my tastes, but because you lied to me, David. You lied! You said you were allowed to go out on dates, and you're not."

"Yeah," I said, sighing. "I did lie to you, Christina, but basically I was lying to myself. I just happened to hurt you, too, and I'm sorry for it." Her arms were crossed, but her expression had softened.

I just realized that I hadn't thought about our competing class ranks for a number of days. Who was ahead at this point? In the face of all the drama, none of it seemed to matter much. Just then, two girls walked up to either side of Christina. The three stood together like a triumphant Japanese anime power trio.

"Oh, hello, Cassie and Shirley," I said. "Did you all help Yaro pick out something to wear?"

"He already has an awesome tux," said Shirley.

"He *owns* it, David," said Christina, though I could tell the attempted put-down lacked malice.

"That was a nice soliloquy, David," said Cassie. "And you're right. You really did embarrass Christina."

"It's hurt her rep," said Shirley.

"To be fair, though, it probably plunged when she asked me to the dance in the first place," I said. She hurried away without responding, as if standing near me for another second would put her status at risk.

The rest of the week went relatively well. Jean was for the moment neutralized, and I seemed to have managed to defuse the situation with Christina. Pretty much everything seemed to be on an upswing. Or maybe I only felt that way because I was having nightly email chats with Betty. We had even considered switching to a chat app, but I was worried that it might crash my stalwart but ancient Asus.

The one problem was that I wasn't getting as much sleep as usual. Betty and I were emailing late into the night, and I had trouble sleeping afterwards. I found myself going over the things we'd talked about, or wondering what I could have or should have said. The worst was the time when I told her about my whole thing with Mr. del Pino's socks and she wrote back, "He's going to think you have a foot fetish."

"I do. I want to put lo mein all over your feet, Betty." I began to panic as soon as I pressed send, but even though I tried to cancel the email as it was "sending," it was too late.

She replied almost immediately with an "LOL," but it was the most risqué thing I'd ever said to her, and I couldn't stop worrying about it for the rest of the night. Needless to say, our work on the skit was becoming a token activity at best.

As we continued emailing each other throughout the week, I wondered what it would be like seeing her in real life on Saturday at Chinese school. The prospect was making me more and more nervous.

After all, we knew each other better now. In a lot of ways, I now knew her better than Chun, YK, and Andy. I liked her more, too.

But what if Betty looked closer at me and didn't like what she saw? Or what if I couldn't be funny in person?

The morning of, I clipped my nails, flossed my teeth, and washed my face twice. After my father and I went our separate ways in Chinatown, I ran my fingers through my hair and checked my face in the reflective metal panel of an ATM to make sure there weren't any boogers in my nose.

All clear. I was ready to see Betty.

As I rounded the corner to Chinese school, trying my hardest to look indifferent, I heard someone yelling at me from across the street.

"David, hold up!" Chun shouted out. He had YK and Andy with him. The three of them were fast-walking in a group to meet me, looking suspicious as hell.

"Are you guys selling drugs or something?" I asked.

"What? No!" said Chun. "Listen, Andy needs a favor from us today."

"What kind of favor?"

"The kind where you get paid," said Andy. "Let's go." Chun was already moving.

"Where are we going?" I asked, feeling a little lost.

"The Grand Street stop," said Chun.

"I just came from there!"

"Then you know the way," said Andy as he walked by me.

Exasperated, I asked YK, "What's going on?"

"Andy managed to get four of the artist edition iPads reserved at the midtown Apple Store. The limit's supposed to be one per person. We have to help him pick them up."

I wasn't about to ditch Chinese school and Betty Jung for a scam trip to the store. Sure, Andy was a friend, but this was a little too much to ask. I'd been waiting all week to see this girl. I'd even admitted to her that I was "psyched" to hang out. Not that the guys needed to know any of that. But still.

"This seems really shady," I said. YK came in closer to my face.

"He's paying us $100 each for one hour of work."

Whoa! "Sounds good to me!" I said. You could really do something with a hundred bucks! I could actually find a way to make up for my absence to Betty by buying her something. Fifty bucks would cover that, right? Betty wanted to go into international finance, so she should be happy that I was choosing to get paid. I just wish I could've texted her to explain what was going on.

I suddenly realized that this was the first time I'd ever played hooky. It's not as if Chinese school was real school, but I still felt bad about cutting class. The other three guys acted as if it was no big deal, though, so I decided to keep my concerns to myself.

Andy, Chun, and YK trusted me enough to bring me along on their little expedition. There was no way I was going to let them down. Plus, $100!

We got out at Rockefeller Center to transfer to the F train. I glanced at Andy, who looked stoic as a granite mountain, but his eyes were alive as he peered into the tunnel looking for the train, which was taking forever to come. A man in a wheelchair on the opposite platform began playing "The Star-Spangled Banner" on a sax.

Listening to it, I suddenly began thinking about how hard it was for my parents and Auntie Zhang to work every day of the week as they did, from dawn's early light to twilight's last gleaming. I only had a small hand in it.

I guess you could say our American journey was still in the preclinical study phase. Who knew how our family would do in the long run, when things got real, when I was an adult and out of medical school. Would my parents and Auntie Zhang still be working at Tung's Garden? They'd all be in their 60s by that point.

Our train finally arrived, and we squeezed in front of the tourists to board. We rode until the 57th Street stop on Manhattan's east side.

As we emerged from the station, the seriousness of the task ahead became apparent to all of us. Andy made immediately for the Apple Store, his eyes trained on its cube-shaped entrance. I hadn't been up in that area, near the southern end of Central Park, since a class field trip in sixth grade, when I'd eaten my first grilled pretzel. I remember the rocky salt kernels had scraped the roof of my mouth and the back of my throat.

When we were about 50 feet away from the store, Andy grunted and waved for us to huddle tight around him. Reaching into his front right pocket, he pulled out a wad of bills in a manner that suggested familiarity with the counting of off-the-books income.

"Holy shit!" said Chun.

"Where'd you get all that money from?" I asked.

"What the hell, man!" said YK.

Andy flexed the bills and counted out eleven $100 bills for each of us.

"Dai lo!" Chun and YK both yelped out in unison. "Dai lo" is a Cantonese phrase used by low-level street gangsters in old Hong Kong films. It literally means "big brother."

"Ni men jiao wo 'da ge,'" Andy replied. Given the wad of cash in his hands, nobody had any objection to calling him "big brother" in Mandarin instead. The money in our hands made all of us—well, everyone except Andy—a little crazy. I got so nervous, I folded the bills over and over again until they were reduced to a wadded-up polyhedron in my hand. Chun kept looking from side to side, acting all shifty. Was he thinking of bolting?

Reading Chun's mind, Andy said in English so there would be no misunderstanding, "Look, you go in with me, buy an iPad, then give it to me when we're back outside. After that, the change is yours. Should come out to 97 dollars each."

We all nodded anxiously and followed Andy into the cube and down the circular stairs into the subterranean store. He stopped halfway down.

"This is important to remember. Don't do the Apple ID. Say you don't have one. And you only have cash." We mumbled okays, then made our way to the sales floor.

Something was definitely up in one section of the store. We saw a line of about 30 depressed-looking middle-aged Chinese people lined up behind a velvet rope. They looked like the kind of tired and hopeless Chinatown people you sometimes see waiting to board buses bound for casinos in Atlantic City and Connecticut.

In comparison, we probably looked like we belonged on the Asian edition of a Disney Channel show.

Following Andy's lead, we walked right by the less-fortunate Chinese. Andy approached the first available Apple customer rep, and we lined up behind him.

"Hello," said Andy with a fake openness I'd never suspected he was capable of. "The four of us are picking up some items. Separately, because we aren't together. We each have our own preorder."

The too-skinny white dude looked at us warily. I chose to smile.

"Do you have a reservation number?" he asked Andy.

"We each reserved online earlier this week, but when we came late last night to pick up the items, they were already locked away in the storage cage. We spoke to someone on the phone earlier today, and he assured us that the items would be left outside the cage for pickup this morning." He gave his words a small lilt when he said "left outside the cage."

The dude nodded and went to the backroom.

Andy turned to us and growled, "Tell him your real name but remember: absolutely no Apple ID!"

"All right," I said. My hand was in my pocket, further mulching the bills he had given me.

The dude came back holding a plastic basket laden with boxes.

"This was the only thing outside the cage, so it must

be for you four gents. You're lucky because these are the last four artist edition iPads currently in our inventory. I can check you out here if you'd like."

Andy gave his name while rocking on his heels.

"What's your Apple ID?" asked the dude.

"I don't have one," said Andy. The dude turned his head slightly.

"You don't use Apple Music or Apple TV?" the rep asked, his brow furrowed. "You've never bought an app before?"

"Nope, not from the Apple store. I've been strictly Android until now. This is my first Apple product. I'm ready for a change."

The rep scanned one of the iPads with his phone and began to type.

"I see. Normally, you'd have to use an Apple ID to even reserve these, but you were able to place an order through a co-branding partner." He squared his jaw. "Well, I hope you know that you're going to have to register an Apple ID in order to activate the iPad," the dude said. "It's easy enough to do—let me know if you need any help with that." Because Andy was paying in cash, he ended up having to walk over to a station that had an actual register in order to get change, which seemed to unnerve the rep even more.

I stepped up next.

"What's your Apple ID?" the dude asked.

"I don't have one," I said.

Apple Dude sighed and looked us over. Then he cast his eyes over at the old Chinese people. "Well, that's a shame," he said half to himself.

Andy must have miscalculated something, because after the purchase, my change came out to about $130. Well, if he had misjudged the other way, it might not have made the trip worth it to me or the other guys.

When the four of us had finished paying and were on our way out, iPads in hand, Chun turned to me and whispered loudly, "Look at those suckers!" He tilted his head at the old Chinese people.

"Why are they suckers?"

"Because they're waiting for the same iPads that we just got!"

Feeling giddy and rich, we jogged our way up the stairs and out onto the street. As soon as we hit the open air, Andy collected our iPads and slipped them into a single black canvas bag. I asked him what the deal was with the old Chinese people.

"Sometimes the store gets surplus shipments," he said.

"Is someone paying them to stand there and wait?" He shrugged.

"They wouldn't do it for free."

YK spoke up. "I don't know about you guys, but I'm going straight to the bank with this."

"Then there'll be a record of you depositing money," said Chun.

"So what?"

"Someday, if you ever get audited and they pull up your bank records, they're going to ask you where that money came from and why you didn't pay tax on it. I am not shitting you guys about this. You'll have to pay back the income tax and a penalty on top of that."

"Shit, you're paranoid, Chun," said YK as he shoved both hands in his coat pockets.

"I'm paranoid? You know the IRS racially profiles people of Chinese descent for auditing, right? They think we're extremely shady."

"Didn't we just do a shady deal?" I asked.

Andy shrugged and zipped up the canvas bag, his mind still focused on the task at hand. "I'm going to FedEx," he said as he sauntered off. We watched him melt into the crowd.

"How much money do you think Andy's making off of this?" asked Chun.

"A lot more than he paid us, that's for sure," I replied

"So what?" said YK. "At least he cut us in on the deal."

"He got us cheap!" said Chun.

"I'm gonna go back to Chinese school," I said, getting a bit antsy myself now that the job was done. I'd noticed it was still early enough to make snack time and see Betty!

"Don't go," said YK.

"That would be so lame," said Chun.

"I have to," I said.

"You just want to see Betty," Chun chirped cloyingly.

"No," I said, annoyed at how easily he'd hit the mark. "I have to meet up with my dad right around there afterwards anyway, so going back makes more sense than hanging out with you bozos." It was a weak answer, even I knew that, but the others already seemed to have lost interest.

Chun rolled his eyes back, let out a zombie groan, and tapped YK's shoulder. "Let's go to the movies," he said.

YK leaned back. "I'd rather go shopping," he replied.

"Bye, guys," I said as I left them to do whatever.

The train ride back to Chinatown was quick, and I had to wait a few minutes to enter the school at snack time. Kids were coming and going everywhere, and I blended in as if I'd been there the whole day. Excellent timing.

I waited for some cold sesame noodles, searching surreptitiously, head lowered, for Betty. Somebody slapped my right shoulder.

"Hey!" I grunted as I reached up reflexively to soothe the affected area. Betty glared at me. How did I miss seeing her?

"David! Where were you?" Wait. Was she wearing mascara?

"What do you mean?" I bleated.

"We were supposed to work on our skit! And where are your jackass friends?" She *was* wearing mascara. Lipstick, too. And a sweater that showed off her chest a little. She looked sultry and angry.

"I'm sorry I got here late, Betty." I said, venturing to pat her lightly on her left elbow with my right hand. "Look, why don't we get some food, sit down, and talk about the skit? Don't worry. Everything's going to be fine."

I once read this short story where a mother told her son before his prom that women like men who take charge and have a plan. It hadn't worked out for the poor guy in that particular story, but Betty seemed to believe me.

"All right," she said.

I was so glad that she didn't look mad anymore that I left to fetch her a straw for her bottle of green tea. We sat down at a smaller table built for two.

"I could have drunk right out of the bottle," she protested.

"Then you would've ruined your lipstick," I replied. "It looks nice."

Betty actually blushed. "I could always have reapplied it. Not a big deal." I circled her face in the air with my right hand. "Any particular occasion?"

She shook her head. "I wore it because I felt like it," she said. "I can look pretty when I want."

We were both quiet for a little bit. I was hesitant to talk. She tugged at the bottom of her sweater a few times, and I was so nervous I couldn't stop touching the bridge of my nose.

To break the awkward silence, I blurted out, "I can still put lo mein on your feet." What in the world made me double down on the one comment that had been tormenting me for the last few nights? To my relief, though, she cracked up.

"That's so gross, David!" she said through a smile.

"For real, though, Betty, I'm sorry I wasn't here to work on our skit." She shrugged.

"I guess it doesn't matter that it's not done today since we're missing more than half the cast anyway." She paused to give me a meaningful look. "Where are Chun, YK, and Andy, anyway?"

I couldn't lie to her. Not about this. "They're at the Apple store," I said. "Well, they were. We went there to pick up these special iPads so that Andy could do some kind of deal."

"How much did Andy pay you?"

"We each got $130." She punched my arm again. "Ow!"

"Why didn't you cut me in?"

"I knew nothing about this plan until right before we left! Anyway, there were only four iPads, so a fifth person wouldn't have worked." She shook her head and bared her teeth as she bit delicately into a vegetable spring roll. "I...I could give you half the money I made," I offered.

"I don't want money from you," she said with her mouth full. "Women are fully capable of earning their pay."

"Of course you are," I said.

She finished her spring roll with another bite. When her mouth was once again mostly empty, she said, "Right now, we should focus on putting together a great show."

"I don't care if it's great," I said. "I'm just a little tired of looking stupid up there." I sipped some lemon tea from a drink box.

Betty set down her chopsticks and looked at me.

"Listen to yourself. You're such a negative thinker. Instead of not wanting to look stupid, you should want to look smart. It's been proven that if you think positively, you can make your whole life better."

The way she was looking at me made the area around my mouth itchy. I wiped my face with a napkin. Her combination of intrusiveness and concern was annoying, but I could tell she really cared about what I said and what I thought.

"I can't help it," I said. "I grew up surrounded by negative reinforcement. Back in elementary school, my mother used to say I was stupid whenever I got a B, and she wouldn't stop nagging me until I had all A's. Now the pressure is on for me to get into an Ivy League school." Betty hid her left hand under her right.

"What's going to happen if you don't?" she asked.

I chuckled. "There's no alternative," I said.

"Which Ivy do you have to get into?" Betty asked.

I shrugged. "Any one of them," I said.

Her eyelids stirred. "Come on, they're all different. Which one do you like the most?"

"I honestly don't know," I said. "They all look the safe to me. Oh, I mean they all look the 'same' to me." Her face crinkled with disappointment at my answer.

"David, were you lying to me when you said you wanted to be a doctor?"

"No, I do. Honestly."

"Well, then you should care about where you're going to spend four years of your life," she said.

"Don't your parents pressure you to get into a school known for being good despite the geographic location or how the actual experience may be?" I countered. She put her elbows on the table.

"It's just me and my dad," she said. So, Betty didn't have a mother. That couldn't be easy. "He gives me a lot of independence," she continued, "but I also have a lot of responsibilities. The one good thing, though, is I get to go out at night if I want to."

"You mean on dates?" I asked cautiously.

Her face flushed. "If someone asked me, I might consider it." Whoa. I felt like I was sort of leading her on. Or she was leading me on?

"You know I'm not allowed to go on dates," I said.

She coughed. Well, I thought at first she was coughing, but she was really trying to stifle her guffaws. "Yeah, you told me about that dance and that girl, remember? So why aren't you allowed to date?"

"My mother thinks dating will hurt my grades. And therefore, hurt my chance of...well, you know."

Betty rubbed the back of her left ear. "Oh man, I'm sorry, David," she said. "I know some kids who are in a similar situation, but a lot of Chinese parents aren't like that anymore."

"I guess mine are holdouts." I suddenly noticed that our shoes were touching. She must have pushed her feet toward mine.

"It must suck."

"It's okay. It's all kind of abstract anyway. I don't even know who I'd ask out if I were able to."

"Really?" she asked as she looked down.

"Yeah."

She scratched both her elbows. "Would you need to date a Chinese girl?"

"You mean, for my parents?"

"Yeah."

"Probably. Well, the right kind of Chinese girl." I dropped my voice. "My mother sometimes says she doesn't like Cantonese people." Betty frowned.

"Why not?"

"She's from a Shanghainese family. They think every

other kind of Chinese is second-class."

"Then why are you at a Chinese school that's mostly Cantonese?"

"My mom got in a fight with the people who run the Chinese school in Shark Beach. You'll probably end up reporting to someone who lives there after you go into finance."

That joke didn't make her smile at all. I'd always heard that girls will keep smiling if they like you, so this was worrying.

"It sounds like your mother doesn't get along with 'her kind' of Chinese, either."

"That would be true. Though she did marry my dad. He's not Shanghainese. He might even have Mongolian blood."

"Who's your mom to say that anyone's low-class anyway? Look at your family. You run a restaurant. That's not exactly white-collar work. Aren't you suburban Chinese supposed to have real jobs? Office jobs? Doctor and lawyer jobs?"

"That's true, Betty." I shrugged. "I'm living the paradox of Chineseness. I'll bet you are, too."

"What do you mean 'Chineseness'?"

"You know how when your parents are immigrants, they only bring over selective parts of Chinese culture, some of which are outdated? And then they force them on you as if they were...talismans."

She sighed with feigned exhaustion. "Do you play Dungeons & Dragons, David?"

"No. Why?"

"There are talismans in that game."

"I'm sure there are, but you know what I'm talking about, don't you, Betty? I mean, your dad forces you go to Chinese school, just like my parents do."

"Actually, I made my dad bring me here!" she protested. I must have looked shocked because she burst out laughing.

"If I didn't have to come," I said, "there's no way I would be here right now."

Betty pulled her feet away from mine. "Be honest with me, David. It's okay. You want to be a doctor because that's what your parents want, right?" She punctured me with her words.

"Yeah, of course they want me to be a doctor. But it's also genuinely what I want to do."

Betty tilted her head. "If they somehow didn't want you to be a doctor, would you go against their wishes and become one anyway?"

"Sure. They wouldn't be able to stop me."

"Then here's what I don't get. They don't want you to go on dates, yet you accept that without question."

"That's not entirely true. I thought I explained to you earlier. I needed a tux," I said. "A nice one. One I couldn't buy on my own or steal. Sure, I could have snuck out to the dance, but I wouldn't have looked nice. And that would have been a dealbreaker."

I suddenly had a vision of me sneaking out of the house and riding the subways through tunnels all night with Betty. I'll bet she didn't think I needed to wear a cummerbund to hold her hand.

Sounds of clanging started up. Kids were pushing in their chairs. This meant it was almost time to leave.

I didn't know if or when Betty and I would be alone together again, so if I wanted to say something, I had to do it now. It was actually a gift that the other guys weren't around.

Mustering all my courage, I blurted out, "Betty, you'd probably say no if I were to ask you out, wouldn't you?"

"You think so?" she asked. Her face gave nothing away. She paused a beat before remarking, "Looks like snack time is over." She stood up.

"Let's touch base on the skits soon," I said, immediately matching her tone and trying to pretend as if the previous exchange had never happened. "I'm pretty certain the other guys will be here next week."

Why the hell did I say, "touch base"? That was dumbass TV office talk!

Betty lifted her chin and nodded. She had me all figured out. Though our conversation had been brief, I'd told her more about myself than I'd ever told anyone else.

"We saw your friend, YK," said my father as he opened the door to Mr. Yeung's truck.

"You mean just now?"

"No, a little while ago. He was hanging around outside a restaurant. Was he in Chinese school today?"

"I saw him there," I said evenly.

Mr. Yeung handed the Game Boy to my father and said, "Checkmate!"

"Where!" my father demanded. Mr. Yeung slid a finger casually across the screen.

"See?"

"You smeared the screen," my father complained. He tried to polish the device clean by rubbing it over his chest like a bar of soap. "You learn a lot today, David?"

"Of course."

Mr. Yeung asked me in Mandarin, "How old are you?"

"Shi liu sui," I replied, making sure to hit the "sh-" sound hard. Cantonese people sometimes let it slide to an "s-" sound when speaking Mandarin. Taiwanese people, too. "Ni de ka che duodale?" I asked.

"Ai ya!" said Mr. Yeung. "You want to know how old my truck is?"

"Yes," I said. It would have been incredibly rude if I had asked Mr. Yeung, an elder, how old *he* was.

"It's younger than you! But it knows Chinese better!" Both my dad and Mr. Yeung seemed to find this hilarious, laughing uproariously.

The Game Boy slipped out of my father's hands in the process, and the battery compartment broke open. I spent the entire drive to Jersey watching four double-A batteries skipping around the rumbling floor of the cab like jittery minnows.

CHAPTER TWELVE

At the end of yet another school day, my mother asked
how I did, but she wasn't satisfied with hearing that
there hadn't been any quizzes or tests.

"Well, what about Harmony?" she asked.

"Still 'TBA.'" My mother snorted as our car rolled to
a red light.

"When are they going to make up their minds?"

"I don't know. Their site doesn't mention anything
about it, and even Mr. Wald doesn't know."

"That's the guidance teacher?"

"Guidance counselor."

"You asked him?"

"Of course!"

I considered asking for my phone back, but now was
not the right time. I had to wait and catch her when
she was unaware or compromised, and my mother was
almost never in either of those states.

"So where do *you* want to go to college?" I was emailing with Betty again. It was easier to write things than talk in person. Our nightly typed conversations had a light tone and left me wanting to know more about her.

"I'm not sure," Betty wrote back. "Maybe Macaulay Honors or City College."

"Those aren't Ivies," I wrote.

"But me thot was Ivee skool!"

I burst out laughing and had to cover my mouth so I wouldn't wake up my parents.

"You know those are good schools, right David?"

"Yeah, I know."

"Did you ever think that the Ivy schools your mother wants you to go to are like the nice tuxes that Christina wanted you to wear? Expensive and impressive on some level, but maybe not a good look overall?"

She was right, of course. "I understand that, Betty, I really do. But I wouldn't want to end up being hounded by my mother about working on transfer applications. It'd just be easier if I get into one of the Ivies right off the bat."

Saturday rolled around again once more. The night of the Dames Ball had come at last. Not that the dance mattered to me. Throughout the week, most of the school had been buzzing about it, but I largely put it out of my mind. I told both Scott Sima, who was going with a group of friends, and Yaro to have a good time, and both reiterated how sorry they were that I wasn't going.

I didn't care, though. Another Saturday meant that I

was going to get to see Betty again. After a further week of carefree conversation over email, it was time for me to show her my serious side by working on our skit.

That was the plan at any rate. I was about a block away from Chinese school when Chun ran up to me on the street. I heard him panting before I saw him. Chun usually looked fairly sharp and well-groomed. Today his hair was crazy and his face dripped with sweat.

"Yo, yo, yo! Dave! Hold up!" I immediately felt a little panicky. Wait, we couldn't be ditching Chinese school a second time in a row, could we?

"Whoa, now what?" I asked.

"We have to help YK's family move. I've already been at it for a few hours." He probably would have been more agitated if he weren't so clearly exhausted.

"Move? Like leaving their apartment?"

"His landlord forced his family out, so we have to help take their stuff over to Confucius Plaza." He meant the colossal subsidized-housing complex near the Manhattan Bridge, where a vast population of elderly Chinese lived. On hot days, when everyone had their windows open, you could hear all the mah-jongg tiles clacking inside from the street.

"We're going to skip school two weeks in a row?" I asked.

"Yeah, no Perfect Attendance certificate for you this year," Chun replied, his voice dripping with sarcasm.

Despite how much Chun and YK liked to dig at each other, it was nice to see that Chun was there for YK in bad times. Which must mean it was pretty serious. Man, Betty was going to be pissed. But I hoped she'd understand. It was pretty obvious that if I didn't go help the guys out, I wouldn't be a real friend.

We walked back the way we'd come, heading as quickly as we could for the corner, which, once we turned, would put us out of sight of the school.

"David!" I heard a voice bark out from somewhere behind me. Was that my calligraphy teacher, Mrs. Ma?

"Shit, someone saw me!" I said. We tried to make a run for it, but a bunch of suburban Chinese and other tourists were blocking the sidewalks, oblivious to anything that couldn't be bought or eaten.

I was just cutting to the street to get around a unit of middle-aged people chatting in German when I felt a hand on my shoulder.

"David!" I turned around.

It was Betty. She looked stunning in a sky-blue dress I hadn't seen before that was probably too nice for Chinese school, and definitely too nice to wear for someone like me, if that's what was going on. She was wearing mascara and lipstick, again. The morning sun bathed Betty in translucent gold, and she looked as if she'd stepped out of a book of whitewashed Chinese fairy tales.

"Hey," I managed to mumble, too awestruck to say much more. I might have forgotten to breathe. Betty's beautiful and angry eyes flashed.

"Where are you and your delinquent friends going this time?"

"We have to help YK move," I said. Chun glanced back at us, shook his head derisively, and kept going. "The landlord threw his family out," I added as I scurried to keep up.

"Oh, no." She softened right away. "Can I come, too?"

"I'm sure he could use more help," I said. I pointed at her dress and said, "That's probably going to get dirty, though."

Betty slapped my hand down.

"It doesn't matter. Let's go," she said.

Chun glanced back at us again and rudely poked his right index finger through his left fist. Betty flipped him off, and he smirked.

YK and his parents were living in a small walkup on the Bowery, just above Canal Street, one of the busiest arteries in Manhattan. The west end of Canal leads to the Lincoln Tunnel and from there to New Jersey, while the east end of the street becomes the Manhattan Bridge, which reaches into Brooklyn, Long Island, and beyond.

I could see YK in a gathering of residents on the sidewalk in front of the building. He was clearly in a state of distress. I didn't even bother asking him if Betty could join us or not because it was apparent that he needed all the help he could get. Betty and I stopped to talk with him as Chun headed inside.

"The landlord tried to break our leases in court, but that didn't work, so now he's changed his tactics. He came in this morning, shut off the pipes in the basement, and removed the building doors. Now there's no water and anybody off the street can walk right into our building," said YK. "It's not safe here anymore." His glasses slid to the end of his sweaty nose, and he pushed them back up.

"You should sue him!" I said.

"We'll sue him after we get our stuff out." He nodded his head at Betty. "Thank you for coming."

"No problem," she said. "It's the least I could do."

He looked at us both. "If you need to use the bathroom, just hold it until you get to Confucius Plaza."

We both nodded.

I stood back and examined the building. It was dirty, and probably would have looked better covered in scaffolding. With a gaping hole where its door should have been, it looked like a toy house in a birdcage that had been shat on and chewed up. Every window was open and screaming.

The three of us followed Chun up the wooden staircase that made up the building's fragile core. Each step gave a little too much, as if it might be booby-trapped. On the landing between the first and the second floors, we met Andy on his way down. He was bear-hugging a cupboard that sounded as if it were filled with ceramic bowls and plates. Having worked in a restaurant for as long as I have, I'd recognize that sound of glazed items scraping against one another anywhere.

Sparing us little more than a glance of acknowledgement, he rightfully turned his attention back to the stairs below.

"Are you allowed to take out the cupboards?" asked Betty.

"We're taking everything we can," said YK. He looked at Betty and muttered, "That jerk of a landlord." He would've cursed if Betty hadn't been there.

On the street-facing side of the fourth floor, Chun strolled out, one of those enormous, ugly, red-and-blue woven plastic plaid bags that FOBs are so fond of in each hand.

"Got half your porn stash here," he said to YK. "The rest of it has wet spots that still need to dry off."

YK tried to kick Chun, but he scampered away, the stairwell groaning under the staccato of his footsteps.

"I'm sorry he used that kind of language in front of a girl," YK said to Betty.

She shook her head and said, "Don't worry, I've heard it all."

When we entered the living room of YK's apartment, I couldn't believe that he and his parents managed to live in a place that was so tiny and basic. They all dressed so well, I had no idea they all shared one closet.

Betty must've been thinking the same thing when she said, "YK, I thought your family was pretty well-off." His face shriveled as if she'd just shaken salt on him.

"We have to save money," YK offered as an excuse.

"Why are you moving to Confucius Plaza?" I asked.

"My grandparents are going to take us in. Temporarily."

I picked up a heavy cardboard box that had apparently once held bags of salted melon seeds imported from China. Betty picked up a box next to it.

"That one's a little heavy," YK warned her.

"I can tell," said Betty as she hoisted it. He gave her an admonishing look. She added, "I'm half barbarian. I can handle it." He shrugged and slung three nylon carryalls around his neck and shoulders. We walked downstairs.

As we exited the building, I looked around for a spot

on the sidewalk where we could put down our stuff until the van came. YK, however, continued walking down the street.

"YK, where are you going?" I asked.

"Confucius Plaza! I told you!" YK called over his shoulder.

"Where's the moving van?"

"There's no van!"

Shit! That meant we had to walk down the east side of the Bowery and Canal intersection, probably the single most pedestrian-unfriendly stretch in Chinatown—and there was plenty of competition for that particular title. We'd also have to cross five ramps and bridge-entrance lanes with quick-change traffic lights, all while laden down with YK's belongings.

My hands were slippery with sweat. I shifted the box to my right side.

"Are you all right, David?" asked Betty.

"I'm fine," I said.

That Saturday, it seemed as if everyone was out driving at once. We stopped for traffic twice before finally making it to safety on the other side of the street. YK was already way ahead. In the distance, Confucius Plaza, a complex of semi-circular buildings that looked like broken brick cogs, towered over the street. Walking by the ground-level storefronts and into the courtyard, we ran into Chun, who was already on his way out again.

"You guys," he warned us, "If the guard asks if you're helping someone move in, say no. Moving is only allowed on weekdays." Chun glanced over his shoulder.

"In this wing, it's an old white dude. He's pretty harmless."

I'd always known where Confucius Plaza was, but I'd never been on its grounds before. Signs were posted everywhere warning that eating and smoking weren't allowed in public. How could Chinese people comply with that, I thought to myself. Especially the elderly? From what I'd seen, smoking and eating in public were the sole pleasures that remained for elderly Chinatown denizens. I'll admit, though, that the courtyard was remarkably clean. The few senior citizens in evidence held umbrellas against the sun and were reading newspapers. They looked remarkably dejected.

"Which way?" asked Betty with a can-do lilt in her voice.

"To the left," Chun said. "Go to the 18th floor on the 20 block." Chun left us to head back for more of YK's stuff.

A security guard was sitting at a banged-up metal desk by the elevator entrance. If he were Asian, he would have fit right in with the unhappy people out in the courtyard.

"Wait," the guard called out to us. He held up a trembling hand. "Are you two moving in?"

"No, no," I said slowly, trying to think of a plausible excuse. "My cousin and I are bringing medicine to our grandfather."

"Well, all right," he said, giving us the kindest of smiles. What a dumb bastard.

We found the 20 block and took the elevator up to the 18th floor. The car rattled on its way up. It sounded as if rocks were pelting the walls.

"This thing is pretty beat up," I said.

"I wish we had an elevator in our building," said Betty. "We live in a walkup, too, but it's a little newer than YK's."

"That's his old building. This is his home now." She wiped sweat from her forehead. I pointed at a grease smudge across the right side of her dress, and she shrugged.

"Confucius Plaza's a big step up for YK," Betty said. "Better facilities and a better building overall. His old place was built in the 1870s. Confucius Plaza was built in the 1970s."

"How do you know all that?"

"I've lived in Chinatown my whole life, David!" She seemed exasperated. "My uncle was one of the construction workers who built this place."

"So you've actually been here before?" She couldn't believe I'd asked.

"Yeah, I have, Jersey Boy! I go to school with a bunch of people who live here. When you grow up in Chinatown, there's no way you're not going to know some people in Confucius Plaza. As soon as people get off the waitlist, all these extended families move in together."

"Yeah," I said. "Well now I also know someone who lives here!"

She smiled. "That's right! You're getting some Chinatown cred, David!"

Our car slowed dramatically and jiggled up the last two feet to our floor before the doors jerked open.

The air in the hallway was thick with the smell of good food and Tiger Balm. We looked up and down the corridor. Only one apartment door was ajar, propped open with an institution-sized canister of canola oil. That had to be it. Betty and I staggered inside with YK's stuff.

The place was filled to the gills. YK's grandparents were apparently adherents of that old-school Chinese maxim "Never throw anything away!"

That's not to say the apartment was disorganized. Single-file pathways wormed their ways through the towering piles of junk, just like in those hoarding shows.

I followed YK's lead along the appropriate path, which ran parallel to a red sofa preserved in a cloudy plastic cover. I finally caught up to him in a room that was about 100 square feet max. How were he and both his parents going to fit in there, even without their stuff? As it was, bags were heaped in all the corners, and half the room was already filled with stacked boxes.

Betty asked, "Where should I put this down?"

YK looked around hopelessly. "Anywhere it will fit. We'll deal with it later."

She hoisted up the box and slid it on top of a stack already four boxes high. I tried to lift the box I was carrying to go on top of hers, but I struggled. Betty came to my rescue by hurrying to support one of the bottom corners of the box, and we got it in place. The too-tall stack slowly tilted to one side until it came to lean against a window frame.

"Is it all right if we block the window?" I asked YK. It didn't have a view of anything, anyway.

"If the ceiling light works in this room, it won't

matter." He leaned over to flick the switch. A milky color leaked across the ceiling as the bare bulb slowly warmed. "Sure, block the window. Block all the windows."

"I think we're gonna have to," said Betty.

We were just making our way back to the door past the covered sofa when we ran into YK's grandmother. Only about four feet tall, she couldn't stop smiling and talking to us in Cantonese. She grabbed both of my hands and cupped my cheeks, even though I was the only one who couldn't understand what she was saying. Whatever it was, it certainly made YK and Betty crack up.

"Guys," I said, "what did she say?"

Hearing me speak English made YK's grandmother respond in kind. "Thank you," she said, grabbing my hands again and squeezing them hard. The unabashed sincerity was almost too much to take. Then she said something else in Cantonese that immediately prompted protests from both YK and Betty. YK's grandmother broke away from me, pushed past YK, and ran off to the kitchen.

"She wants to cook something for us," Betty said with embarrassment, the proper manner in which such a favor should be received.

"Should we wait?" I asked.

"Let's keep moving stuff," said YK. "We'll be back before she's done," he said.

It was funny. In one sense we were skipping Chinese school, but in another, this was real-life Chinese school. I was getting a lesson in intergenerational immigration and community.

Betty and I ended up going back to the elevator while YK stayed to help his grandmother figure out her new (i.e. YK's old) microwave. I didn't realize how sore my arms were until I hit the elevator button, which failed to light up, though we could hear the cars clanking in the shaft. Betty and I settled in to wait.

I said, "Your dress is getting all messed up!" She looked down and touched the smudges.

"Well, this can always be washed. As far as our skit is concerned, it's probably toast now."

"You have to admit, though," I said, "this is way more fun than Chinese school."

"I guess you could call it fun—for us at least. YK doesn't look like he's enjoying it. Plus there's going to be a price to pay in Chinese school. We're going to be so behind."

"That's no big deal, Betty," I said. "What I like about Chinese school is precisely that I don't have to try to be perfect all the time when I'm there. I worry about my class rank every minute of every day during the week. Seriously. Every single day, all week long. I don't need that all weekend, too."

She gave me a hard look and touched my arm. "I thought we were supposed to love learning. It's not all about grades."

"I wish you were my mother," I said. She withdrew her hand quickly.

"That's a weird thing to say."

"Are you calling me 'weird'?" That was one of my least favorite words, especially when applied to me.

The elevator doors burst open without warning,

and Andy stepped out holding a box stuffed with wall scrolls. I could see a wok and a rice cooker through the stretched-out diamonds of the mesh bag tangled over his right arm.

"Hey, maybe the two of you can move the couch together next," Andy said as he turned his back on us and headed down the hall. "It's a job for a twosome."

"We can't move a couch," I said.

"Yes, you can," he said, continuing down the hallway, not even bothering to turn his head over his shoulder to address us directly. Betty rolled her eyes at him. She was willing to help YK as much as she could, but I got the feeling that Betty had had it with obstinate Chinese men telling her what to do. We boarded the elevator, which jerked to a stop every other floor on the way down as well.

We ran into Chun in the lobby. "Come over here, you guys," he said tilting his head. Chun put down his box, and we regrouped in an alcove behind the elevator, out of earshot of the security guard. "Andy says you two are going to grab the couch."

"That's what he said, but won't it be too heavy for us?" asked Betty.

"Naw, it's light. It's a two-seater with a wicker frame. Take the cushions off and you'll be fine. Here's the thing, though—stash it in the community room. We'll have to find a way to get it upstairs later without going past the security guard."

"You know, I have to leave at 3 o'clock," I reminded Chun. "That grocery truck isn't going to wait for me."

"Yeah, I know. We should be done by then." He

picked up his box again and heaved it up to his chest.

"I can keep helping," volunteered Betty.

"That would be cool," Chun said as he walked off.

On our way out we glanced at the security guard. He had nothing to do except stare at the door and scratch himself.

As it turned out, Chun and Andy were right. The couch wasn't heavy at all, just bulky and a little prickly. Betty and I could carry it even with the cushions still on it.

The only problem was the couch was unraveling at the seams, so wicker strands where the weave was fraying would jab our hands if we weren't careful. This added yet another level of difficulty to the proceedings, because it meant we had to hold the couch a few inches away from our bodies as we walked. Since I didn't have many opportunities to be a conventional gentleman, I volunteered to carry the front end and walk backwards down the stairs of YK's old building. At each turn in the landings, the middle of the couch frame would bang against the two posts on the handrail, fraying it some more.

Having finally made our way out the front door, we proceeded to waddle awkwardly toward Confucius Plaza, trying to maneuver around YK's angry fellow evictees, who were pacing the sidewalk. Our wicker boat pitched about, but we managed to steer our way across Canal Street and past the perilous Manhattan Bridge entrance. It was a little easier than our earlier trip because no drivers wanted to dent their cars by hitting a couch.

As we approached the Confucius Plaza housing complex, I noticed YK and Chun standing in front of the courtyard entrance. They were in the midst of a yelling match with the security guard.

Chun spied us and surreptitiously waved us on. We kept moving down the block, pretending we had nothing to do with either YK or Chun. It was pretty obvious that trying to move the couch in right now was just going to make matters worse.

"Betty," I said, "I think we should keep going south. We can check back later to see if the coast is clear."

"Sounds good," she said. "I'm not surprised the guard caught on to us. It wasn't too hard to figure out we were moving in a ridiculous amount of stuff."

"Guess we *don't* all look alike to him," I said. This got a smile out of her. It was worth moving the couch just to see that.

"He's with Chinese people all day. He must study their faces because he's bored," I persisted, hoping to keep the smile there.

I couldn't tell whether or not it was working, though, because I had to keep glancing behind me to make sure I wasn't about to step into a pothole.

"Now there's an idea for a skit," I continued. "Sworn Chinese brethren helping a friend move from one apartment to another."

"You're being too bro-y, David!" Betty yelled. "I've been working way harder than anyone else in the group on the skit." She tried to kick me, and the couch pitched and rolled.

"Betty, you're going to make me drop this thing!" I yelled.

She cut it out, and we continued south. I wasn't sure how far away from Confucius Plaza we should go, but we walked until we came upon the larger-than-life bronze statue of Confucius himself near the end of the block. It's a major Insta spot for tourists and suburban Chinese, who take pictures with the sage after eating and shopping. Apparently all you need to prove your filial piety these days is a picture through the Lo-Fi filter.

When we reached a point about 20 feet away from the statue—out of range of the queue of photo-takers—I said, "Let's put the couch down here for a sec and take a rest."

"Good idea," said Betty. "Maybe we should photobomb people!"

"It's no fun photobombing people you don't know," I said, as we set the couch on the ground, and immediately dropped onto it. It felt good to finally sit. Plus we were sitting next to one another. On a couch! Betty pulled her arms behind her back.

"My arms," she moaned. I sat back and stretched out my legs. The couch that had scratched both of us mercilessly while in transit now in fact made for a comfy seat.

"Oh man," I said, "I hope no one from Chinese school sees us."

"If anyone sees us, they're cutting class, too," Betty said matter-of-factly.

I wasn't worried about running into my father and Mr. Yeung because I knew they were perusing the distributors blocks away from us, north of Canal Street. I couldn't think of anyone else I might run into.

Although there were quite a few people on the sidewalk, there was also plenty of room for them to walk around us, which is what they did. Once in a while, we'd get a quizzical look, but, typical for NYC, no one actually said anything. Two people sitting on a couch on the sidewalk wasn't among the most unusual sights in the city.

Betty turned, put her knees on the couch, and tried to look back to check for any sign of YK or Chun. My eyes dropped to her butt. It was right there. Who could blame me?

"Shit," she said, "Chun is still arguing on the sidewalk." Betty slid back into her seat, and smoothed down her dress. The bright blue color was now polluted with stains and smudges. My own clothes were dirty, too, but it's harder to see dirt on jeans and a black jacket.

I leaned back and crossed my ankles. There wasn't much space between Betty and me on the couch. I could have tried to hold her hand, but she was texting.

"I'm just letting the guys know where we are," she said, apologizing for ignoring me.

I slid down a little bit more in my seat.

"Betty?"

"Yes?"

"When did you figure out that you liked me?" She laughed.

"What makes you think I like you?" she asked.

"We wouldn't be emailing each other—and you wouldn't be writing back—if you didn't like me." She crossed her arms and looked at me.

"Can I ask you something?"

"Yeah."

"Do you legit like Christina Tau? If you could date her, would you?"

"It's true she's cute," I said. "Well, everyone says she is. But we're so different. I have a feeling she wouldn't be happy with anything about me beyond one dance. Maybe not even while it was happening."

"Wouldn't you want to do anything you could to make a girl happy, though?"

I had a sudden flashback to going over tuxes with Christina and her friends. Their idea of putting together a partner for her started with the uniform, not the boy.

"A girl should be happy with me the way I am!" I blurted out. "Maybe I'm not so great, but having money wouldn't make me any better."

Betty was thoughtful for a moment. Then she must have seen something, because she lifted her chin and tilted her head and pointed with her eyes. She wanted me to look at what was happening behind me. I turned to see an extended family of suburban Chinese haphazardly placing their shopping and leftovers bags at the marble base of the Confucius statue to pose for a group picture. It was clear that this was a post-meal excursion because several of them were holding bags of leftovers.

I wondered who'd won the fight to pay the check. That struggle—one that can involve grabbing wrists and even such trickery as "going to the bathroom" to slip a credit card to the cashier—is a cherished Chinese ritual. It also ensures a subsequent gathering to battle again so the person who'd "won" before can pretend to lose and enjoy a free meal.

This particular group seemed to have three generations to it. Grandparents with wispy hair and wizened, preserved-wood faces. Parents with sharp clothes and expensive glasses. Kids my age in Harvard and Princeton hoodies.

Yeah, prove you're smart by wearing those sweatshirts, jackasses, I thought to myself.

After taking two pictures each (the minimum) from five different phones, the group separated along generational lines.

One of them, a young woman in a Harvard hoodie was walking right by our couch when I suddenly realized it was Christina, minus the major makeup she usually wore. At just that moment, she turned her head and stopped.

"Is that really you, David?" Given her tone of voice, it was clear she'd make a great detention supervisor.

"Hi, Christina," I said.

"I thought you weren't allowed to go on dates!" she practically yelled.

"This isn't a date. It's a couch."

"You're lying again, David!"

"He's not lying," said Betty. "And this is indeed a couch, not a date." Christina twitched with anger.

"Who the hell is that homeless half-breed?" she asked me.

Betty lazily raised her right middle finger at Christina.

"She's more Chinese than you!" was the only thing I could come up with in the heat of the moment. But I could feel my face becoming bright red. I was so pissed, I was breathing with my mouth.

Betty, on the other hand, had no problem rising to the occasion. "What the hell's *that*, David?" she asked loudly.

"That's Christina," I said. "Christina Tau."

Betty laughed hard. "Is that a real hoodie," she asked Christina, "or did you buy it on Mott Street? Don't you see they misspelled 'Rutgers'? That's where you're gonna go, right?"

Howling with anger, Christina angrily dug out her phone.

"I can't wait!" she yelled as she held up her phone and clicked multiple pictures of Betty and me in burst mode. Christina should have demonstrated more restraint. Didn't she know that burst mode eats battery power?

"Hey, Christina, isn't the Dames Ball tonight?" I asked. "I hope you have fun with Yaro. I hope going with you doesn't hurt his popularity too much."

She yelled back something unintelligible as she rejoined her family, which had already begun walking off, oblivious to the issues of its youngest members.

I threaded my fingers together in frustration. I still couldn't believe she'd called Betty a "homeless half-breed!" I could see Jean saying that, but I'd never taken Christina for an out-and-out mean-spirited—not to mention racist—jerk! I was still staring after her, violent thoughts dancing like shadow puppets in my mind, when Betty touched my shoulder, causing me to jump slightly.

"Do you think I got a little bit too mean, David?"

"No," I said. "Christina's the one who started it.

That was so messed up. I'm sorry she said those things."

Betty rubbed her mouth. "You shouldn't apologize for the girl who wanted you to wear a tux." I laughed.

"Seriously," she continued, "I didn't mean to put down Rutgers or anything. I know a bunch of people who go there."

I held up a hand. "You don't need to defend Rutgers," I said. "It's a decent college. It can handle a joke."

Betty sighed and leaned back. The couch creaked. "David, is that what all you uptown Chinese Americans are like?"

"What?" I said. "I don't live uptown."

"That's a metaphor, David! Uptown means rich and suburban!"

"My family's not rich."

"You've got more money than any of your three buddies! Or me and my dad! You own a restaurant! The rest of us would probably just be working there..."

"Betty, we go to the same Chinese school! And right now, we're sitting on the same busted-ass couch out on the street!" I was getting a little frustrated.

Betty looked me over. I folded my right leg over my left knee and shrugged. "True," she conceded. "You don't wear very nice clothes."

"Are you ready to fit me for a tux, too, Betty? Because, honestly, I don't have anything as nice as that dress you're wearing. Well, the way it used to look." I suddenly thought of something from Dr. Wu's class, and I screwed up my face to remember it better.

"David, are you all right?"

"'Fine words and an insinuating appearance are seldom associated with true virtue,'" I said.

"What?"

"That was supposedly one of Confucius's sayings. Dressing up may mean you're hiding something."

Betty swept her arm out to the statue of Confucius in a robe with loose sleeves. "Well, that guy's not dressing to impress, that's for sure."

"And about our restaurant," I persisted, "yeah, sure, my family owns Tung's Garden, but it's no cash cow. We're not like, featured on the Food Network. We don't even have our own Insta account." Her mouth tightened.

"Are you guys like the Chinatown restaurants that rip off their workers?"

I was floored by the thought. "What are you talking about, Betty?"

"They steal tips from the wait staff and make them work overtime for no extra pay."

"We would never do that! Our employees are like family. Uncles and Aunties." That was no exaggeration. "Our chef, Auntie Zhang, I've known her my whole life."

"I didn't mean to insult you, but I had to ask. You know, my father was hurt while working in a restaurant," said Betty quietly. I moved closer to the edge of the couch so I could turn to face her.

"You never told me that. When was this, Betty?" I asked.

"Oh, years ago."

"Hey, I remember there was a collection for him a while back. Was that what it was for? May I ask what happened?"

She looked me in the eyes. "He was a waiter, but his boss basically forced him and some of the others to install a ventilation system. My father lost his footing on a ladder, and the whole thing crashed down on him. He could have died."

"Did he go to the hospital?" She propped up her head with her right hand.

"He didn't have health insurance. His boss helped him find a doctor, but I'm using the term 'doctor' loosely. After he was patched up, he was fired. The asshole boss even claimed that the back wages they'd owed him had been used to pay the doctor. Can you believe that?"

"That's bullshit!"

"He's fine now."

"That doesn't matter!" I waited for Betty to respond. Since she'd unlocked her life to me a bit, I decided to push the door open further. "Was your mom around at the time?"

"No," she said. "She'd already left us to join a Chinese monastery upstate." My eyebrows rose.

"She divorced your dad to become a Buddhist nun?!"

Betty began to pick at the cuticles of her left hand.

"They never actually got divorced. She just left. I was mad at her for a while, but then I realized she'd had a hard life, too."

I wanted to cry for Betty. She and her dad didn't have any money for college tuition. Macaulay was free if Betty got in, but City College was probably going to break the bank. That beautiful blue dress, now all dirty, was probably her most expensive outfit.

No wonder Betty could come off as pushy and controlling. She'd had to take control of the situation after her dad got hurt. I was relatively lucky. I worked with my parents and Auntie Zhang, and I could rely on any of them for almost anything I needed. Not to mention the grad students who delivered our food.

"Are you in touch at all with your mom?" I asked softly.

"Only through my aunt, her sister. I'm glad that she seems happy now. My father refuses to go up there, though. He doesn't believe in religion."

I felt a hard slap against the back of my head.

"What the hell?" I yelled. It was Chun.

He nodded as he examined the situation. "Do you guys think you're on some bootleg Chinatown version of *The Bachelor* or something?" Chun pointed at Betty. "Answer my texts! Let's move, already. That jackass guard left when his shift was up. What a committed servant."

Andy sauntered to the front of the couch and regarded Betty and me. To judge from his slightly raised eyebrow, he was doing a full if silent assessment of our body language.

Chun patted the back of the sofa. "There's free juice and cookies in the community room that we can plunder once we get there. Oh, and YK's grandmother made something for us."

Amazingly, we finished moving the last of YK's stuff about two hours before Chinese school ended. There was no point in going back to classes at that point, so the four of us plus Betty drifted over to the arcade on the southern end of Mott Street.

The videogame and pinball arcade there, Chinatown Fun, had recently reopened after being shut down for several months. Word on the street was that the other businesses had collectively lobbied Chinatown Fun's landlord to drop a proposed rent hike because its customer base of shiftless youth had begun to prowl the neighborhood looking for other idle amusements, including shoplifting, vandalism, and roughing each other up. This was, naturally, bad for the neighboring businesses, which meant it was bad for tourism. Which meant it was bad for Chinatown. As a result, the landlord had essentially been forced to relent, and Chinatown Fun had reopened.

Though I'd walked past the place a handful of times on those rare occasions my family had gone to eat in Chinatown, I'd never been inside.

As soon as I entered the darkened space and was surrounded by those loud game sounds, though, I knew I was going to have a blast. Andy and I played a rebooted Space Invaders game that projected onto a giant screen on the wall. Then I let Andy play solo for a while, so I could join Chun in a few frenzied rounds of Dance Dance Revolution A20. Betty watched us dance from the sidelines, cracking up at our antics.

We had just stepped off the machine to get some more tokens for a rematch when three kids walked right up to Chun and pushed him into a corner. They were all speaking Cantonese, so I couldn't understand what they were saying, but it was clear they weren't being friendly. Chun answered them coolly and walked backwards to a vacant area in front of some pinball machines. The biggest kid confronting Chun kept pointing a finger in his face, nearly touching Chun's nose. Chun said almost nothing, his face blank.

Betty was no longer laughing. Her face too had gone very still and serious. Her blue dress looked clean and purple in the lights of the arcade, her face, otherworldly.

"What's going on?" I asked her.

Betty cradled her elbows. "They're saying he's either with them or against them."

"Oh."

"They're sort of a gang."

"I can see that, but they're all smaller than us. We could probably take them."

She leaned toward me, almost mouthing the words more than uttering them. "You don't need to be that big to pull a trigger."

"They have guns?" I asked, matching her tone.

"If they don't, their older brothers do."

Keeping his hands in his pockets, Chun began responding to the gathered youth with what seemed to be wisecracks. He never took his eyes off of the biggest kid. Andy didn't know Cantonese, but he could tell that Chun needed some backup, so he went over, unbidden. He took up a position behind one of the smaller kids, who flinched as he looked up at Andy's immobile face.

YK, who'd gone to get some more tokens, lingered by the change booth as he evaluated the situation. I was about to join Andy and Chun when Betty pulled me back.

"Let go of me," I said, trying to shake her off.

"Don't get involved," she said. "YK has the right idea to hang back. If you head over there, things are just going to escalate."

"We're bigger than those twerps, and there are more of us!" She punched my arm.

"There are more of them just a text away! Goddamn suburban Chinaboy! You don't know how it works here! This is just yelling. It'll all be over soon."

Just like she said, the three kids stepped away shortly thereafter, striding out of Chinatown Fun as if on an errand.

Chun walked over to me and coolly ran his fingers through his hair.

"Ha, didn't think you had it in you to dance so well in that last game, Dave," he said as if nothing had just happened.

"Chun, are you all right?" I asked. He shrugged.

"What do you mean? I know all those guys from high school. They're harmless."

"Are they trying to get you to join their gang?" I asked.

"That dumbass little outfit? We could beat them all up, just you and me!" He patted his wallet. "I need more tokens," he declared, then went to join YK at the change booth. I saw them talking to each other in the slow, assured manner of men of the world.

Andy tapped my shoulder.

"Dance Dance," he said. "Let's go." We stepped up to the game stage together. The introductory music blared out, and I smiled at Betty, who gave me a withering look that somehow nevertheless managed to look super cute.

"You and me, next!" I yelled at her as the booming soundtrack started up.

"I don't play!" she yelled back.

CHAPTER THIRTEEN

I groaned as I eased into the truck cab. Mr. Yeung laughed.

"You move like an old man! Slower than me!" He started up the truck as soon as I was belted in and we began to move.

"My legs are sore," I said.

"From what?" my father asked.

"From sitting all day." Anything but, actually.

Andy had kept feeding tokens into the dancing game for close to an hour and a half. I think we all witnessed the beginning of an addiction.

I guess I didn't have to keep playing it with him, but Chun and YK were having a two-man Cantonese summit meeting about the gang kids, so we were sort of stuck at Chinatown Fun. Plus I'd wanted to show off in front of Betty a little bit.

Mr. Yeung flipped down a sun visor and handed me a little square packet.

"David! Put this on your leg!"

"What is this?"

"Japanese medicine patch! Puts the heat right on there. Boom! You feel better."

"No thank you, Mr. Yeung." He continued to hold out the patch, one hand on the wheel.

"Hey! Take it!"

"No, thanks."

"I'm going to crash the truck if you don't." I grabbed it, and my father began to laugh.

"Mr. Yeung's very funny, right, David?"

"Not really."

"Hey, I got you to take it, huh, David?" said Mr. Yeung.

While we were sitting at the early dinner with Mr. Yeung, my mother got up to answer the phone. It wasn't a food order, and although the call itself was brief, it seemed serious. She came back with an angry smile, though she didn't mention anything about what the call was about.

Once Mr. Yeung was gone, however, she immediately began to yell. "David! How come you've been skipping Chinese school?"

"When?" I asked, trying to keep my voice steady.

"That was the Chinese school secretary! She says she hopes you feel better because you haven't been in school for two weeks now!"

"There's got to be some mistake," I said calmly. "My friends and I have been working on a skit. Sometimes we go into an empty classroom to write and rehearse. Principal Ho must have missed us."

mother and told her I wasn't going to class. Did someone call you?"

"No, I didn't hear anything. Maybe a late April Fool's prank?"

Chun! I was going to kill that guy!

Betty and I exchanged good nights. I printed out some MCAT study pages, but I had to update the software driver. While searching the downloads folder for the update, I came across the picture that Al had given me of Christina's friend Jean being busted for shoplifting. I printed it out and put it in my MCAT pile. I wanted to remember to bring it to Chinese school so I could show Betty and share a laugh about the company that Christina kept.

I guess I should have been more concerned about the pictures Christina had taken of Betty and me, though. Christina's screaming was burned in my memory, but by Monday morning, I'd forgotten about all the snaps she had taken with her phone.

As I approached the bus stop, I saw that Jean was holding up a tablet to Percy, Fred, and Grace. They all seemed mildly amused. Were they checking out pictures from the Dames Ball?

"I didn't know you were into the exotic, David," said Percy.

"What the hell are you talking about?" I asked, immediately on edge.

"He's into exotic girls," said Jean, once again happy to have found something that would get a rise out of me. She twirled the screen over so I could see.

On display was a slideshow of pictures of Betty and me sitting on YK's wicker couch, the images advancing every two seconds. Betty's expression went from annoyed to cool all while holding up her middle finger. My face didn't change much, though I noticed I'd crossed my arms and legs in a defensive posture.

"That's your girlfriend, right?" asked Jean. "I didn't know you were into white girls, David."

"What's wrong with white girls?" asked Al. Everyone ignored him.

"I don't see her color," I said, regretting my words immediately.

"You don't see her color? Of course you do! You didn't want to go to the Dames Ball with Christina Tau because she's too yellow for you! Who's the racist now?"

I was getting so mad, my tightening grip nearly crushed my bag. Then I remembered that I was carrying that printout of Jean's mug shot!

I could shut her up right now. Just make one more assholic comment, Jean, just one more...

"David, why is this girl's dress so dirty? Does she wear clothes from the trash? Is she homeless, or something?"

I tore open my bag and furiously searched through my papers. Jean and her friends began laughing, confused by my actions. Then I pulled out the shoplifting photo. I presented it to her with both hands. "*Your* clothes are looking a little dirty in this picture, Jean!"

She craned her neck and blinked, then grabbed the printout in a panic.

"Keep it," I spat out. "I've got a digital copy."

Fred and Grace remained where they were, but Percy walked over and took the picture from Jean's hands.

"Wow, that really is you, Jean," he said. "What the hell happened?" She didn't answer him and focused on me instead.

"How did you get a hold of that, David?" she asked. I think it was the first time I'd ever heard her speak quietly.

I purposely looked in every direction but Al's to protect him.

"I have my sources, Jean," I said. "Now how about you stop showing my picture around or I'll start showing yours." She was so nervous she began to hiccup.

"Everyone already has these pictures," said Jean. "Christina sent them around to her friends." I nodded slowly.

"That's too bad for you, then."

"Honestly, most of Christina's friends don't care about pictures of you, David, but you *have* to get rid of that picture of me!"

"No I don't." I caught a look from Al. He looked happy. "I'm not the only one who has this, you know." Jean mashed her lips around.

"Who else has it?"

"Jean!" yelled Percy, probably channeling his dad. "You'd better answer me, goddammit! You stole something at the mall?! When?" Fred and Grace, their curiosity aroused, stepped in to have a look at the picture.

"It's nothing, Percy!" said Jean. She turned her back

on me, grabbed Grace by the arm, and walked away.

After homeroom, Christina Tau accosted me in the hallway.

"You have to delete that picture of Jean now," she ordered.

"Who the hell are you to tell me to do anything?" I asked. "And thanks for sending around pictures of me and saying racist things to my friend."

"Jean has nothing to do with any of that! Blame me, not her!" Christina cleared her throat. "And I'm sorry I went off on you in Chinatown, but I was mad when I saw you with that girl." She was being honest and seemed pretty desperate.

"Jean was the one throwing your pictures in my face at the bus stop, though," I said. "She's been taunting me regularly, by the way. But what do you care?"

Christina grabbed my arm and searched my eyes looking for some sense of decency. "Look, it's true, Jean was busted at the mall, but she took the rap for me, too. We were both shoplifting, and we went out separate exits. They picked her up, and she didn't rat me out."

"Sounds like you owe her big time," I said.

"The security company was supposed to delete her mug shot. That was the deal she made. She paid for everything."

I crossed my arms. Listening to this was going to make me late to Mr. del Pino's biology class, and that guy hated tardy students.

"I'm glad I have a little memento of the event then," I said. "Seems like it's pretty valuable."

She wrung her hands. "How much do you want for it?"

"Never mind money," I said. "Did you put those pics online?"

"No, I just sent them to friends. Honest."

"Tell your whole crew to delete them all. And I want you to post an online apology on your Insta account to Betty Jung, J U N G, for your racist and demeaning remarks."

"I will."

"Before the school day's over."

"So we're all supposed to be friends from now on? Is that what you want?"

"No. I just want you all to leave Betty and me alone. They can all ignore us if they want to, too. That's fine."

"Ok, done. Let's shake."

I shook her hand. It was cold and smooth as polished stone. Christina straightened up.

"Now I want to see you delete that picture," she said.

"First off, I don't have a phone anymore thanks to you. Secondly, you'll just have to trust me," I said. "I'm sticking to our deal. But if things fall apart, I'm going to post Jean's picture online and tag all of your friends."

"You'd better not!" she yelled after me.

I yelled back, "Think of it as a trust exercise."

Christina must have sent out some all-points bulletin, because not only did her allies not bug me again, they all seemed a little scared of me.

"We're all screwed," Betty emailed me Tuesday night. Alarm bells went off in my head. She couldn't have known what had happened with Jean and Christina.

Aside from my Chinese school buddies, we didn't know any people in common. I'd been planning to surprise her with a link to Christina's apology, but she got me first with the subject line to her otherwise blank email.

"What do you mean?" I wrote back.

"There's a new principal at Chinese school. That phone call you got was no prank. I got one today, and I pretended to be my mother," Betty replied.

Damn, I thought, that explained why someone from the Chinese school had called to ask where I'd been. Old Principal Ho would never have had the initiative to chase down absent students.

"What happened to the Ho?"

"The board threw his ass out on Friday, the day before we helped YK move. They told the kids that Ho was sick on Saturday. New guy's named Gao."

Gao. That means "tall."

"Is he a big guy? Does he live up to the name?"

"Heard so. Apparently, he's ex-military. Worst of all, he's from the hood. Kid from Chinatown returns to kick some ass. It's going to be a nightmare."

That got me sweating. One of Principal Ho's most endearing qualities had been that he was the hapless foreigner. His accent added a comic tinge to everything he ever said, especially when he was irritated. Needless to say, getting away with stuff was a breeze. But a Chinese American? There's no way he wouldn't know what was up. This Gao dude would probably put an end to our smoking on Day One.

"One good thing, though," Betty wrote. "We get another week to work on the skits. This Saturday,

Gao's apparently gonna hold some big assembly to talk about changes."

"How did you find all this out?"

"I know kids who work in admin in the school. Advantage to actually living in Chinatown vs. the suburbs."

Nice dig, Betty.

"I'm richer than you, though."

"Ha!"

"I'm burning Benjamins right now, just for kicks."

"Did you hear about the hospital internship yet?"

I sighed. "No. Still TBA."

"Don't worry. I have faith in you! Good night, David."

"Bye, Betty."

School was stimuli-free the rest of the week. I still didn't have many friends, but I also felt like I had no enemies. The whole Christina thing had finally blown over.

Jean was silent and sullen at the bus stop, which was a nice change. It meant I could ponder the more difficult MCAT questions without interruption or agitation.

Al and I didn't nurture our budding friendship, either. Having already executed our joint plan, there wasn't anything more to tie us together. He worked his phone, indifferent to everyone.

Waiting at the bus stop now was painless. I hadn't realized how tense I'd always been, bracing myself for some bullshit from Jean. I discovered to my surprise that I no longer had red lines in my hands from gripping my books like a shield.

The only anxiety I felt now was the possibility of seeing someone else's name after the Harmony Health internship post on the board.

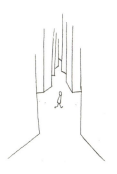

CHAPTER FOURTEEN

I walked to Chinese school on Saturday, thinking about how I could defend my friends and protect Betty from the new and terrible principal.

As I approached the school, I saw a big man in a suit with a crew cut in front of the steps. He stood as straight as a statue, but statues usually had kinder faces.

Watching him greet the younger children who were being dropped off at the school and shake hands with their parents and grandparents, I realized with a sinking feeling that this was probably going to be much worse than I ever could have imagined. It was obvious that this guy was going to change the culture at the school to one focused on learning and discipline. The sharp gleam in his eyes as they collected data gave it away.

That call home had probably been just an opening salvo, a notice of intent announcing that he wasn't screwing around. You cut my school, I call your parents. Given my multiple recent absences, I was probably already on a special list of known delinquents. We all probably were.

It seemed unfair that Chinese school was becoming a stressful place just as the social anxieties of high school had finally been neutralized.

Principal Gao's massive head turned my way, and he blinked to initiate a facial-recognition subroutine.

"You're David Tung, aren't you?" he boomed in English with a menacing familiarity.

"Yes. Are you Principal Gao?"

"That's right. I'm glad you're finally back." As I nodded and began to move past him, he put out an arm to block me. "David, do me a favor. Wait out here with me for a bit and then let's walk into school together. I'd like to talk briefly with you in my office before classes start."

"Okay." What else was I going to say? "No"?

I stepped a few paces back to give him some room to do his thing.

"Stand here, right next to me," he said, gesturing to the space beside to him. "Can we do that?"

I swallowed and obeyed. I couldn't bring myself to ask him why he needed me to be there, so I just stood there uncomfortably, shifting from foot to foot, my hands at my sides. I wished I had a phone to occupy myself with. Instead, I had to squint into the sky and pretend to study the scaffolding across the street, or the pigeons, or the departing parents, in order to avoid having to look at the faces of all the kids coming past us. I concentrated on keeping my back straight.

Principal Gao had spoken to me in English, but he

used Mandarin to greet all the other students, parents, and caretakers who passed, speaking with the hard "r"s and "sh"s that northern Chinese use. There was no trace of that soft-hiss Mandarin—characteristic of native Cantonese speakers like old Principal Ho.

Maybe he figured that speaking to me in my native language was a way of letting me know that he had my number and knew exactly who I was and what I was up to. Someone who never applied himself when learning Mandarin. Someone who had to shape up or be shipped out.

As Chun approached us, his jaunty walk became an anxious stutter step. He looked terrified. All of us knew from many years of experience that there was no other way into the building, but that didn't stop Chun from swinging his head around frantically, searching everywhere for an alternate entrance that only quantum theory could provide.

Catching sight of Chun, Principal Gao pointed mysteriously at his own left eye and, in Mandarin, barked out: "You're Chun, right?"

Chun lifted his chin. "Yeah, that's me."

"We called your house and left a message. Nobody called back. Why?" Chun made a dopey face.

"Our answering machine has problems," he said in English.

"Are you a problem, too, Chun?" Principal Gao replied in English, working his jaw. I could see the muscle there tense.

"No."

"All right, get inside." Principal Gao pointed in the

direction of the entrance, in case Chun had forgotten where it was. My friend glared at me as he sauntered in. Did he think I had pointed him out to the new principal?

Andy was next.

"Hey fatso, why do you want to come to my Chinese school?" he called out, again speaking Mandarin. Andy was taken aback.

"I...I don't know how to write and read so well," he managed to reply, also in Mandarin.

"Then during snack time, you can sit with me in my office and we'll do some extra work. You don't need to be eating any more food." Andy slumped a bit and shuffled into school.

YK was the final victim. As usual, all he had with him was the box that held his precious stash of collectible cards.

"What's in that box and why are you bringing it into my school?" Principal Gao roared in Mandarin without bothering to say hello or to introduce himself.

"It's nothing," said YK, cool and slippery as sesame noodles.

"Give it to me," said Principal Gao, holding out his hands. YK handed it over immediately, pretending he didn't care. The big man popped open the box, eyed the contents, and closed the lid again with a hard slap. "Now why in the world would you be bringing in cards for toddlers to school? I know you can't possibly be playing during class time."

"No."

Principal Gao leaned over YK. "And you sure as hell aren't selling these cards on school property, are you?"

"Never even crossed my mind. In fact, these cards belong to a cousin of mine. I'm meeting him after school to give them back to him."

Principal Gao gave the box a few hard shakes.

"You can pick this up after school, YK. I'm glad you decided to come today."

Deflated, YK trudged up the stairs.

Did I say that YK was the last victim? That wasn't quite true. I was.

After the last of the kids had entered the brick building, Principal Gao shoved YK's box into his left armpit and put his right arm around my shoulders. His fingers probed my shoulder joint for weakness. "Let's go to my office, David. There's something I want to talk to you about."

I had never been to the principal's office before, not in Chinese school and certainly not in regular school.

The horror writer H.P. Lovecraft once said that the oldest and strongest emotion was fear, and that the oldest and strongest fear was fear of the unknown. I had no idea what Principal Gao wanted with me, and that lack of knowledge made my abdomen as tight as an oak-tree trunk.

Mrs. Lim, the Chinese school secretary, regarded me with sympathy as we walked into the administrative offices. Pushing up her glasses, she asked Principal Gao if he needed anything. He said no, though he followed this up with a query about whether all the teachers had gotten his memo about the assembly. Mrs. Lim nervously assured him that they had before turning away.

Principal Gao gave me a gentle nudge, propelling me into his darkened, windowless office. I had to put my hands out to feel my way in before he hit the light switch.

He closed the door behind him, and it shut with a gentle click. "David, have a seat," he said, gesturing to a stuffed chair the color of a dirty tangerine. He parked himself in a black ergonomic office chair and placed his right hand on a white circle that had been branded into the desk by a hot mug. Each of his fingers tapped a different part of the circle. "I wanted to talk with you because you're very important to us, David. I hope you know and appreciate that."

"What do you mean, 'important'?" I asked.

"Well, you come from a more privileged background than nearly every other student here." He planted his elbows on the desktop and pushed his hands together into a prayer position. "I'll bet your parents have big plans for you. They probably want you to go to Harvard or Yale so that you can eventually become a doctor, right?"

Principal Gao didn't wait for me to respond. He already knew the answer.

"They don't want you to end up working in their restaurant forever, do they? I'll bet you already work there, what, 20, 30 hours a week." He paused to nod and make a two-handed welcoming gesture. "I know what you're going through. My parents wanted the same for me. The difference is that I didn't have the wherewithal to apply myself. I still live with that shame. Every day.

"But not every kid has to blow it like I did. Now that I'm here, I'm making it my mission to motivate every kid to meet their parents' expectations. And I'm going to need your help to do so."

"My help?" I asked. He seemed as surprised as I was that I had spoken up.

"Well, David, I was hoping we could share your story with some people."

"But I don't have a story." Principal Gao exhaled slowly but powerfully enough that I could feel his breath in the region of my throat.

"Of course you do! You come to our school even though there's a Chinese school right in your town in New Jersey. Your parents wanted to send you to a better school, a place that would provide their son with a top-notch education in Chinese language and culture, one that's embedded in the native habitat. And they expect this enrichment program to improve your overall learning experience. Isn't that your story, David?"

"Okay," I said, mostly because by then I just wanted to say things that would make him happy.

"I have really big plans for this place," he continued, as if confiding in me. "I'm a former student who's going to kick everything up a notch. I was named to this position because I shared these big ideas of mine with the board of directors. They know they've been on the wrong track. And now they've hired me to correct it."

His elbows slid apart, and his hands formed a knuckle-and-nail globe.

"I have this idea for starting a brand of Chinese language and culture schools. Tri-state area first, then nationwide. I know that sounds overly ambitious, but I think there are a lot of opportunities out there. These days, people are eager to know about China and the Chinese language and culture." He broke his hands up and tapped his right fingers against the desktop. "Even white people want their kids to learn Chinese."

"In Chinatown?" I asked.

"Yes, of course. Sure, Rosetta Stone is out there, but what we can offer is interaction with the real thing. Chinese instructors. Chinese food. Not only will participants in our immersive program get to learn Chinese, they'll get to experience *being* Chinese." He slid his hands into his lap and out of my view. "David, I don't expect you to understand any of this. It's a little insider baseball. But one thing I do want you to know is that I plan to make you a bit of a star."

He smiled at me as kindly as he could, but there was no warmth in it. This meeting was going in a most unexpected direction. It almost felt like an inappropriate internship interview. I twisted in my seat.

"I want to produce a series of videos," he continued, "testimonials from you about how you grew up in the suburbs and how you find that you're really getting in touch with your roots. How you think that learning Chinese is good for everyone in terms of becoming a global citizen." My head was exploding. The only thing I could think to say was the one thing about Chinese school that Betty had been hammering into my head for the past few weeks.

"But we haven't finished writing our skits for Mr. Chen's class," I said. Principal Gao gave a dismissive wave with his right hand.

"Oh, don't worry about that. I cancelled the show.

I mean, why have a bunch of kids in bad costumes fumbling through their lines on stage? It's not good for the performers. It's not good for the audience, either. It's just a big waste of everyone's time. What I'm going to do instead is find the funding to bring in professionals so that we can have a big show for the kids, the parents, and the press. But save that for the relaunch. First we have to come up with new branding." I wiped my sweaty palms on my knees.

"Why do you want me in the videos?" I asked. "Chun, YK, and even Andy are locals, real Chinatown kids. Not me." Principal Gao laughed. Hard.

"C'mon, David, you're smarter than that! I want to bring people *in*, not alienate them! Chun is a pseudo-gangster! YK is a little too designer-y. And Andy, that guy looks like Chairman Mao! You, on the other hand, are the perfect candidate. Not only do you represent the demographic I want to hit, you look like an assimilated American kid from the burbs. Someone people can trust!"

YK is too "designer-y?" What the hell's that supposed to mean? I wanted to ask, but I'd just thought of a more pressing query. I took a deep breath and shifted in my chair.

"What about Betty?"

I appeared to have caught him off-guard with this. "Betty?" he repeated, his voice devoid of recognition.

"She's the best Mandarin speaker in the whole school."

Principal Gao rubbed his nose and tried to look at his own eyebrows. Only when he'd managed to locate her in whatever files he held in his head did he return his attention to me.

"Betty is...different. Maybe too different." He tapped his desk with both index fingers to make a point. "I'm trying to avoid distracting people from what it is that our school can offer."

"She's half white," I said. "Wouldn't that appeal more to white people?" Principal Gao shook his head and made a deep, low sound in his throat, the kind that typically precedes big admissions.

"White people want the real thing," he said.

"I'm not the real thing," I said.

Principal Gao leaned back in his chair and regarded me carefully.

"You've got the right look, David, and the right background. Of course you're the real thing. Plus, never fear, you'll be compensated well. Say $200 per ad. What do you think?" The principal stood up, walked over to me, and shot an open hand to me. "We can talk about all the details later."

I stood up and shook his hand, not because I agreed with anything he'd said, but because I wanted to mark an end to the discussion and leave as quickly as possible.

When we were done shaking, he didn't let go of my hand.

"Where are you going now, David?"

"I have that performance class. With Chen lao shi." Principal Gao nodded.

"Take me there, I want to sit in on that."

Thankfully Principal Gao didn't sit right next to

me, planting himself instead at the back of the room, where he sat in stony silence and seemed to record everything he saw and heard. Everyone was too freaked out to goof off in any way. The whole class worked industriously on what I now knew to be our doomed skits. It was pretty obvious that Principal Gao hadn't yet told Mr. Chen that the show was going to be cancelled, and I sure as hell wasn't going to spill the beans. If I passed a note to Chun telling him the news, I knew for sure he wouldn't be able to help himself from yelling out, "The show is cancelled?!"

For the most part, my pals and I restricted ourselves to helpless looks and speaking in whispers. It wasn't even fun sitting with Betty, who threw herself into writing out our skit in longhand. We avoided looking at each other for fear we might crack up. After all, the principal's presence made the classroom comically oppressive. A cartoon dungeon with us hanging by our hands that were shackled to the walls.

Just my luck. Principal Gao decided to sit in on my Confucius philosophy class as well.

Snack time was the first place where I could speak freely with everyone.

"First of all, you guys should know, there's not going to be a show. Principal Gao cancelled it, so let's stop work on the skit immediately."

"The show is cancelled?!" yelled Chun. Luckily, his outburst was mostly swallowed up by the ambient sounds of kids talking and eating.

"Shut up, Chun!" I growled.

"That's bullshit!" said Betty in a low tone. "I worked hard on that thing!"

"If you think that's bullshit, just you wait. That's only the tip of the iceberg."

"What else did he say to you?" asked Chun. "You were in there for a while, man."

"Did he chew you out for cutting?" asked Betty.

"Did he throw away my box?" YK asked.

Andy had no questions. He just stared at my forehead, trying to read my thoughts.

"He wants me to do video ads for the school," I said.

"What?" asked Chun. "That doesn't even make sense! Why you? You're not even from here."

"He wants to franchise the school, kinda like McDonald's," I said. "He thinks he can take it nationwide."

"That's the dumbest thing I ever heard," said Chun. "Every Chinese kid is already in a Chinese school." I shifted and crossed my legs.

"He wants to make Chinese school for white people."

"Huh?" Betty spluttered.

"Well, to be fair, they got more money," Chun proffered.

"David, did he throw away my box?" YK asked.

"He still has the box," I said.

"Shee-it. Selling Chinese school to white people," Chun said with a chuckle that smacked of admiration.

"I can see it working," said Andy.

"I guess that's why he needs the least chinky Chinese kid in the school," said Chun, giving me a glare and shredding my Chinatown credentials in the process. I slid down in my chair.

"I never said I was going to do it," I said.

"Like hell you're not," said Chun. "How much are you gonna get paid?"

"It doesn't matter because I'm not doing it."

"You should do it," said Betty.

The bell rang early. As we prepared to head back to classes, Principal Gao got on the intercom and explained, again in Mandarin, that the auditorium in the basement was now open for seating for the assembly. The five of us got up and headed out of the cafeteria.

Fast-walking to the front of our pack, Andy turned to address us.

"I looked at the third-floor fire escape," he said. "The door handle is alarmed again." Andy patted the cigarettes in his shirt pocket and sighed.

Just then, Principal Gao swooped down upon us. He walked right into the middle of the group and pointed at Andy.

"What have you got there, tubby?" he asked.

"My phone," said Andy.

"I was waiting for you in my office. Did you forget we were going to skip snack time and study together?" Something must've gotten caught in Andy's throat because he started gurgling but no words came out. "I'll see you after the assembly, then, Andy. I hope you like what I have to say."

Principal Gao danced down the stairs to the auditorium. We let a dozen smaller kids go ahead of us before we followed.

Apart from the shows our class staged, we rarely went down into the basement auditorium, which held about 150 cushioned folding seats with swing-up tables. Mostly it was rented for meetings by Chinatown associations or other groups. The local police precinct used it to hold their monthly discussion forums with the community.

As the students continued to file in, Principal Gao leapt on stage and adjusted the microphone.

"Let's go, let's go," he said in English, his voice strained with an impatience that an educational professional really shouldn't have.

We sat down in a row in the middle. YK swung up his table and put a notebook on it. We all stared at him.

"I hope you're not planning on doodling while Principal Gao talks," said Chun.

"What?" YK asked. "I'm going to take notes. He might say something important." Chun slouched down sideways and managed to kick YK's seat from below.

"You're a kiss-ass!" Chun accused YK.

"He's got my cards," YK hissed. "I don't want to give him any reason not to give them back."

Principal Gao let out a sigh that was so bass-heavy it blew dust loose from the PA speakers.

"I'm just going to start, and you guys can fill in anyone who misses anything," he declared in English. He wanted us to understand every word. "So, first of all, I want to congratulate all of you for being here and trying to improve your language and culture skills, whether you came voluntarily or not. I know that back when I was sitting where you are now, I would much rather have been at home watching cartoons instead of being in Chinese school. In fact, I would have even preferred doing homework for regular school.

"Most of the time, in fact, this was the last place in the world I wanted to be. My parents wanted me to come here, though. They were worried that they were losing me and that Chinese culture was going to die in my generation. That wasn't the case, clearly, since here I am! But the fear is still there. Your parents are worried that you are all going to forget your proud heritage."

A boy near the front let out an audible snort.

"You!" said the principal, pointing into the crowd. "Get up here!" The boy complied, but as he ascended the stairs, it seemed as if gravity had suddenly gotten five times more powerful than usual. "Stand over here, center stage!" said Principal Gao. He wasn't using the microphone now. He didn't need it. The boy complied. "You're Carl Ching, aren't you?"

YK's number-one customer nodded and mumbled something inaudible. I could see that Carl was just beginning to register how much trouble he was in.

"Do you have any friends here, Carl?"

The boy mouthed "Sorry" to Principal Gao so quietly—at least in comparison to Gao's naturally booming voice—that it was almost a form of pantomime.

The principal turned to the audience. "Who are Carl's friends? Raise your hands!" Nobody moved. No one was stupid enough to risk getting dragged up on stage. "Carl! Show me who your friends are! Point them out for me!"

The boy pointed a shaky hand at a girl next to his empty seat.

"Jessie!" the principal boomed. "Are you friends with Carl?"

The girl shook her head emphatically. Principal Gao pointed to others near Jessie.

"Are any of you Carl's friends?

They all shook their heads. Carl looked as if he wanted to die.

"Nobody wants you here, Carl!" the principal declared even as he turned his back on the child. "Go home! I'll be calling your mother later."

Carl stumbled off the stage and scurried out of the auditorium.

Principal Gao returned to the podium and continued cheerily as if he hadn't just scarred someone for life.

"I'm your new principal, but I wanted to gather you all here to say that the important thing is that it's a new day for everyone. We all need to adjust our commitment level to the school, to our teachers, and to each other. As a part of that, I'm cancelling the next school performance by the older students. I'm sure you worked very hard on it, Chen lao shi, and I appreciate that."

I looked over at our teacher. He was stunned. He'd found out at the same time as the rest of the school.

"Are there any questions?" Principal Gao asked.

No one dared to even blink.

Before the day was over, Principal Gao managed to corner Andy, confiscate his cigarettes, and make him do

10 pushups on the newly vacuumed rug in his office.

"At least it didn't smell too gross," Andy said.

In order to get his cards back, YK also had to do pushups as well, in addition to promising not to sell things on the premises.

Chun was the last person that day to visit the office. After the last class let out, there was still no sign of him, so we waited for him on the sidewalk. I thought it was a little strange that Betty was waiting with us. Her MO was usually to run away from Chinese school as soon as it was over. Maybe it was my imagination, but I got the feeling she wanted to tell me something, but couldn't find a way to do so with the other guys around.

Chun came out at last, feet stomping, arms crossed.

"Principal Gao patted me down," he growled. "As if I would come to Chinese school with a gun. As if I would have a gun at all!" He turned to Betty. "Nothing happened to you, I see. How come?"

"I'm a girl," she said. "I'm also a good student."

"You're also white," said Chun. "Principal Gao wouldn't dare mess with white people. Cops would be all over his ass for something like that."

"Hey Chun," I said, "Lay off of Betty."

"I'm all right, David," she said.

"Yeah," Chun said noncommittally.

"I feel bad for Carl," said Andy.

"He didn't deserve that," said YK. "He still owes me money, though. Now I'll probably never get paid."

Chun spoke up again. "I still can't believe Dave gets to be the school mascot."

"How many times do I have to tell you?" I said.

"There's no way I'm gonna to do it," I said.

"You'd be stupid not to," said Betty.

"Dave's stupid, anyway," said Chun.

"Whoa," said YK, "that's mean."

"I don't care," said Chun. "It's just fucked up that Joe Suburb, who's probably even whiter than Betty on the inside, is going to represent our school. Which is in Chinatown! He's not even Cantonese!"

"I'm not Cantonese, either," said Andy.

"So what?" said Chun. "You're working class. Actually, you look like an illiterate Chinese peasant!"

"I'm glad the show got cancelled," said Betty. "Now I don't have to work with an asshole like Chun."

Chun scratched his sides.

"The feeling's mutual, Betty White!"

She turned and left hastily. My three friends stood around, hands in their pockets, looking at nothing. If I said nothing about Chun's awful behavior, I'd be just like Percy, Fred, and Grace at my bus stop.

"Do you really have to be such a jerk, Chun?" I asked. "A racist jerk?"

"I was only kidding," he said. "If she can't take a joke, she shouldn't hang out with me. That goes for you, too, Davy Boy."

He'd never called me "Davy" before, and he said it with a sneer. All four of us were quiet for a while.

"What a bullshit day," YK finally said. He shifted his box of cards to his other arm and waited for someone to dismiss him. Andy yawned.

I was already late for my rendezvous with my father and Mr. Yeung.

"See you guys," I said to my feet as I walked away. I looked, but I didn't see Betty anywhere.

I didn't tell my parents about how Principal Gao wanted me to do video ads for the school until Sunday morning when we were at the employees' table prepping vegetables.

My mother laughed out loud.

"Why would he want you? Your Chinese is terrible!" I sighed.

"He knows that, but he says I'm the right person to do it, anyway. He says I have the right face and voice to get white people to go to Chinese school."

"How much is he going to pay?" my father asked.

"He's offering $200 per video," I said. "He emailed me a contract yesterday." I had really wanted to email with Betty about it, but she hadn't replied to my messages. Either of them: the one in which I pretended nothing happened or the follow-up that apologized for the shit that Chun had said.

My father looked at my mother.

"If he does enough of those video ads, it could pay for some of his college expenses," he said. "Let me see the contract, David."

"It's on my laptop at home. If I had my phone back, I could show you how much money they could pay me in the next few months," I said, emphasizing the words "money" and "pay." I proceeded to ask, "Mom, can I have my phone back?" I was going for directness over innuendo. She gazed at me with reptilian eyes.

"Are you going to call Christina Tau?"

"Definitely not. Anyway, the dance was last week."
My mother grabbed her purse, opened it, and dangled
my phone.

"No girls, David!"

"I know." She shook her head as she handed it back
to me, already regretting her lenience. I plugged my
phone into the long power cord by the employees' table
that all the grad-student delivery guys used and waited
for my phone to come back to life.

"I don't like it," my mother told my father. "David's
going to make the school a lot more money than
whatever they end up paying him."

Auntie Zhang said something in Mandarin about
how I should be paid according to the number of views
rather than a one-time fee.

"Huh, huh, huh," said my mother as she nodded.

No one asked if I actually wanted to do the ads. I'd
be happy with the money, of course. It could pay for
a new phone and a decent service plan with unlimited
texting. I assumed that I would still be texting with
Betty. I hoped her email silence didn't mean she was
mad at me. But the way Chinese school had ended
on Saturday made me feel as if all my personal bonds
there had been chopped off like the knobby ends of
string beans.

My phone buzzed. It had finally finished booting up.

There was one text, from Yaro about our last 20
Questions game. He said that the man had survived
an apocalypse but had become very lonely when he
couldn't find any other survivors. He decided to commit
suicide by jumping off the building, but when he heard

the phone ring, he realized that he wasn't alone in the world, after all. No wonder I hadn't been able to solve it in 20 questions!

I opened the email from Principal Gao and handed the phone to my father. Good thing the power cord stretched that far.

Once his eyes had honed in on the $200 figure, he was unable to read the rest. He made a motion to hand my phone to my mother, but she waved her hand. She didn't need to read it to understand.

He handed my phone back, and picked up his knife again. I read Principal Gao's email again, opening up the attached contract. It didn't seem like a legal document to me. As I puzzled over it, a new email rolled in.

Betty?

No. It was from "Harmony Health Oncology Internship." The subject line read, "Interview Scheduling."

That could only mean one thing! I was a finalist for the hospital internship! Dr. Vivian Lee, whose headshot made her look like a good witch, wanted to meet me for an interview! Problems at Chinese school? What problems? What's Chinese school, anyway? I was in the running for that goddamned internship! My grades and my desperate essay must have shown how serious I was!

At first I was too excited and relieved to form words so I stood up and held my phone above my head in triumph.

"David," said my mother, "stop fooling around."

"Email!" I stammered out, unable to say more. "Hospital! Internship!"

"What?" asked my mother, looking alarmed. My father stared at me hard.

I lay down my phone between them and pointed at the sender and the subject line.

"That's great, David!" yelled my mother. She got up, came around the table, and hugged me. She never hugged me. That's how excited she was. "Hey!" she yelled at my father and Auntie Zhang, while rapping her knuckles against the employees' table. "David got the Harmony internship!"

"Not yet!" I managed to say.

I called the hospital and made an appointment with Dr. Lee's scheduler to go in on Tuesday at 3:30 p.m. That way I'd be home way before the dinner rush.

Later that night, I feverishly began prepping for my interview with Dr. Lee by watching more of her online talks. I'd seen most of them already, but repeated viewings sure wouldn't hurt.

Wow, I thought, I should email Betty and tell her the good news.

I typed out an excited email to her, telling her about the internship, but I began to have second thoughts. She'd parted bitterly from me and my friends at Chinese school, and she and I had had zero quality time together that day. I wanted to reconnect in some way, so I trashed the opening to my email and began it a new way, with an explanation of how I was definitely closer to her than Chun.

I sent the email, then brushed my teeth. By the time I'd gotten into bed, Betty still hadn't written back. I felt good, though. I had shared something with her that I wasn't planning to tell anyone else outside my family. It's not like I needed praise from her or anything. I just wanted her to be happy for me. I wanted her to be happy.

CHAPTER FIFTEEN

Monday morning, when I got up, I saw that Betty still hadn't written back. Was it possible I'd made her feel badly by being too self-congratulatory in that third email? Or maybe she was grossed out when I told her how close I felt with her? Maybe she blamed me for getting her mixed up with Chun in the first place.

The fact that she hadn't written back took away most of the pleasure I'd felt from being reunited with my phone. And from finding out that I was a finalist for the Dream Internship of My Young Life.

Walking to my bus stop, I breathed in the clean, crisp air. I'd never heard so many birds.

Thankfully, waiting for the bus was now almost a delight. Jean and her friends gave me a wide berth, and Al and I exchanged nods. We both had our headphones on.

When I got to school, I couldn't help smirking to myself as I walked head down by the notice board with its "TBA" mark. I did however swing by Mr. Wald's office to tell him the news.

He laughed. "I already knew. The hospital called last week to verify all your information and your latest grades."

"I can't blow this now," I said.

"Even if you don't get it, and I'm not saying you won't, being a finalist is worthy of putting on your college application. In fact, if you don't get it, I suggest you consider volunteering there this summer regardless. Remember what I said about showing that you're serious about pursuing your interests?"

"That's a good idea."

"Congratulations, David."

"Oh, Mr. Wald?"

"Yes?" He smiled slightly anticipating my question.

"How many other finalists are there?"

"There can't be many, David," he said in a measured voice. "But you're the only one from this school."

Wow! I'd beaten out Christina! That put a spring in my step. Maybe even two springs.

I spent the rest of Monday at school having imaginary conversations with Dr. Lee. I thought it would be obnoxious for me to say in the interview that I aspired to get into an Ivy League college. But then again, she was Asian. She knew the deal with parental expectations. She had to.

If she asked me how I'd become interested in the medical profession, my plan was to spout some Steve Jobs quotes from my essay. That alone would demonstrate both my powers of recall and how sincere

I was. "Your time is limited, so don't waste it living someone else's life." That was one of my favorites. During the interview, I planned to tell Dr. Lee, "If Jobs could have continued living his own life, he would have been able to do so much more."

I imagined her nodding at the wisdom of one so young.

My classes seemed to float effortlessly by. Man, I knew it wasn't cool to be all high on myself, especially before the internship was even in the bag. Then again, it was the first time I felt good about myself at Shark Beach High academics-wise. Despite my relatively lowly class rank, I'd managed to become a finalist for the big Harmony Health internship!

Whatever euphoria I was feeling ended as soon as I got off the school bus, though. My mother was grim when she picked me up.

"Did you call a girl with your phone?" she accused.

"No!"

"Mr. Yeung brought his daughter. She's waiting for you at the restaurant! I never should have given your phone back to you."

"Mom, I have no idea who you're talking about."

She shook her head with annoyance and wouldn't even look at me.

Whoever this girl was, she was going to make me lose my phone yet again!

When we entered the restaurant, my mother hung back and followed my lead. As I continued walking I saw Mr.

Yeung sitting at the employees' table with my father. Sitting next to him, calmly sipping from a can of Coke, was Betty.

I felt the world shudder to a stop.

"Betty!" I yelled out. "What are you doing here?" I was too surprised to sit down.

"Hi David," she said. Straightening up, she put her hands around her soda can, and cleared her throat. "This is my dad."

The three adults were silent as they closely monitored our discussion and potential body movements. I remained standing, as did my mother, who seemed poised to throw in an arm to block any type of physical contact between Betty and me. My dad sat at the far end of the table looking puzzled. Mr. Yeung sat between them, his eyes more tired than ever.

"Wha—What are you doing here, Betty?" I could hear my question echo in my head. She tilted her head down and turned her eyes up to me.

"I wanted to tell you that I'm not going back to Chinese school."

"We go to Chinese school together," I explained to the three adults, who all nodded solemnly. "I'm so sorry that Chun was an a-hole to you, Betty."

"No, that's not the reason, David." She shifted in her chair and pushed away the soda. "I'm transferring to a school in Hong Kong. I was accepted into a program that includes an internship with HSBC Bank."

"You mean, not until junior year, right?"

"Yes, but I have to leave now. The fiscal year in Hong Kong ended March 31, and there's government funding involved, which means they have to start spending it."

"Now? This month?"

"Day after tomorrow," she said.

"When did you find out, Betty?"

"I found that everything was set about a week ago. The last thing I was waiting for was the visa from the Chinese Embassy, which is always a little dicey," she said. "But now I have it."

I swallowed spit that tasted sad. "That's amazing, Betty," I said. "That really is. You'll still be working on the IB, right?"

"Yes."

"It's just one year in Hong Kong, right?" I asked, my voice getting unnaturally high as I tried to control my emotions.

"It could extend to senior year."

I must have unconsciously stepped closer to Betty because the next thing I knew, my mother had slammed a chair from behind into my calves. "Ow!" I yelled.

"Sit down and talk like a gentleman, David!" she admonished. I cringed into the chair. Well, making me sit with a girl was quite a change in behavior for my mother. She must really admire Betty's father to have allowed this arrangement.

"I wanted to say goodbye to you in person," Betty said.

"That's nice of you," I said. After having been so high on myself earlier in the day, I was now freefalling. The only girl I cared about in the world was going away. "Do you know anyone in Hong Kong?" I heard myself ask.

"My dad's cousin is there," she gave a wan smile.

"I've never met her, but she's someone who lived in New York for a while before going back. I'm thinking about interviewing her for my independent study on gentrification in Chinatown." As my body started to come out of shock, I could feel blood beginning to flow again.

"Betty," I said, glancing at Mr. Yeung. "I had no idea that Mr. Yeung was your dad." She shifted in her seat.

"He's always been my dad, David."

"But your last name is 'Jung,' not 'Yeung.'" Betty glanced at her father and my parents before continuing.

"'Jung' is my mother's name. It's German. It sounds like 'Yeung' if you pronounce it right. That happens to be a coincidence."

I felt terrible. "I've been pronouncing it with a hard 'J' this whole time. You've never corrected me."

"I don't have time to correct everything you do, David."

I snorted and she continued talking. This supervised meeting with Betty was going better than I might have imagined.

"Oh, and congratulations on getting to the next stage for that big hospital internship. I started writing a reply—to all your emails—but I figured I should just say it in person." She shrugged.

"If I get the Harmony Health internship, I won't be going back to Chinese school, either. I'll have to be at the hospital on Saturday and Sunday afternoons."

"I'm sure you'll get it!" Betty said, slapping my shoulder. I felt my face heat up. "Wait, David, what about your friends at Chinese school?" she asked.

I said, "You're my friend, Betty." I paused there because I felt my insides tighten a little. If I had said "best friend," I might have cried.

"You're my friend, too, David."

My mother cleared her throat.

"I like hanging out with the guys," I said, "but they're not always the greatest people in the world. Chun was really a jerk to you that last time. You never deserve to be treated like that." I watched Betty blink.

We looked at each other, and I could tell that we had become the highlights of each other's Saturdays— every day, for me, really. Betty had wanted to see me in person at least one last time, and I was grateful that she had made the effort, regardless of the consequences. Or my mother.

"You both stay for dinner!" my mom nearly yelled. "We have so many fresh vegetables your father helped bring, Brandy!"

"Betty!" I said. My mother shook her head.

"I'm sorry—Betty!"

The dinner invitation was surprising, as well as the apology to Betty. Maybe Betty talking about HSBC Bank had earned my mom's respect. Maybe Betty's demeanor alone was impressive. Or maybe seeing us together made my mom think about those Chinese soap operas.

"Thank you for the offer, Mrs. Tung," said Betty, "but we should go. I still need to pack so many things." She stood up and brushed the pleats of her blue dress. It was the same one she wore the day we helped YK move, and it looked as good as new.

"How about some food to go?" my mother said,

nearly pleading. "David! Go pack some food!"

"We cannot accept," said Mr. Yeung as he centered his cane and rose to his feet. "Really, we just ate." Betty smiled.

"It's true, we're really full right now," she said. "Your food looks wonderful, Mr. and Mrs. Tung." My parents gave her big smiles, and they looked genuine. They must really like her! Both of them hounded Mr. Yeung until he finally accepted a few containers of food. A good host forces guests into a corner until there is no other way out, protecting the guests' humbleness. A good guest relents at the very end to allow the hosts to display generosity. It's a stressful win-win.

Because Mr. Yeung had come with his daughter, it made this visit a little more formal than usual. To mark the occasion, we at Tung's Garden had to adhere to Chinese decorum and follow our guests out to the parking lot to see them off. Even Auntie Zhang came out.

My parents, Auntie Zhang, and Mr. Yeung walked out first, exchanging chit-chat. I trudged next to Betty a little further back. I wanted to ask her when she'd be back.

But instead I grabbed her left hand with my right hand like I'd never let it go. I felt her respond in kind. We fell even further behind our parents.

I wasn't able to turn my head to look at her face. If I did, I would fall apart.

Our parents were getting closer to the truck. Once Betty got in, I felt for certain I'd never see her again.

Maybe I should kiss her now. No. That would be cheap.

I felt our pulse in our tight grip.

Our parents had just about reached the truck. Betty and I were so in sync that we let go at the same time. Our arms were at our sides by the time our parents turned around to check on us.

Betty didn't linger for even a moment, opening the passenger door and hopping up in the cab. Her window was down. While her dad made his way to the driver's side, I yelled up, "I just got my phone back!"

She smiled at me. "I just got rid of mine! I'll have another one in Hong Kong!"

Our ancestors decreed that there are to be three rounds of waving goodbye to esteemed guests. The hosts make the first waves as the guests board their vehicle. The second occurs as the engine starts, and the seatbelts go on. The hosts make the third and last waves when the vehicle backs up and pulls away.

I kept my arm up as long as I thought Betty could see it.

Walking back, I recalled Betty's story about her dad getting hurt while working for that restaurant owner. He was permanently disabled. What was Mr. Yeung going to do without Betty around?

What was I going to do?

I wondered if Mr. Yeung had ever told my father that he, too, had a kid in Chinese school. Maybe not. Through all the years we had known Mr. Yeung, all those rides in his truck and all those meals at our restaurant, he'd revealed nothing about himself. At the same time he hadn't asked about our private lives, either.

It must have been so hard for Betty to ask him to drive her to see me. She would have had to consider his busy schedule, the cost of the gas, the time it would take to get out here and back.

But Betty had also mentioned that her dad was at least open to the idea that his daughter could go out on dates. She was an A student and an awesome daughter, too, I was sure. It made sense that Mr. Yeung would do almost anything for her.

"Dad," I said as we were walking back inside, "did you lie to me about how Mr. Yeung hurt his leg, or did he lie to you?"

"What do you mean, did I lie?"

"Well, I know he didn't hurt himself doing movie stunts." My father looked stunned.

"He didn't? What happened?" I told him the story and he shook his head. "No restaurant should treat its people like that."

He held the front door open and Auntie Zhang walked in. My mother waited to the side for me. I asked her what she thought about Betty.

"She's very nice."

"She works with her father, you know," I said. "Just like how I work here with you." My mother made an agreeable-sounding grunt and rolled up her sleeves, getting ready for another night of Tung's Garden.

"I like her a lot, mom," I said. She nodded in silence.

Later that evening, I swapped some late-night emails with Betty. She was writing on her dad's computer, which was older than mine.

"We've switched places," I wrote. "I'm writing to you on my phone, and you're on a laptop."

"We didn't really switch," she wrote. "You're not going to Hong Kong. I am."

"I wish I could go with you."

"You can't. You have to get that hospital internship! Hey, isn't your interview tomorrow?"

"Oh, shit!"

Betty promised to write from Hong Kong as soon as she had a phone. We tried to keep things cheery as we signed off.

She was going to find someone else. Or rather, someone else was going to find her. Someone smarter and better looking than me. Richer, too. Well, that last part wasn't exactly a high bar. HSBC had wealth-management operations, right? Some billionaire's kid was going to sweep her off her feet under the guise of teaching her about the twisted ways of international finance.

I had one thing going for me, though. I'm sure that no one had ever held her hand the way that I did. I knew that she was still thinking about it, just like I was. No matter what happened from now on, though, I had to be awesome in that Harmony Health interview tomorrow. Oops, I meant later on today!

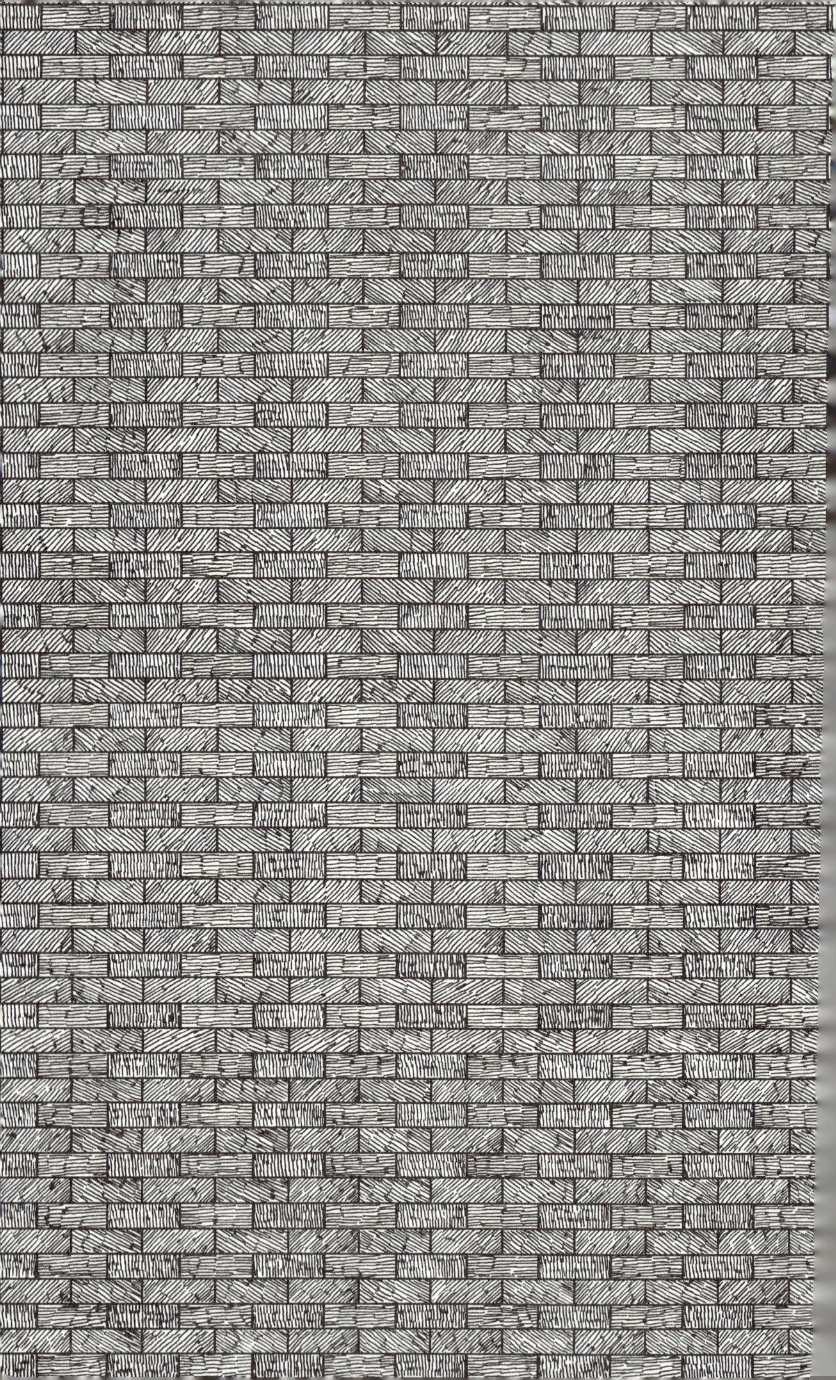

CHAPTER SIXTEEN

I woke up in hyper-focus mode. Interview day. I went to the car, stashed the shoes that I only wore to weddings behind the passenger seat, and hung my father's old dark blue sports jacket on a side hook. The material looked cheap, and the morning light highlighted scuffs on my shoes, but there was nothing I could do about it now except brush off some lint, which I did.

I pictured myself wearing this get up to the Dames Ball with Christina Tau. She would have died of embarrassment after shrieking, "Florsheim!"

Yet these were a genuine reflection of who we are. This was how my family dressed up.

To keep things simple, I wore only my white button-down shirt and ironed wool slacks to school. Miss Muntz joked that I must be going on a date. I said that I was trying to air out some of my nice clothes that had been in storage.

At lunch, Benson Gong asked if I was going to a funeral.

"No way," I said.

"You look so down," he said. I'd thought Benson was going to comment on my clothes.

It was true, though. Dread was perched on my shoulders like evil crows. And Betty was going to Hong Kong.

No! I couldn't think about that. Well, I could as long as it didn't totally cloud my mental facilities. I had to stay sharp!

Betty, I'm about to go to my interview at the hospital, and you've made me forget everything I've ever learned about cancer.

I felt a little short of breath as I tried to understand my feelings. Even if I got the internship, a perfect score on the SATs, and won a spot at Harvard, Yale, Columbia, UPenn, Cornell, Dartmouth, Brown, or Princeton— vaguely in that order of preference—Betty was probably out of my life forever.

I hadn't realized how seeing her at Chinese school had sustained me all this time. No way could this hospital internship, which I wasn't going to get anyway, compare to Saturdays with Betty.

I barely heard the final bell of the day. I couldn't think clearly.

I almost boarded the bus at the end of the day before remembering that my mother was picking me up in the school parking lot.

As I approached the car, I was mildly freaked out to see that the sports jacket was no longer hanging off the rear side window.

"Mom!" I said as I opened the door. "Where's

the jacket?"

"Oh, I put it across the seat. It was blocking my view."
She hit the gas before I even had my seatbelt on. This was
my first job interview, really, and it had both of us jittery.
I was her kid, after all, which meant that whenever I did
anything, her reputation was also on the line.

I reached back and grabbed my jacket. It didn't look
wrinkled. I took out my tie from the front pocket and
let it unfurl. I slung it around my neck and measured a
length of two fists at the fatter end.

"You sure you know how to tie it?" my mother asked.

"I'm sure," I said. I flipped down the blind and
aimed the mirror at my neck. I came up with a knot
that looked good enough. I buttoned my top button and
tightened the tie knot.

When we pulled into the hospital's parking lot, I told
my mother she could come inside and read magazines
if she liked, or have a snack at the cafeteria, but she
refused. Chinese superstition holds that it's bad luck to
enter hospitals and funeral parlors. Instead, my mother
parked and busted out a Chinese newspaper.

"I'm going to pray!" she said.

"You're not religious," I said.

"Don't tell me what I believe!" she snapped.

I smiled and shut the door on her. A gray phantom of
myself in the window's reflection fell away as I left.

I was surprised that I could simply walk into the
hospital, enter the elevator, and head up to the fifth
floor. I thought security would be tighter. Chun once
told me that way back in the 80s, when Chinatown was

a bullet-ridden warzone, rival gang members would go into hospitals to "finish the job" if an enemy was being treated there.

I was about 15 minutes early. Dr. Lee's office, according to the floor map, was on the near side of the rectangular layout. I decided to walk the other three sides to kill time.

The hallways were empty, but I could hear activity behind various closed doors. Every other minute it seemed a coded announcement would break over the PA speakers. A thin South Asian man in scrubs texted as he leisurely walked by, not even glancing at me.

As I came around the first corner, a rattling sound coming from deep inside a room with an open door drew my attention. A middle-aged white woman was pushing an instrument with a bad wheel across the floor.

"Who are you?" she asked when she noticed me standing outside. I didn't recognize her accent.

"I'm here to see Dr. Lee," I replied. She lowered her head and went back to cleaning up. Had someone died here? Was that why the room was empty? I got creeped out and left.

As I continued my walk, I focused on measuring out my footsteps evenly. Someday I might really be a doctor, walking down these same halls. I nervously touched the knot in my tie with both hands to make sure that it hadn't somehow come undone. How did people who wore ties every day get used to it?

Soon enough I stood outside the oncology administrative offices. I was about to enter when I stopped short, filled with panic. All of my anxieties converged in that moment. Shit! How was I going to impress Dr. Lee? Maybe my 1550 SAT score was just par for the course. I should have studied up on more SAT vocabulary words with which to dazzle her! I'd also been slipping on the MCAT test questions lately!

I was beginning to sweat profusely, so I forced myself to remember what I'd learned online about the two basic rules of an interview: 1) never answer a question with a question; and 2) if you really don't know how to answer, say what little you know with a dose of humor.

Wait. What did I know and what did I not know? How was I supposed to answer that? Are you answering a question with a question? No. Uh, yes.

I rubbed my arms. This was no time to doubt myself. Procrastinating would cause me to lose my nerve. I marched forward with determination, sailing right by the reception desk in the process.

"Excuse me, may I help you?" I stopped in my tracks and turned. An Asian woman sitting at the desk had lifted her head and was giving me the eye. She looked like she could be Dr. Lee's older sister.

"Hello," I said. "I have an appointment to see Dr. Lee."

"Oh," she said with exaggerated nods. "You must be one of the finalists for the internship."

"Yes, I am. Can you give me any tips about her?"

"I can only think of one thing." She stood up, revealing a badge that read, "Dr. Vivian Lee." "Don't piss her off!" She laughed hard and clapped. "You're very funny, David! I couldn't tell that from your application."

I played along as though I had known all the time it was her. Dr. Lee wasn't wearing makeup, so the good witch looked instead like a nice mom.

We shook hands. "You're funny, too, Dr. Lee."

"Oh, please," she said. "Let's duck into this office here." She gestured with her head.

We walked into an office that was nearly bare. A PC without a monitor sat on the desk. She closed the door behind us and scooted to the seat behind the desk. I sat on a plaid cushioned chair that somehow didn't seem appropriate for a job interview.

"We just lost a doctor," said Dr. Lee. Reading my face, she quickly added, "Oh, no, he didn't die—he moved to Los Angeles. That's where I'm from, by the way. This was his office. We don't want to go into mine. There's too much stuff in there. It's got books and journals all over the place. It looks like the children's section of the public library! Only those books make more sense."

I nodded, wondering if I was supposed to laugh and when I'd get a chance to say something. She was one of the most outgoing and expressive Asian Americans I had ever met.

"Do you want some water? Or coffee or tea?"

"No. I just came from school." What did coming from school have to do with being thirsty or not? I immediately thought to myself. You sound stupid, David!

Now that the door had been closed for a few seconds, the odor of an institutional cleaning agent was taking hold.

"Well, all right," said Dr. Lee as she flipped open a folder. "Yes, um, I really like that you already know you want to be a doctor, and you say it's not just because that's what your parents want you to do." She sounded a little skeptical.

"They don't oppose it, that's for sure," I said. "But as I stated in my essay, I was really moved by the health challenges that Steve Jobs faced."

"Yes, I remember what you wrote. Well, my parents, they encouraged me into the medical profession. But luckily I wanted to do it as much as you seem to. Plus it turned out I was good at it." She scratched her chin. "Well, sort of good at it."

"I know you wanted to be a vet at first," I said.

Dr. Lee smiled. "Wait, how do you know that?"

"I heard you mention it in one of your lectures."

"It's true, I did. When I was very young, younger than you."

"Then you realized that you'd have to tell people their pet was going to die, and you didn't want to do that."

She nodded sadly. "I've changed a lot since then. Nowadays, I have to tell people that they or their loved ones are dying." She straightened up. "But it's something that must be said. If you can't handle all aspects of your job, you probably shouldn't do it. You have to be all-in, ya know?"

I thought about my family toiling away at Tung's Garden. "Immigrants have to be all-in with their third or fourth choices, though," I replied. Shit, now it sounds like I'm trying to prove her wrong!

"Oh, what do you mean, David?"

"I'm just thinking about my parents. Running a restaurant wasn't at the top of their list."

"Yes, I see your point. But the ultimate goal of immigrant generations is for their children to pursue whatever they want to, right?" Dr. Lee hesitated, and I was about to raise a slight objection but managed to stop myself. "You talk about your Chinese American heritage in your essay, David."

"I did."

"I'm Korean. Our parents are way more strict."

"Really?"

"With boys, anyway. I know you live in Shark Beach. That school is majority Chinese."

"Yes, that's true."

"It's an expensive place to live. When my husband and I were looking for a home, we wanted to be in your school district, but we were completely priced out."

"But you're famous, Dr. Lee." She smiled and leaned to one side in her chair.

"Well...we could have bought there if we had really wanted to, but we decided on Summit instead. The school systems are pretty much comparable, but at a lower price. Also, and this is key, it's closer to the H-Mart in Paramus."

I nodded although I couldn't help but remember my mother complaining about how overpriced H-Mart stores are. "Everything is twice the Chinatown price!" she had said.

I shifted in my seat and my hands crawled up to check my tie knot. Still tight.

"Any questions for me?" asked Dr. Lee. Wow, she

didn't want to ask me anything else? I mean, she hadn't even asked me any cancer-related questions! Had she lost interest in me as a candidate already? Good thing I had come prepared for this phase of the interview. You have to ask insightful questions to show that you have a high level of interest in the position and that you care about who your boss is and what they've accomplished.

"What was the most unexpected thing you discovered after enrolling in medical school?"

"Ah, David, that's such a good question. Well, I'd have to say it's been a whole bunch of things." She put her elbows up on the desk and sucked in her lips as she looked up into the air. "I guess first of all, I found that you will put in all that time throughout school and the residency, and it will be really tiring. At times you'll feel like you're not getting any sleep at all. And yet medical school is also energizing because at the heart of it, you're learning how to save peoples' lives."

"Got it. Um..." She held up a finger and continued.

"Nutrition. That's one thing they don't teach you in medical school. If people just ate better and exercised regularly, the average life expectancy in this country would go up at least five years. Seriously." She seemed to be looking at my throat. Was my tie uneven? "I'll bet your mother makes you eat brown rice at the restaurant."

"She used to, but now I just eat it on my own. Pardon me, Dr. Lee, but could you tell me what I would be doing here? That is, if I'm lucky enough to get the internship?" She fingered a C-major chord with three fingers of her right hand on the desk.

"In all honesty, David, you would be doing a lot of admin stuff. Delivering envelopes and packages. You'd be pretty busy on Sundays in particular. Amazon boxes come in, and you'd have to help distribute them to doctors and patients. I promise that you wouldn't be emptying any garbage cans, but you also wouldn't exactly be assisting in surgery, either. The important thing, though, is that this internship would be a foot in the door and a window into our world. It would allow you to see the reality of how a hospital works, and what it is that doctors can or cannot do. Plus it could lead to a letter of recommendation." She raised an eyebrow and added mischievously, "But only if you're the best intern ever."

Her phone buzzed in her pocket.

"Do you need to get that?" I asked.

"It's not important. I can tell from the ring." She made a gesture of dismissal with her right hand. "Anything else you want to tell me, David? Are you still stoked to save the lives of superstars like Steve Jobs, as you wrote in your essay?" She swiveled in her chair and something fell to the floor. "Oops, what's this doing here? I hope nobody's looking for it."

It was a cane. It didn't look too different from the one that Mr. Yeung used. It was battered, but it had endured and still looked reliable.

Dr. Lee stood up and laid it across the file cabinets behind her.

I thought about Betty saying she had a lot of responsibilities. She'd been talking about helping her father deliver goods.

I thought about my father showing me his ripped-up palms.

I thought about my mother as a young girl, locked in a room and studying.

I thought about tireless Auntie Zhang. What if she were ever to fall ill?

I took a deep breath that filled my lungs, and spoke. "It's true, Steve Jobs was an amazing person. Maybe he was even a 'superstar.' But everyone deserves superstar care because everyone is a superstar. To someone." I felt as if I'd just said the most important thing I'd ever realized. I was almost gasping for breath.

The left side of Dr. Lee's mouth folded inward.

"Very good, David," she said.

I felt fine about my interview until I got into the elevator. Then, as the doors shut, I recalled how Dr. Lee had sighed when she shook my hand. "Nice try," she seemed to be saying in retrospect.

The elevator stopped on every floor down. As we took on more and more passengers, I shuffled to the back to yield space. By the time we reached the lobby, I was standing in a corner under the only dark light bulb.

I trudged out the hospital doors. Why the hell hadn't Dr. Lee asked me about my grades or how I was doing in my science class? Aren't those pretty important things you'd want to know about when hiring an intern? Why didn't she talk about the MCATs with me or throw out a few terms to see if I knew my stuff? I had studied all those stupid acronyms she'd talked about in her lectures, and she never even gave me a chance to use them! What was the interview for? Was it all just a personality test? Maybe she wanted to see how tall I was? Make sure I didn't smell?

I was mad at myself, too, for not simply bragging about how much I was learning in high school and the awesome grades that I was getting. I shouldn't have waited for her to ask about that stuff. I should've shown initiative. I should've done so much more.

Everything had gone wrong, beginning with me failing to even recognize Dr. Lee. The whole interview was just the universe's joke on me. Why had I babbled on about pets and fourth choices of immigrants!

My mother saw me coming and, by the time I was still a good twenty feet away, had already unlocked the car. I threw open the passenger door and dropped into the seat.

"How did it go, David?" she asked.

"I think I screwed up," I managed to say before bursting into tears and folding up my body. I couldn't hear everything she said, but I felt her rubbing my back.

Despite my distressed emotional state, I knew we were still headed for the restaurant to put in a work shift. So I tried to modulate the amplitude of my sobs to zero before we got there.

CHAPTER SEVENTEEN

I woke up Wednesday morning feeling relieved. The whole uncertainty of maybe getting the internship was gone. I definitely wasn't getting it. Maybe I was meant to appear in those online ads for Chinese school after all. Maybe I would like it.

I wanted to tell Betty everything so badly, but I didn't want to clog up her inbox when she was on her way out of the country to her new life. I also didn't want to bring her down.

I showered and then rattled my toothbrush through my numb mouth, thinking the whole time about how Betty was probably already up in the air.

I thought good thoughts for her and missed her sorely. I even imagined her walking by my side as I left the house.

At the bus stop, Al came up to me.

"David, I wanted to tell you that I'm moving away

this summer."

Why was everyone saying goodbye to me?

"Al, what's going on?" I asked. He rocked back on his heels.

"In my old school district, I would probably make valedictorian, but I don't even rank in the top 10 here."

"What about the computer classes here that you wanted to take?"

"It doesn't matter. No college is going to care about my coursework if my class rank isn't in the single digits."

I looked him in the eyes. "Did you get into the summer coding class?" I asked.

He lowered his head. "Nah, I didn't make it," he said. "Really sucks." He was clearly disappointed, so I changed the subject.

"It's probably been hard making friends here, huh." He rubbed the back of his head.

"I don't care about that so much. I just wanted to be the best programmer in my school. It's become pretty clear to me that I could never be that in Shark Beach. There are some real computer geniuses here, and they're all competitive as hell."

"Al, aren't you just as competitive? Didn't you just say you wanted to be the best?" He swung his backpack to his other arm.

"Not all the time. I share some stuff. Didn't I give you a little something?" He smiled briefly and coughed into a fist.

Indeed he had. That picture of Jean had the potential to derail her life. In retrospect, I was proud of having calibrated its use to what Mr. Cohen would call a "measured response." I had diplomacy skills even though I was mainly a dishwasher.

That night at the restaurant, my mother came into the kitchen, interrupting me as I was cleaning buffet trays. Someone important was here and wanted to see me. My mother seemed nervous. What was going on? I washed my hands hastily and dried them as best as I could with a damp towel. Auntie Zhang watched me and shook her head. I was no help in the kitchen at all. I couldn't even wash my hands properly.

Could it possibly be Betty? Had she changed her mind and never boarded that plane?

I came through the swing door cautiously. I was shocked to see Dr. Lee. She was wearing an unbuttoned light coat over a suit.

"Hello, David," she said. "I'm glad to see you working so hard. Your parents must be so proud of you." My parents both seemed uneasy. Nothing was more disturbing to them than an Asian adult who spoke English with no accent.

"Hi, Dr. Lee," I said, trying to channel my nervousness into being upbeat. "Um, these are my parents."

"Yes, yes, I've met them already. Listen, David, I've been at a conference all day, and while I had a short break, I made a difficult decision. There were so many wonderful candidates. I didn't call because I wanted to ask you in person if you would be my intern."

"What?"

"David, I want you to be my intern!" she boomed,

bending her knees a little bit and holding out her arms. This display of emotion was foreign to my parents, who seemed uncomfortable. "When can you start?"

I felt my insides crinkle. I got the Harmony Health internship! I really did!

"I guess I could start this Saturday," were the words I managed to get out.

"You need him the entire weekend?" asked my father.

"Three hours on Saturdays and Sundays," said Dr. Lee. "We can add other days when the summer rolls around. It won't interfere with your dinner rush hour, I promise."

"Please stay and eat here, Dr. Lee!" my mother commanded.

"I'm sorry, Mrs. Tung," said my new boss. "I have to get dinner started. Every once in a while, I do get to cook, and tonight's the night."

My mother said something urgent to Auntie Zhang, who immediately skipped into the kitchen.

"It would be great if I could be there from late morning to mid-afternoon," I said. "There's a bus line that goes almost directly from the restaurant to the hospital and back."

Dr. Lee rubbed her hands.

"We can make that work," she said. "See, David, it was meant to be. Your teachers love you and told me so many great things about you, but do you know what really got me? You said that everyone was a superstar to someone else, and that really affected me. I had never thought of patients in that way. I know that everyone is special but, yes, you're right: They are superstars. Would you mind if I reference that in the future?"

"Please do," I said. "Will I get royalties on that?"

Dr. Lee and my father laughed, cuing my mother to join in.

Auntie Zhang came out of the kitchen bearing a delivery bag.

"Dr. Lee, you have to take this food home," my mother ordered. She forced the bag against the doctor's side. "It's the best things that our own family eats. Better than the buffet tables."

Dr. Lee took the bag and bowed awkwardly. "Thank you!" The fact that she didn't protest at all surprised all of us. "Oh, I also have more good news, David," said Dr. Lee. "Mila Pharmaceuticals is supporting the internship, so you'll get a stipend of $700 at the end of the cycle. Isn't that great?"

I could get a new phone!

"Wow, that's incredible!" I said. I took out my phone to begin writing myself an email. "What should I bring the first day, Dr. Lee?" I asked.

"Well, just a Social Security Card or your birth certificate. We need to process your employee ID."

"We're all American citizens!" declared my mother. "We're proud to be!"

"Of course you are!" said Dr. Lee. "It's strictly for administrative purposes." She took a breath. "Well, David, we'll see you soon. Welcome to the Harmony Health family."

My parents and I followed her out the door. We had intended to walk her to her car, but we didn't have far to go. She had parked her white Lexus in front of the restaurant in a no-parking zone. Well, she had physician plates, and you can park anywhere with those! We waved goodbye to her, and she waved back.

When we got back into the restaurant, my mother hugged me and my father grabbed my shoulders from behind. It was a celebration with restraint because we still had more work.

Before I went back to the dirty buffet trays, I emailed Betty the news. I wasn't sure when she'd get my message, but I wanted her to be the first to know that I had done it.

I watched videos of Dr. Lee's presentations all night. That's my boss, I thought.

On Thursday morning, short on sleep yet alert enough to fly a jet, I sprinted from the school bus to the board outside Mr. Wald's office. The "TBA" was gone! They hadn't put in my name yet, though. That blank space was so dramatic. I still couldn't believe I was the one who had bagged the internship!

In homeroom, the usual boring announcements by the head secretary were in progress when the principal got on the microphone.

"On behalf of Mila Pharmaceuticals and Mila Pharmaceuticals CEO Furman Yen, Shark Beach High School is proud to congratulate David Tung for being awarded the inaugural Mila Pharmaceuticals oncology internship at Harmony Health Systems. David was selected for the internship from more than 200 applicants. Let's give him a hearty round of applause."

I don't know if people in other classrooms were clapping, but my fellow homeroom denizens gave me a raucous hand. I was surprised, to be honest. Even Percy and Percy II were clapping, and I thought they both hated me.

As I walked into the hallway at the bell, people who'd never spoken to me before came up to congratulate me. I think everyone knew I was smart, but today was the first time they thought I was special.

I couldn't believe what people were saying to me.

"You did it!"

"All right, David!"

"You killed it!"

I'd never heard such congratulatory words meant for me. My old friend Yaro sought me out for a high five and a fist bump. I showed him that I had gotten my phone back and told him that 20 Questions was back on.

Scott Sima found me in the hallway and carried me on his shoulders to the internship notice board. The whole track team came out, too. It seemed as if the whole student body followed us to Mr. Wald's office. I had to duck at some points to keep my head from smashing against light fixtures and ceiling sprinklers. I felt like a kid again.

"I'm gonna be late for Mr. del Pino's class!" I yelled.

"Mr. del Pino's right here, David!" said Scott. I looked over, and my biology teacher was standing against the wall, making room for the surging crowd. He gave me a thumbs-up.

Brett Hau, our current class valedictorian, gave me a wary nod in a gesture that said, "game recognize game."

Everyone shouted out each letter in my name as the bemused Mr. Wald plugged "DAVID TUNG" into the grooves of the bulletin board. After he'd slid in the final "G," he dashed back to his office and came out with the football.

"David," he said, "I want you to squeeze this! This is a big, big victory!" He reached up and put it in my hands. I squeezed that football as if it could make all my wishes come true. Well, more like one very big wish.

In our school, winning a prestigious internship was apparently a bigger deal than being named homecoming king.

Miss Muntz even started off her class by saying that nobody was more "wonderful" than me. Not a single person snickered. I would've.

The first negative reaction was of course from Christina Tau, who eyed me all through English class. She caught up to me when class was over.

"I still can't believe they picked you, David," she said as we filed out. Hallway traffic came to a standstill as students observed what they hoped to be a testy confrontation. "The last time I checked, my class rank was higher than yours." She must have really wanted this internship, maybe even more than she'd wanted to go to the dance with me.

"It's about more than class rank," I said. "Dr. Lee never even asked about my grades during my interview," I said. "What did you talk about in yours?"

"I didn't have an interview!"

"You weren't one of the finalists?" She stomped off. Yeah, we had a truce, but I hadn't forgotten what she'd called Betty, and I didn't care how mad I made her.

"This isn't over, David!" Christina taunted me from

a distance.

I could only laugh. She was right. Our class ranks were so close at the top end, we would probably be locked in battle through the last test of senior year.

But I'd won this early round, the one for the big hospital internship.

I was feeling so confident that during lunch, between receiving pats on the back, I spent my free time writing an email on my phone to Principal Gao. Not only was I not going to do videos for Chinese school, I wouldn't be coming back at all.

My mother picked me up at the bus stop in time to see other kids, even Fred and Percy, talking to me.

"So, you're popular now!" she said.

"Not really. Well, maybe. My internship was announced over the intercom." My mother smiled.

"You're popular at the restaurant, too. You have a special guest waiting for you."

"Did Dr. Lee come back because our food is so good?"

"No, it's Principal Gao." My blood ran cold. Wow! That was creepily fast! I'd only emailed him a couple of hours before.

"Why is he at the restaurant?"

"He says he just wants to talk to you. He's a very charming young man."

As we headed to the restaurant, I kept repeating to myself, he's got no power over me, he's got no power over me.

It's true: outside Chinese school, he was just some

dude. Which meant I had nothing to worry about. So why were my guts fossilizing?

At the restaurant, I let my mother go in first. Principal Gao was sitting at the employees' table with my father. The "charming young man" stood up and nodded politely to my mother. He then turned to me and gave me a big smile with a friendliness that was undermined by a glaring set of eyes.

"Well," Principal Gao said when the four of us were seated at the table. "I understand that David doesn't plan on returning to Chinese school."

"I'll be interning at a hospital," I said. "Harmony Health, that is."

"I've gathered that from your email, David. Congratulations, that's a remarkable achievement. You're going to go on to do amazing things."

"Thank you."

"I was just talking with your dad here about how we're really going to miss you at the school." My father nodded to affirm the truth of the statement. "You were an integral part of the community. I know your many friends will be disappointed they won't see you anymore."

"I do have a Facebook account, so I'll still be around if someone needs me," I offered.

"Of course, of course. But I'd like to remind you of the role I saw you playing in terms of the development of the Chinese school. I still believe that we can maintain this aspect of our relationship."

I looked over to my father. He was turning his

near-empty teacup clockwise, 90 degrees at a time. My mother had her right hand on her just-filled cup, steam seeping out through her fingers.

"What are you talking about?" I asked Principal Gao.

"You could still do videos for our school even if you're not attending," he said. "We could work around your schedule on the weekends. We could even come film you at the hospital to show people how well-rounded you are."

"Wouldn't that be a little dishonest?" I asked.

"How so? You attended our school for more than eight years. You have an established record with us." Principal Gao dropped his voice and bowed his head slightly as if inviting intimacy. "We could really use you, David."

"Well, Betty is dropping out of Chinese school, too. She's in Hong Kong now. Seriously, Principal Gao, it might be cool to do a Zoom video with her. A Hong Kong skyline in the background would add even more authenticity." He opened his hands wide to show how generously minded he was.

"You and I both know that Betty's Mandarin is excellent. But her heritage might confuse people."

I looked again to my parents. They showed no reaction apart from fingering their teacups.

Sure, they had just met Betty for the first time the other day, but they'd known her father for years. Didn't my parents have anything to say to counter Principal Gao's shallow and insulting dismissal of her?

I get it, though. Betty wasn't super special to them. Even if they didn't like what Principal Gao was saying about her, it certainly wasn't disturbing enough to them to confront him. After all, the man was an educator. And a guest at Tung's Garden.

I was the one who had to stand up to Principal Gao. Because I was the one who knew and loved Betty.

Pressing both of my palms into the table, I leaned toward the principal. I wanted him to hear every word.

"No. I'm the one who's confused. I'm supposed to get into a good college, but I'm also supposed to work here to help out the family. On top of that, I have to go to your school to learn some token amount of Chinese. All this just to make everyone happy. Everyone except me. Now, by some miracle, I've managed to get this internship. Something that I wanted and worked hard for. And I'm not going to compromise my time at the hospital in any way because it's the one thing I want to do. It's the one thing in my whole life that's for me!"

I was now standing. And shaking. Principal Gao regarded me with caution and kept his voice steady.

"Whoa, David, let's calm down, buddy."

"And don't you ever talk about Betty again! You hear me, Gao?"

My parents, who must've been a bit taken aback themselves by my conduct, sprung into end-the-embarrassment mode.

"David must be tired," said my father.

"He's had a long day at school," my mother explained.

"I've had a long day at life!" I yelled. I tore across the dining room and charged into the men's room.

This is exactly what a meltdown feels like, I told myself. This is a meltdown. Feel. It. I ran the cold faucet and splashed my face. I held my hands to my closed eyelids and felt hot tears.

Then I rinsed my mouth out a few times and shuddered. Slowly the halts in my breathing eased.

I wasn't the most-stressed Chinese American kid out there. All of us probably had parents with outsized expectations. I'm sure that Christina, Jean, and Percy, to name a few, felt the weight of their parents' expectations on their miserable backs all the time just as much as I did. That's probably one of the reasons why Al couldn't stand our school. He didn't know that the students there were bred to fight with their claws out for those extra points, lifting that B-plus to an A-minus to an A.

I couldn't explain the situation to Al because we spoke different languages. I was trained to battle for grades. He only wanted to learn.

But every arena has rules. One of them was that as much as Tung's Garden might have been a source of annoyance to me, it was my family's domain. My parents were allowed to harangue me here, but not an outsider like the principal of my Chinese school. A guest had to behave like a guest.

I washed up one more time and dried my forehead.

Though I was ready to leave the bathroom, I hesitated. I had no idea what I was going to say to Principal Gao once I went back out.

Of course when I finally did emerge, he was still sitting there. But something had changed. He looked a little adrift.

"I know you're under a lot of pressure, David,"

Principal Gao said as he made a gesture of conciliation with his arms. "You're a high-achieving kid, and I can't ask you to take on any more." I stared at him directly.

"Are you going to put Betty in your videos?" He smiled slightly and tapped the table with his right index finger.

"I think I'm going to use the entire school. Everyone. All the students will get a minute or two to talk about the school in the end. All of our kids are great."

"They are," I said. His face broke out into open admiration.

"You have the heart of a fighter, David," he said. "I didn't know that. You're not a quitter, like Chen lao shi." Principal Gao shifted in his seat. "Can you believe he didn't even have the courtesy to give a two-week notice? Very unprofessional."

Soon thereafter we said our goodbyes. No one followed Principal Gao to the parking lot.

"That was unexpected," I said.

"I talked to him a little bit," said my father.

"What did you talk about?"

"I just told him how Dr. Lee liked what you said about everyone being a superstar to somebody," he said. "The principal really understood, I think."

"Yeah," my mother chimed in. "He thought you were going to be the superhero of the school, but now he knows that everyone there is a superstar!"

"Everyone," said my father.

My dad had stuck up for me against Principal Gao! And my mother wasn't mad at me for flipping out against an authority figure!

"You two are my superstars," I told them.

CHAPTER EIGHTEEN

It's already been a few weeks since I started working at the hospital, and I've pretty much settled into my role. I'm basically like a mail-delivery guy who can also run little errands. Dr. Lee keeps saying she'll have more time to talk to me about her research after her next big conference is over, but I've looked at her schedule and there always seems to be another event she'll have to prep for. Whenever we do have more extended chats, she's always friendly, but also somewhat stressed.

Maybe I'll have to invite Dr. Lee and her family to our restaurant to get her some down time.

About two weeks after I started at Harmony Health, Christina Tau landed an internship at another hospital a little farther away. I hadn't applied for that one, because working there was only feasible if you had a car, but her Infiniti could crush those miles. So in a way things worked out for both of us.

When I heard the announcement in homeroom, I

took the risk of being late to Mr. del Pino's biology class to find Christina and congratulate her.

"I knew you'd get something great," I told her. She touched her left ear, highlighting a diamond stud.

"Well, I'm not getting $700 out of it," Christina said. But she was smiling. Her injured-noblewoman-of-ancient-China act was done.

"You know where that $700 is going?" I waved my prehistoric phone at her. She laughed.

"Oh, my god, I had that phone in seventh grade, I think! You win, David!" I was about to wave goodbye when she told me to wait.

"I wasn't very nice when you got that Harmony Health internship. I'm sorry."

"Christina, it's all right," I said with sincerity. "Hey, now that we're both on our way to the Ivy League, maybe we can meet up in the cafeteria and go over MCAT questions. If they're not too hard for you."

She laughed hard enough for me to feel her breath on my face.

"Yeah, you're on," she said. I turned to go.

"Yaro was a fun date at the Dames Ball," she called out.

"That's great," I said, and genuinely felt good for her and for him.

Surprise, surprise, Jean and Percy have broken up. She isn't at the bus stop anymore these days because she's now dating a junior who can give her a ride to and from school. The whole atmosphere at the bus stop has changed as a result. Mornings are fun now because I hang out with Percy, Fred, Grace, and Al, and we all show each other stupid videos on our phones. We all laugh pretty hard because we're trying to offset anxieties over upcoming finals.

I've kept up with what's going on with my old Chinatown crew, too. YK apparently froze up in front of the camera, so they're going to save him for later in the year, after he's gone through some media training. Andy pooled the money he made from his iPad deals and is now going for bigger fish—buying Tiffany jewelry and selling it to buyers in China. Everything he's doing is completely legal, he assures me.

It would be out of character for Chun to say he missed me, but he does often ask when he can come to visit our restaurant. Apparently, he's always wanted to learn the restaurant business. Oh, and he has a girlfriend now. The way he puts it is he wants to come over, check out our restaurant, and then stay over—presumably with his girlfriend—in the extra bedroom of our house. I can just imagine how much my mom would love that.

I told him that he had to apologize for the racist things he said to Betty, and he actually did, copying me on the email.

I'm glad that he did, and that she accepted.

Because she's sort of my girlfriend now.

Sometimes wishes do come true! When I squeezed Mr. Wald's football, back on that day my internship was announced, I wished that Betty would come back to New York as soon as possible and in a way that didn't hurt her future career.

I emphasized the second point when I told her about my wish.

As it turned out, when Betty landed in Hong Kong, an immigration officer scanned her passport, and two people showed up to escort her immediately to an unmarked side office. She was told that her visa had been cancelled, no explanation. Betty had to wait about two hours for a flight home, so the officers got her a bowl of braised pork on rice and let her watch TV.

"Oh my God, David, that food was so good, it made me laugh," she said. When she got back, Betty called my cell from JFK using a stranger's phone. At two in the morning.

HSBC Bank felt so badly about the situation that they gave her a part-time administrative-assistant job at the Chinatown branch.

Someone at the bank eventually told her that her Hong Kong job had been a casualty of the latest change in the trade dispute between the U.S. and China.

Speaking of long-running disputes, my mother loosened her restrictions on me a little bit after having a long talk with Mr. Yeung. That visit by Betty actually worked in her favor.

Of course my mom will never admit Betty is my girlfriend. She still insists that we're just friends.

We're not allowed to hang out at night. Oh, and Betty has yet to see our house. Heck, my own family barely sees our house.

But most Saturdays, Betty will catch a ride with our dads to our restaurant, and while our parents eat an early dinner together, we'll walk down to the multiplex next door and see a movie. I always worry that my bus from the hospital will be late, but that thing runs on a tight schedule. I usually get to the restaurant right before the truck pulls in and Betty, my dad, and Mr. Yeung all pile out.

We are so innocent, Betty and I. The most we usually do is hold hands. We agree only to kiss if the movie is bad, so we try to find stinkers. Sequels are pretty good bets. Luckily, the only theater in town is a multiplex, so there are plenty to choose from.

I will never forget *The Expendables 4* because that's when we had our first kiss. We waited until the meathead guy walked away from the shootout, then we turned to each other because we knew that whatever happened next on the screen didn't matter.

Betty had offered her cheek to me but I put my hand up, turned her head gently, and kissed her lips. Our tongues bumped, and we both pulled back, snickering. She wiped her mouth with the back of her arm, like my saliva was disgusting, and it hurt my feelings.

"Booger," she whispered, although the film was loud as hell.

"What?" I asked. She pressed a napkin into my hand and tapped the left side of my nose.

"You have a booger, David!"

"Oh, damn," I said as I moved to fix the situation.

That was how the first one went.

It's much better now.

When we return to the restaurant, our faces washed and stinking of foaming hand soap, my parents force us both to eat something. The adults generally spend another hour talking about real and imagined events in the recent and distant past over empty plates and a Game Boy chess game abandoned after a dozen moves.

The adult conversation always continues as we walk out to the parking lot. My parents and Mr. Yeung come to a stop and yap some more. Betty and I provide directors' commentary on the scenes we just watched, cracking each other up.

One of the adults always suddenly exclaims something about the time, and then Mr. Yeung wobbles to the truck. Betty and I share the most awkward, restrained hug, and then she hops up into the cab.

We go through the three-wave ritual before her face in the window flashes by and the truck is on its way back to the city.

I walk back in to the restaurant with that afterimage of Betty floating in front of me.

I know for sure that we're going to get married one day.

Because that's what you do after you finally have a girlfriend, right?